Rule of
THREES

RULE OF THREES

Marcy Campbell

chronicle books
san francisco

To my favorite three: Rick, Lily, and Whit

Library of Congress Cataloging-in-Publication Data available.

ISBN 978-1-7972-0123-8

Manufactured in China.

Design by Mariam Quraishi.
Typeset in Bembo.
10 9 8 7 6 5 4 3 2 1

Chronicle Books LLC
680 Second Street
San Francisco, California 94107
Chronicle Books—we see things differently.
Become part of our community at www.chroniclekids.com.

Also by Marcy Campbell:

Adrian Simcox Does NOT Have a Horse

One Big Thing

In between forkfuls of spaghetti, my dad said it was time to play our new family dinner game, "One Big Thing."

"Let's hear something important that happened to everybody today," Dad said.

I still didn't see the point of this game. It seemed like a game other families needed to play, families who barely ever saw each other. We ate dinner together almost every night, unless Dad had a late meeting or Mom had to show a house. I honestly wondered if Mom and Dad had secretly been reading parenting blogs together. *How to talk to your tween! Keep your middle schooler engaged at dinnertime!*

"Do we have to keep playing this?" I asked.

Mom said, "We told you, Maggie, we just want to make sure we talk, really talk, like always—"

"—Even though you're in middle school now and might think you're too cool for your old parents," Dad finished. He leaned forward. "So, Mags," he said, "tell me something good."

I sighed, my brain scrolling through the snapshots of my day. There were some good things. My choir teacher had me sing a solo verse of this *Lion King* song we're working on and said I sounded great. And I'd gotten matched with a lab partner who seemed like he probably wouldn't throw dead worms, or anything else, on me. That was kind of neutral, I guess. Oh, but Rachel . . . she seemed really distant at lunch, and also wants us to call her Ra-*kell* this year for some reason.

I knew Rachel's family wasn't playing any dinner games. They didn't even eat in the same room, preferring to spread out to the different TVs around the house with their plates balanced on their knees. And at my other BFF Olive's house, her baby brother was usually crying or flinging sweet potatoes against the wall. I was lucky. As an only child, I didn't have any trouble getting my parents' attention.

"Does it always have to be a good thing," I asked, "or just a big, important thing?"

"It doesn't necessarily have to be something good," Dad said. "I mean, like, you remember last week when Mom had that house deal fall through, which was pretty bad, but still important."

"Did something bad happen at school today, Maggie?" Mom cut in, her eyes going wide.

"No, geez, I'm just trying to figure out what to say." They looked disappointed, like I was ruining their game again, and I knew right then that if I did have something bad to report, I'd have to do it in a kind of good news–bad news sandwich, like Mom did at her open houses. I'd been to plenty of them, so I'd seen her in action, witnessed her camouflaging the not-so-nice qualities of a fixer-upper. She might point out the "gorgeous natural light," then quietly mention that the appliances could use some "updating," and then she'd end by gushing loudly about the "solid oak floors!" It was a compliment sandwich. Good-bad-good.

Three was the best number of details. You didn't want to overload a person's brain with too many.

"Well?" Mom said, tapping her fingers against her glass.

"You go first. I'm still thinking," I said.

She wiggled her eyebrows. "I listed a new house, on Briarcliff!"

"Bravo!" Dad raised his glass in the air, and Mom and I clinked ours against it.

"That's awesome, Mom!" I said. Briarcliff was a street by the golf course with a bunch of McMansions, which typically sold for a lot of money. That meant more commission for my mom, even though often, the houses weren't so great on the inside. Mom always said you didn't have to have a lot of money to have style, and sometimes people with the most money didn't have any of it.

"What's it look like?" I asked cautiously, and Mom made a pukey face. I pictured crazy-patterned curtains puddling on all the super-cold marble floors, endangered animal heads hanging on the walls.

"Maybe you can help me stage it before it shows, Maggie," Mom said.

"Sure!" I replied, but I wasn't going to touch any dead animals.

"One more thing," Mom added. "I got an offer on that little bungalow around the corner, for just under the asking price, so, fingers crossed."

New mansion listing—but it's yucky—and an offer on the bungalow. Good-bad-good.

"Well, I went to work today, and had a perfectly normal, no-surprises day," Dad said, and raised his glass again, though Mom and I didn't clink it this time.

I cocked my head at him. "Is that supposed to be something *big*?"

"What's bigger than having a perfectly normal day? I consider that a big success." Dad winked at me, and Mom shook her head, laughing.

"Oh! I just remembered!" I said, my arms goose-bumping with excitement. "There was this announcement about a contest at school where we compete to decorate the hallways or something. Mr. Villanueva is supposed to give the details at an assembly this week."

"Well, that sounds right up your alley," Mom said.

It sure was. Mom and Dad had prepped me all summer about how important it was to get involved, as soon as possible, at my new school, because it would make me feel more comfortable there, more like I belonged in middle school rather than back in elementary school. What better way to get involved than by doing design, something I already knew and loved? Plus, it was the perfect next job for the BFFs. This was big, all right.

"You should call Grandma and tell her about it," Mom said.

"Just what I was thinking. I'll call her right after dinner." I popped the last buttery hunk of garlic bread into my mouth, washed it down with some milk.

"Help me with these dishes first?" Dad asked.

Mom and I cleared the table while Dad filled the sink with water, then Mom went to check her phone for texts. People always liked to bother her about house listings during dinnertime.

"Wash or dry?" Dad asked.

"Wash," I said. I always said wash. Dad knew not to make the water so hot that I couldn't put my hands in it. I dipped my fingers into the suds. *Ahhhh . . . just right.*

I started washing the spaghetti bowl while Dad loaded the dishwasher with the plates and cups and silverware.

"So, this contest sounds pretty cool," he said.

"It is! It's going to be awesome. I'm just hoping we get a good location to decorate. And that Olive and Rachel are as excited as I am."

"Why wouldn't they be?" Dad asked. He pulled a yellow checked towel from the drawer.

"Well, Rachel is acting, I don't know, just kind of different."
I scrubbed at some dried sauce on the edge of the bowl. "She's
just . . . acting like she wants to do different things and have new
friends and stuff since we got to middle school."

"That happens," Dad said.

"It happened to you?"

"Sure. I made different friends as I moved through school,
depending on what kinds of sports or clubs I was involved in. But
I kept some of those old friends, too. I still talk to a friend I met in
kindergarten, in fact. That might be the way it goes for you, too."

"Yeah, but I like the friends I have."

"Of course you do. No one is saying you need to go out
looking for new friends, but if you meet some people you hit it
off with, sometimes new friendships just happen naturally, and
sometimes old friendships might move a bit into the background."

I handed him the bowl, and he dried it off. I didn't want my
friendship with Rachel, or Olive, to move into the background.

Dad must have noticed I looked worried. "Everything looks
worse at night," he said. "You'll feel better in the morning. All
you have to do is just keep being the great girl you are, and the
right friends will be attracted to that."

If he was Mom, he'd be grabbing his laptop right now to
email the school counselor, or texting Rachel's mom to discuss
the situation, or getting me to make a ten-step plan for dealing
with changing friendships. But that wasn't Dad's style.

We finished the dishes while he hummed a song I recognized from a Beatles movie we saw recently, about a marketplace and life going on.

"I better call Grandma," I said. "Mom says not to count on her being very alert after seven p.m."

"You shouldn't count on *me* being alert after seven p.m. either," Dad said, swatting me with the dishtowel. "Or before seven p.m., for that matter."

I grabbed his towel and swatted him back before running upstairs to my room.

-•- ✦ -•-

It took Grandma five rings to pick up.

"Hello?"

"Hi, Grandma, it's Maggie."

There was a pause, and I glanced at the clock. It wasn't seven yet, only 6:45.

"Oh! How are you, sweetie?" she asked, her smile coming right through the phone.

"I'm fine. How are you?"

My grandma wasn't like my friends' grandmas who constantly complained about all their aches and pains and how things cost too much and how kids didn't act like they were supposed to anymore. In fact, Mom said she sometimes wished Grandma would complain more, just so she'd have a heads-up when something was wrong with her, especially now that Grandpa had died.

"Oh, I'm doing very well," Grandma said, "just looking through some seed catalogs, thinking about putting some Cardinal flowers along that shady part of the fence next spring."

"Grandma, it's not even fall!" I laughed.

"No harm comes from proper planning," she said breezily. It was something she said a lot, something I'd taken to heart. I always put lots of planning into my room designs. Grandma had taught me I should measure the rooms and sketch out just where everything should go, so there wouldn't be any surprises.

"Grandma, guess what? The school is going to have a contest where we get to decorate hallways and stuff!"

"Hallways? What about the . . . the metal . . . containers . . . where you put your bags . . ."

"The lockers?" I asked.

"Yes, lockers. How are you going to design around those?"

"Ummm," I said. I didn't have any idea, not yet. I didn't even know any details about the contest. "There might be some classrooms, too, not just hallways," I said.

Grandma wasn't saying anything, and I felt my excitement droop like the philodendron on my bookshelf I was always forgetting to water. "It's going to be great!" I said, but my heart wasn't quite in it anymore.

"Of course it will, sweetie," she said, then paused again. "It's probably bedtime, isn't it?" she asked.

I wasn't sure if she meant her bedtime or mine, but I said, "Yeah, I should probably go. Do you want to talk to Mom?"

"No, that's okay. It was nice to chat with you, honey, and I'll talk to you soon, okay? Bye, Margie."

I hung up, not sure if I'd heard her right. Did she just call me *Margie*?

Little Red Car

I might not have noticed the little red car pull up outside our house the next day if its brakes hadn't screeched so horribly, pulling me, Rachel, and Olive away from our meeting and over to my bedroom window. The car skidded to a stop just past our place, then backed up, then jerkily drove forward again, very slowly turning into our driveway, the woman behind the wheel squinting at the house numbers painted in white on our mailbox.

"Who's that?" Rachel asked.

The driver was a gray-haired woman wearing large glasses. She stopped the car, pulled a purse onto her lap, and started digging through it. I saw her turn and speak to a kid sitting in the back. I couldn't see his face very well.

"Probably somebody with the wrong address," I said. "Or somebody selling something."

That last part, though, wasn't very likely. No one came to our house selling anything, except during Girl Scout cookie season, but that wasn't until spring. It was barely September. Honestly, no one came to the house unexpectedly at all, except the BFFs and sometimes my dad's basketball friends.

I looked again at the car, noticed a dent in the front left fender. I'd never seen the car before, or the woman, who, although she looked like she could have been somebody's grandma, definitely wasn't mine. She opened her door and while she struggled a bit to get out of the car, her striped top rode up, giving a clear view of her elastic-waist pants, which didn't match the top. Definitely nothing like my grandma, who always dressed very stylishly, even if she was just going to the grocery store. Grandma really loved colorful scarves and had four special hangers for them in her closet.

The boy turned his head then, glancing toward the house. He looked about the same age as me. He was wearing a blue hoodie, and a mop of black hair covered one eye, making him look both goofy and dangerous.

"He's cute," Rachel said, and I gave her a little punch to the arm, but not enough to really hurt. It's just that I was sick of Rachel's newfound interest in boys. She'd never even noticed them in fifth grade. In any case, he actually wasn't cute, not really, but still, there was something about him that made me stare, something that seemed oddly familiar.

I felt that little buzz in my brain that I got whenever something was *off*. You could call it intuition, I guess, but that seemed too fancy and important. It was just a *feeling*, the same feeling I got when I realized a design project I'd been working on wasn't quite there yet.

He looked up toward my window and saw me looking back at him. I quickly turned around. "Break's over," I said to my friends. "Let's get back to our tablescape."

I was so thankful to have our little trio, our design team, together that I didn't want to waste another minute. Rachel had joined the swim team this year, and Olive had to help out a lot with her baby brother, so it was getting harder to meet. When we started the BFFs, in fourth grade, we didn't have as much going on, and there wasn't any pressure. We were just messing around then, redecorating each other's bedrooms. But word got out. Soon, we were helping some friends with their rooms. Then we helped some friends' moms, who actually paid us.

I started adding to my savings account, so that someday I could help pay for college, where I'd study interior design and do this for real. Grandma had told me once, if she'd had it to do over, she would have done just that. But she got too busy raising my mom, and meant to have more kids (though that never happened), and anyway, she said, "things were different back then."

"Olive, could you move the vase a little to the right?" I asked.

Olive did.

"A little more," I said.

Olive moved the vase too far.

"Now back, just a little, just a little. There. Perfect," I said. "What do you think, Rachel?"

"Hmm?" She was sitting behind me, playing with my hair like she'd done ever since we'd shared a carpet square in kindergarten.

"The tablescape, what do you think of it?"

"Oh, yeah, it looks good," she said.

"Are you actually looking?" I asked. She was trying to coax my curly black hair into a bun, and it hurt.

"I'm looking, Maggie, I'm looking, and it looks fine. And also, it's Ra-*kell* now, remember?" She kept her grip on my hair, but leaned forward, looking at my face. "By the way," she said, "I have some new blush you can borrow."

"No, thanks," I replied. I pushed her hands away from my head, let my hair fall.

Rachel laughed and said, "I would kill for your cheekbones. I mean, *hello*, they're one of your best features, and you're not even highlighting them. What happened to 'Using Your Assets'?" she said. "Isn't that rule number, I don't know, five-hundred-and-something?"

Olive giggled, and I shot her a look. They could make fun of my rules if they wanted to, but those rules worked.

"Well, I think it looks fantabulous," Olive said. Everything was fantabulous to Olive. If I'd told her once, I'd told her a million times, it's either fabulous or fantastic, not both.

But she was right; it did look awfully nice. The tall yellow vase Olive had just moved was flanked by a little bronze pig, wings sprouting from its back, and on the other side, a silver picture frame. Grandma had taught me how to group things with her thriller-filler-spiller method. The rule was actually meant for plants that you'd arrange in a pot. The "thriller" was the tall, eye-catching plant. The "filler" was a plant that was pretty and lush, taking up space, and the "spiller" was something that spilled out over the edge.

I wasn't into gardening as much as Grandma was, but the concept still worked. I had my tall thriller—the vase—and a chunky photo frame—the filler. The pig? Well, he didn't actually spill out anywhere, but his wings were spread, and I thought it had a similar effect.

I'd bought all three items at the dollar store, adding them to my overflowing prop box. I was the keeper of the box and the unofficial leader of the team, which meant I always hosted the meetings of our design company, the BFFs, which stood for Best Foot Forward, along with the obvious, Best Friends Forever. Of course Dad liked to joke about whether this meant we were the Best Foot Forwards, or the Best Feet Forward. I also set the meeting agendas. Today: How to Create a Tablescape.

"Remember," I told them. "The rule of threes works because our eyes are more attracted to odd-numbered groupings. It forces our eye to move around, looking for patterns, which makes for a more stimulating visual experience."

"So, we could use fives or sevens, if we wanted?" Olive asked.

"Sure, if we had a big enough table."

Olive was scribbling with her favorite pink pen in her notebook. She was the official notetaker. And Rachel (or Rakell now, I guess? I just couldn't make the name stick in my head) was the one who added the "wow factor" to my designs. The three of us made a great team, perfect complements. Like a trio of knick-knacks on an end table.

Rachel would be the thriller. I would probably be the filler, keeping everything else in place, and that left Olive as the spiller. She was often more emotional than me or Rachel, and I imagined her moods—whether good or bad—filling up the planter, and then cascading right over.

"I *love* the little piggie," Olive said.

"Me too," I agreed, and Rachel added, "Bronze animals are very on trend right now."

"Yes, they are," I said, surprised Rachel knew that. Maybe she actually had read that article from *House Beautiful* I'd copied for her and Olive last week.

The tablescape would be nothing without that pig. Take out the pig, or the picture frame, and your brain would say *you're missing something,* even if you didn't consciously realize it. Add one more item, and your brain would say *too much.*

Three is perfect. Look at us—three BFFs. And there were three members of my immediate family, just me and my mom and dad. They always talked about us being a team, and I knew we were a lot closer than families with a ton of kids. There's one family in our town with *twelve* kids, and I wondered how the parents could even remember all their names. Some people talk about a "third wheel" like it's a bad thing, which I don't get. I mean, think of a stool, a tricycle, my family. Think of our tablescape! Three is balance.

I heard a car door slam, then my dad's heavy footsteps downstairs, crossing the living room floor. The doorbell rang, and Mittens, my cat, came shooting into my bedroom.

"Oh, sweet kitty!" Olive said and scooped her up. "You are such a sweetums," she said, nuzzling her. "Such a sweet little wittle . . ."

"Shhh," I said. I was back at the window. The old woman was standing on our front stoop now, looking the house over with a critical eye, like she was thinking about buying it or something, even though it wasn't for sale. The boy was still in the car.

Olive was being so noisy with the cat that I didn't hear Mom come upstairs. She stood in my doorway, resting her hand on the frame as though she was trying to steady herself. All the blood had drained right out of her face.

"Mom?" I said.

She looked around my room. "Are you almost done?" she asked, kind of breathless, like she'd just run a race instead of running up the stairs.

"Um, well, not quite," I said. I looked at Olive, who shrugged. Rachel had retreated to my loft.

"Hey, Mrs. O," Rachel called down.

"Yes, hi, Rachel," Mom said.

"Actually, Mrs. O? It's Rakell now. R-A-K-E-L-L."

"Uh, okay, sure," Mom answered, not looking at her. She hadn't taken her eyes off me. It was like I'd done something bad, but what could I have done? Put a glass on the coffee table without a coaster? Left my towel on the floor in the bathroom? Nope and nope. I'd only been home from school for an hour. How much trouble could I have gotten in?

Mom said, "I need you to finish up, Maggie, *now, please*," in a tone that made the "please" seem out of place. She leaned closer to me. "We have some family business to discuss."

I didn't like the sound of that. I heard Dad coming up the stairs. Of course, he wouldn't be the one to tell me to finish my meeting or that I was potentially in trouble. It was always my mom who did that type of thing. If they had some good-cop, bad-cop arrangement, Mom was always bad-cop. Maybe that's why me and Dad got along especially well.

He said from the hallway, "Susan, I need you down here." He never called her that. She was always "Sue" or "Susie." Maybe she was the one in trouble.

As Mom left my room, she said, "Robert, I'm *trying*. What do you want me to do?" The two of them moved across the hall to their own bedroom.

"What's that all about?" Olive asked.

I didn't know, but I didn't like this whole using-full-names thing. My dad was always, always "Bob." Outside, I heard the unmistakable thump of a basketball and the clang as it bounced off the rim of the hoop in our driveway.

"It's that kid," Olive said, "from the car."

Olive nodded toward the window, then back at me like she was waiting for me to do something. What was I supposed to do? So the kid had a basketball, and we had a hoop, and it was a free country, and if he was waiting for his grandma or something, which reminded me . . . where was his grandma? Downstairs? In our house? Alone?

I could hear my parents' voices, low and angry, seeping under their door. I heard my mom say, "I *told* you, Robert," and the way she said it made my stomach turn loops like I was right back in second grade and crying on my way to the bus stop. I went over to my desk, grabbed my phone, and turned on some music so we couldn't hear them.

"You don't have to do that," Rachel mumbled from my loft. "I'm used to it." I knew without asking that she was scrolling through *Teen Vogue* on her phone.

"Used to what?" Olive asked.

Rachel didn't answer. I busied myself with our prop box, trying to stuff everything in. I picked up the cheap silver-plated frame, which still contained the photo that came with it, of a boy being pushed on the swing by . . . his father, I supposed? The boy smiled out of the picture at me, like, *Whee, isn't this fun?*

I stuffed him into the box. I put the vase in next, then the pig, who perched on top of everything, smiling away, like he knew the sweetest secret. When I bought him, I thought he was some kind of angel-pig, considering he had wings and all, but when Dad saw him, he told me about this figure of speech: when pigs fly.

"It means something's impossible," he'd explained. "So, if somebody thought something would never, ever happen, they might say it would happen 'when pigs fly.'"

Mom came back into my room while Dad ran down the stairs in a blur. She rubbed her forehead like she had a really bad headache. *Thump, thump, clang* went the ball outside.

"Maggie, do you think you could . . . go to Rachel's or Olive's or something? Just for a bit? While your dad and I get some things . . . sorted out?" *Thump, clang.*

"But I thought we had *family business* to discuss," I said.

"Well, we *did*, Maggie, but you've been goofing around with your little arrangements, and now it's too late!"

Olive sucked in her breath while I went to my desk and sat down in my chair, stretching out my finger to touch the special shell I kept behind my pencil cup. *Little arrangements*, huh? Not cool. How would she like it if I said *for sale by owner*? There were certain things we didn't say around our house.

"You just told me that a few minutes ago, Mom." My skin was feeling all prickly and warm. I wiped my suddenly sweaty hands on my pants. "What's the big deal? Who are these people anyway?"

I tapped my phone to turn the music off, which made the room seem way too quiet. Even the basketball had stopped bouncing.

"I'm sorry," my mom said softly. "I'll . . . explain later. I'll send you a text when you can head back home."

"You can come to my house," Olive said. She was still holding Mittens, but now she brought her over to me and transferred her to the back of my neck. I liked to wear her that way, like a black-and-white scarf, and Mittens seemed to like it, too. She started purring. Her body was very warm, and that relaxed me, like my shoulders were wrapped in a blanket.

"So will you?" Olive asked. "Come to my house?"

Rachel had gotten down from the loft and was zipping up her backpack. She didn't even look up, so it seemed clear I wouldn't be going to her place, which is where I'd normally hang out. Olive's house was a lot more chaotic, with the baby around. At Rachel's, we were pretty much ignored.

"Thank you, Olive," Mom said, as though Olive was babysitting me or something. Mom turned and went back downstairs.

I quickly gathered up my homework, figuring I'd get a start on it at Olive's. I heard the strange woman's voice downstairs. Maybe she was an accountant or something. I remembered once when Mom and Dad had someone to the house to go through some retirement stuff. But this seemed different. And why would she bring her grandson, if that's who he was, to a meeting? And why were my parents acting so weird, and angry? I felt that buzz in my brain again. Something was definitely *off*. Something that probably couldn't be fixed by moving a vase three inches to the right.

That Basketball Boy

The three of us moved through the kitchen with Mittens dart-
ing around and between our legs, almost tripping us. I caught a
glimpse of my parents sitting stiffly on our living room couch,
the gray-haired woman across from them on the loveseat. I
paused, wanting to eavesdrop, but thought better of it when
Mom turned and gave me a look that said I'd better be on my
way. We tumbled out the door.

"Oops, sorry," Rachel said, almost running into the basketball boy.

He was on our front stoop looping the ball around his waist.
Faster and faster it went, but somehow he kept control, so the ball
didn't fly away and shatter one of our windows. He didn't look
at us and he didn't move, so we had to kind of scoot around him,
like he owned the place. Honestly, it was incredibly rude.

It was hot out, and I was already starting to sweat by the time we reached the corner at Maple. When Rachel turned, I instinctively turned, too. I'd been going to Rachel's house for so many years, I could find it in the dark. I knew there were twelve stairs up to her bedroom, and the third one creaked. I knew all the outfit combinations in her closet, or at least I used to, until she went on a massive shopping spree just before school started.

Rachel turned toward me. "I have to work on that group project. With Katelyn," she said. "That's why I can't have you over."

"Oh, yeah," I said. We all just stood there for a minute, then Rachel gave a stiff little wave, and walked off.

Olive headed in the other direction, rattling off the things we were going to do at her place. "We'll have a snack, like maybe some cookies, we have a pantry full of snacks, but you probably remember that, don't you? My mom said she trusts me to make the right choices, so she's just gonna keep that pantry full and trust me to choose wisely and to remember the difference between everytime foods and sometimes foods, which I think is really cool because, like, most moms would never do that in a million years but can I tell you a secret, I eat the sometimes foods all the time."

She finally took a breath. "Is Katelyn the one with the super shiny lip gloss?" she asked.

"Yup," I answered.

Olive's mom was stirring some kind of fishy-smelling soup.

"Oh, hello, Maggie, what a nice surprise," she said.

"Hi," I replied. I tried not to wrinkle up my nose at the soup, but it really smelled bad. All houses had a smell, and Olive's usually smelled like some kind of food I didn't like. Rachel's smelled like her mom's flowery perfume. The houses my mom sold had all different sorts of smells, musty or lemony or sometimes cat pee. (Mom would insist they tear out all the carpeting before she'd even advertise any listing like that.) Really the only house that didn't have a smell was my own, but that's just because I was so used to it, whatever it was.

"Hey, Mom," Olive said. "Hi, Noah-Boa." Her baby brother zoomed across the room toward Olive in his exersaucer, bumping into her legs and laughing uncontrollably.

"He is getting so fast in that thing," Olive's mom said. She turned to look at him while her spoon hung in the air, dripping a thick red sauce onto the stove. "But just wait, pretty soon he'll be even faster, on his own two legs."

She had that weird, faraway look on her face that parents get when they think about kids growing up too fast. My parents got it sometimes, too, usually when I had to dress up for something. Noah gurgled and wrapped his arms tightly around Olive's neck. That's why she called him Noah-Boa. He had quite a grip.

I noticed nothing had changed in the Roselli kitchen since the last time I was over, which was unfortunate. The place was in bad shape. Two of the walls had a terrible mint-green paint that was so old, it might be in style again if they kept it around a few more years. The yellow floral wallpaper on the other walls was pulling apart at its seams and curling up around the stove. The cabinets were nicked and scuffed, doors hanging crookedly, and there were spice jars and plastic containers and baby bottles strewn across the stained laminate countertop. I couldn't help but see the kitchen as a "before" picture.

The BFFs had never designed a kitchen, only bedrooms and a living room once. But I'd love to get my hands on this room. Quartz countertops would be great, but they were expensive, and I knew Olive's parents didn't have a lot of money, especially now that they had another mouth to feed. Another kid in the Roselli house meant Olive had to make do with less of everything, including her parents' time. She said sometimes they were so busy with the baby, they even forgot to tell her good night. That never happened at my house. Still, Noah was pretty cute, I guess, and he wasn't so close in age that he would fight with Olive over who got to do this or that, like Rachel did with her older brothers.

Olive was playing peekaboo with Noah, which set him off laughing again. The kid was so surprised every time Olive came back from behind her hands, like he must have thought for a minute she was really gone.

"Can Maggie and I hang out for a little bit in my room?" Olive asked. "We'll get started on our homework. Her parents are having a meeting at their house."

"Sure," Mrs. Roselli said. "And you're welcome to stay for dinner, Maggie, especially if that would help your parents out."

Would it help my parents out? I didn't know. But I was not going to stay and eat whatever was bubbling on the stove. "No, that's okay, but thanks," I said. I checked my phone to see if my mom had texted yet. Nothing.

Olive opened the pantry, out of view of her mom.

"Choose wisely," Mrs. Roselli said. "Dinner is in an hour."

Olive grabbed two packs of Twinkies, two granola bars, and some red licorice and ran up the stairs. I ran after her.

"Are you going to get in trouble?" I asked, as she dumped the feast out onto her purple flowered comforter, the one splurge her mom had agreed to when the BFFs redesigned the room. I didn't mind the comforter, but in combination with all the other colors in this small space—the pinks and yellows and oranges—I just found it too, too much. It certainly wasn't what I had planned for the room, but Rachel had convinced me that the client, in this case Olive, always wins in the end. She might be right, but the room still bugged me every time I came over.

"How can I get in trouble if we destroy the evidence?" she said. "Have some." Olive slid the Twinkies across the bed.

"I better not," I said. "I don't want to spoil my dinner." I actually wasn't a big fan of Twinkies. My mom told me they sat on the shelves for years.

Olive licked some cream off her finger. "It didn't look like anyone was even making dinner at your house, or even thinking about it," she said.

She was right, nobody was, I realized, as I noticed my stomach jump. I wasn't feeling too well. I pushed the snacks aside and leaned against Olive's pillows. Then I covered my face with a particularly soft, pink one. I could hear Olive unwrapping a granola bar, could hear her mom clattering pots downstairs in the kitchen. It was like covering my eyes had improved my hearing.

Everything felt weird and wrong—not just right now, but these past few weeks. The year wasn't starting out the way I wanted it to. I remembered our fifth grade science teacher, Mrs. Peterson, telling us things would be different in middle school, that lots of things might change, like our interests and even our friendships, and my dad had said the same just the other night.

But I already had the friends and interests I wanted. Of course, everything was perfect back in fifth grade. I mean, for starters, we were at the top of the food chain. All the little kids looked up to us. And our BFF business was really taking off. Plus, my parents hadn't had an argument, as far as I knew, in years. Nothing needed to change. I wouldn't let it.

Olive jiggled my foot. "Are you thinking about Rachel?" she asked. "I know she's been really different lately, and I noticed you haven't been calling her Rakell, which I admit is pretty hard to get used to. I hate when things change, too, you know, my mom always says change is much easier for kids than adults, but I don't know if I believe that, I mean, it seems like maybe one of those things parents say to make themselves feel better when they screw up, you know?"

I did not take the pillow off my face. I felt a little bit like crying, and thought I'd better keep it there, just in case.

Olive jiggled my foot again. "Do you want some licorice?" she asked.

"No," I mumbled.

"Are you okay? Are you worried about that basketball boy?"

"What? No," I said. "Why would I be?" I threw off the pillow, checked my phone. Nothing. I texted my mom: *Can I come home now???*

Five minutes passed. Olive started her math homework. I stared at my phone.

"I'm just gonna take off," I said.

"Oh, okay," Olive said. "See you later. Have a fantabulous evening!"

I said goodbye to Mrs. Roselli and waved to Noah-Boa on my way out, careful not to get so close that he'd wrap me in one of his death grips. Then I stepped outside, and the sun hit me, almost pushing me back into the nice, cool house. The weather felt *off*, too. It was way too hot, considering it was after Labor Day. Then again, it always seemed like our town stuttered its way into fall. There would be a day or two of cooler weather, then we'd take a leap back, right smack into the middle of summer. I always felt tricked, and I didn't like it one bit.

I noticed a dribble of sweat creeping down my back and decreased my walking pace to a stroll. I didn't need to hurry. What was I in such a rush for? My mom hadn't even texted. I didn't want to get there too early and have to edge past that basketball boy to get into my own house.

I noticed a new "For Sale" sign on a brick ranch. The sign said Hartman Realty in big, red letters with my mom's smiling face and cell number. Call Susan Owens. Another smaller metal sign hung below that, which said: "This one's a charmer!"

Mom had all these little signs she could attach below her phone number like: "Great starter home!," "Deluxe Master Suite!," or "This one's going F-A-S-T!" She'd stopped putting up that last one, though, because she felt like, if it was up for more than a few weeks and the house didn't sell, it would be false advertising, like she was a big old liar. She wasn't the kind of person who went around telling lies, not normally, not that I knew of. Although I guess it was true that I'd called her a liar once, screamed it at her one morning in second grade.

That was an unreasonably hot day in September just like this one, so hot that the tears felt like they were sizzling on my face as I walked to the bus stop that morning, by myself. I'd never walked to the bus stop by myself before that day, the day Mom told me after breakfast that she and Dad were having "some problems."

She'd said it really carefully, like it would be a surprise to me, but it wasn't. I was seven, not stupid. I had seen Mom crying in the kitchen for months before that. Plus, I'd been tiptoeing downstairs after I was supposed to be asleep, always finding Dad in the dark on the couch listening to this same singer, always the same guy and same songs. *It's a marvelous night for a moondance.* I remembered that. But mostly I remembered Mom telling me that fateful morning that she and Dad were going to live apart, and that I needed to decide who I was going to live with.

And then she said Dad would prefer I lived with her, and I called her a liar and ran from the house and down the street, to my bus stop. I knew he'd never say that. I also knew, if I had to choose between them, that I'd pick him, which I figured was not the answer my mom, or anybody, probably, expected or wanted.

There were a bunch of family meetings after that, with both Mom and Dad explaining to me that parents argue sometimes, and it's scary, but they still loved me, and it wasn't my fault. I'd never thought it was my fault before they said that, but then I did start wondering what I had done wrong. I wondered if they could read my mind and knew I wanted to live with Dad. It was a totally scary time, waking up and wondering, *Will today be the day I have to pack? Where will I live? Will my dad get an apartment like my classmate Norah's dad had done?* Norah told me how gross and empty her dad's place was. Every day, I'd get up and worry, and eventually I started to think: *Let it happen today.* Better to rip off the Band-Aid quickly than to painfully tug it a few millimeters at a time.

But none of my fears ever came true. And slowly, my parents changed, became more like the in-love parents I remembered from my preschool years. One day, around the time the leaves had all turned colors and the sky became that bright blue dome you only really see that time of year, I saw them, my parents, hugging in the backyard, that brilliant sky behind them.

And everything was like normal again. Mom wasn't crying. Dad wasn't staying up late. No moondances. Just normal, every-day, family stuff. Our meetings were less frequent, but they said I could talk to them whenever I needed to, ask them anything. I was glad *not* to talk about it. And now I couldn't think of the last time I'd heard them argue. Before today.

I stopped walking, dug into my backpack to see if I had a spare pair of sunglasses. I didn't. When I turned the corner toward my house and saw that the red car was missing from the driveway, I picked up my pace, eager to get inside. Mom must have forgotten to text me. They were probably busy making dinner. I'd come in, and Dad would use that silly voice where he'd pretend to be a waiter at a French restaurant: "Welcome to Chez Owens! Tonight, ze chef has prepared ze most delectable spaghetti in all ze land!" I smiled at the thought of it, my stomach grumbling. The nauseous feeling I'd had at Olive's was gone. I was really hungry, and really hoping for spaghetti.

I got to my house and was just reaching out to turn the knob to the side door by the kitchen when Dad opened it. I smiled at him, waiting for his funny voice. But he didn't smile back. And I didn't smell garlic bread or anything. Dad just stared at me, like he wasn't sure if he should let me in. When he finally spoke, he said, in the most un-funny voice ever, "Mags, we need to talk."

I felt like I'd been punched in the gut.

When Pigs Fly

The kitchen light shone behind my dad's head, creating a halo around his black curls. Neither of us said anything for a moment. I wanted to go in, but he was blocking my way.

"What is it?" I asked, wondering if I would finally get the "family business" discussion my mom had promised earlier. Maybe they'd sit me down in the dining room and do the good-cop, bad-cop routine, like when I got in trouble for using my phone after bedtime. Mom would accuse me of breaking the rule, and say they couldn't trust me, and Dad would step in to smooth everything over and insist it must have been an honest mistake, that I needed to text someone about homework, and he was sure I'd never do it again. The truth was usually somewhere in the middle.

Dad was still staring at me. "What is it?" I asked again. "What do you need to talk to me about?"

I had my backpack on, but I felt like I should take it off and hold it in front of me, like I needed to somehow protect my heart. Dad threw a glance over his shoulder toward the hallway, like something was behind him, but I saw nothing except our family photos on the wall, our worn carpeting. Then he finally stepped aside so I could come in. He spoke softly.

"That boy you saw earlier? When you left for Olive's? The one who was waiting outside, wearing the blue sweatshirt?"

"Yes," I said, impatiently. How many strange boys sat on our front stoop? What other boy would it be?

"Well, sweetheart, the thing is that . . . I don't know how to say this so I'm just going to say it . . . he's my son."

Just like that, the basketball boy poked his head around the corner like he'd been summoned. He stood there with his hands in his pockets. A brother?

"That's crazy." I shook my head. "I mean it's possible . . . when pigs fly. Right Dad?"

Dad opened his mouth to speak, but nothing came out. I glared at the boy, and he glared back. Like he was mad at me! Like I'd done something to him!

Mittens sauntered in and did her figure-eight around my legs. The boy smiled at her, so I picked her up before he could get his grimy paws on her. I held her close, feeling her soft fur tickle my chin. It seemed like the room was shrinking around me, and my backpack weighed a hundred pounds.

"You're kidding, right? Good one, Dad. Very funny."

"No, Maggie. I'm not joking."

He looked slumped, bent. My dad—who was actually six-foot-something, who worked as some kind of manager at the power company, American Power, who liked to flex his bicep when he left for work saying he was going to *American Power!* and pretend to zoom out the door like a superhero to make me laugh—he looked very, very small.

"I don't . . . I don't understand," I said.

I blinked. I set Mittens down, and she ran for the kitchen, where I could hear water running into the big spaghetti pot. Oh great, spaghetti. At least one thing I'd hoped for was actually happening, though everything else was going wrong. My eyes went all swimmy, filling with tears, but I could see well enough to notice Mom come out of the kitchen and gently take the boy's shoulders, steering him out of the room.

Dad had reached out to take my little, shaky hands into his big, steady ones. "I know this is impossible to believe," he said. "I know that, but you have to at least let me try to explain."

I closed my eyes, thinking maybe when I opened them, I'd find myself in my bed, realizing this had all been a dream.

He said, "You remember back a few years, when you were little, and your mom and I were having some ... some difficulties ..."

My eyes were still leaking, and his words sounded far away, like I was underwater and he was standing on the shore. I could not listen to this, so I let go of his hands and ran to my room, my footsteps heavy, stomping up the stairs. I closed the door and inched myself into my packed closet, nestling between a dozen stuffed animals. I did not turn on the light. I sat in the dark.

There was no lock on my closet door, but nobody came in here other than me. I had put a homemade door-hanger on the knob, decorated with a sequined skull and crossbones and the words "Health Hazard. Do Not Enter." My parents thought it was funny, and they never made me clean up, as long as the mess stayed *inside* and didn't seep out into my room.

My closet smelled like my jasmine hand lotion and like bubblegum wrappers and a little like old dusty things, like the smell from the boxes in the attic where my parents kept stuff from their own childhoods—their yellowing report cards and sports trophies. They went through those boxes with me once, reminiscing, but Mom got sad when she opened a container with a corsage Dad had given her and saw that the flowers had disintegrated, leaving behind nothing but papery brown flakes. My closet smell usually made me feel comforted and calm.

But not today. I was anything but calm. Were my parents planning to take this kid in, like a stray, like when we found Mittens eating out of a trash can in a parking lot? Who was the woman who'd dropped him off? And why hadn't *she* kept him? Why was this boy here now? Where was he before? And was he staying??? He was NOT sleeping in my room!

My stomach felt all queasy again, like I'd eaten a bucket full of Olive's Twinkies. I realized I actually hadn't eaten anything for hours. I didn't know if I'd ever feel like eating again.

I worked out the math in my head. The kid didn't look much older than me, and it's not like I didn't know how babies were made. Ugh, yuck, so Dad . . . with some other woman who wasn't Mom . . . I felt even sicker.

I heard soft footsteps enter my room. I peeked out the crack in my door and saw Dad's legs.

This kid was what? My half-brother? *Brother* was such a foreign word, a word associated with other girls, like Olive and Rachel, but certainly not with me.

"I didn't think I'd ever meet him," Dad said, from the other side of my door. I could see he was still wearing his shiny leather work shoes. "His mother moved away just after he was born. She wanted a relationship, and I, obviously, didn't."

Dad was speaking quietly, like he was talking to himself, and that was fine with me because I didn't want to hear it. I didn't want to hear it! *Lalalalalala.* I wanted to cover my ears, but instead

I positioned my mouth by the crack in the door. There were things I needed to understand.

"How do you *know* he's your son?" I asked. That would get him. This was all a mistake, never mind the fact that the kid looked an awful lot like my dad, okay? That was just a coincidence. Everybody has a secret twin somewhere, sometimes more than one, who's not even related to them. I'd seen a YouTube video about it.

"We did a DNA test, when he was a baby," Dad said.

I nudged the door open a bit more with my foot. I knew about DNA. We'd actually extracted some from a strawberry in science class last year, but it was weird to think of the same stuff inside me, and Dad . . . and that boy.

I could see all of Dad now, but it was shadowy in my room. There was no more halo behind his head like there had been from the kitchen light when I'd come home. Dad ran a hand over his face like he was trying to sculpt a new, less tired and helpless expression. It didn't work.

"Oh, Mags," he said, "so much has happened today." He started pacing across my small room, three steps one way, then turn around, then back.

"His name is Anthony, but he goes by Tony. He showed up at his school, Bircher, and he was hungry and not looking so good, so Children's Services went out to his apartment and found his mom, who was not doing well at all, and his mom gave them my name, which for the life of me, I can't under-stand, since I didn't think she wanted me to have anything to do with him. But I guess she was out of options. Then the social worker had to check out everything over here."

It was like listening to Olive. I waited for him to take a breath, like I do with her, but got impatient. I pushed the door open some more, until we could see each other, eye to eye, his eyes brown and mine green. I had my mom's eyes.

"How long is he staying?" I asked.

"I don't know. His mom is going to get some help. She's hop-ing to get him back soon."

"What's wrong with her?" I asked.

"Drugs," Dad said softly.

I picked at a loose piece of carpeting. "Why didn't you tell me?"

"I was going to. I wanted to, earlier, years ago actually, after I saw his mom in a store, and so I knew she'd moved back, and I saw . . . him . . . but, Mags, you were too young to understand."

"And what about Mom?" I said. "What about *your wife*?" How could he act so cool and collected when this whole thing was insane!

If he didn't like my tone, he didn't let on. "Mom and I worked this out a long time ago."

"How old is he?" I murmured.

"Thirteen."

"That's a year older than me! How could you and Mom not have told me all this time!"

Dad got up and moved closer to the hallway. He had his back to me when he said, "To be fair to your mom, she didn't know until a few years ago, until—"

"Second grade."

"Yeah, I guess . . ." Dad's mind was working, like he was trying to count backward. He wouldn't look at me. "Listen, this is hard for me, Mags. This isn't . . . I mean, this isn't an entirely appropriate conversation to have, and—"

"Appropriate? Geez, Dad, it's too late to decide if it's *appropriate*. It just *is*."

I remembered the family meetings we'd had back then. All the talk of openness, the encouragement to ask them anything. How our family was like a three-legged stool, and we needed all of us in sync to keep it balanced. All I knew was they were having problems and thinking about a divorce. I didn't know there was another woman in the picture. I didn't know there was a kid!

"Your mom forgave me, you know," Dad said, now looking straight at me.

What was he expecting me to say? I wasn't going to tell him I forgave him. I wasn't that easy.

"Well," he said, "maybe we should just call it a night." He sighed. "Want this open or closed?" He pointed to my closet door while I sank deeper into my nest of stuffed animals. I didn't answer.

"Try and be compassionate," he said, "to Tony. He's been through a lot. You have no idea."

He started walking out but turned back around. "I love you, Mags," he said.

I still didn't answer.

- • - ✦ - • -

Eventually, the sun started to dip behind our neighbor's chimney. My stomach was growling like crazy, but how could my stomach think about food at a time like this? Stomachs were so stupid. Everything was stupid. Still, I could smell the garlic bread, and it was making me drool. Maybe I could just tiptoe down and grab a plate, bring it back to my room.

I went downstairs, walked down the hall, peeked into the dining room. Mom and Dad were sitting in their usual spots at either end of our rectangular wooden table. And there he was. Thankfully, Tony wasn't in my chair, but the one opposite, the one in front of the large window. Outside was the pear tree with the bird feeder I'd given Dad last Christmas. Tony's back was to the window. I wondered if my parents were playing the "One Big Thing" game with him, though it was pretty obvious what big thing happened to all of us today.

My seat, on the other side of the table, always had a clear view of the outdoors so that, during dinner, I could see if any birds came by to eat their own meals. I'd learned to identify the usual suspects, the cardinals and titmice and chickadees, house sparrows, robins, the occasional nuthatch. But now, if I went in and sat down, Tony's big head would be blocking my view.

Meanwhile, Tony's view was of a large mirror on the wall that my mom and I had hung over the summer after we'd painted the room a pale yellow. The mirror brought the outdoors in, made the small room look bigger, but that was an illusion, of course, a decorating trick. So, not only would Tony be blocking my view of the birds, but he got his own view of them, reflected in the mirror. It wasn't fair, none of it. Oh, how I wished Tony himself was an illusion, just a trick of the light.

Tony saw me and stopped eating, his fork hanging in midair. Mom turned around and said, "Maggie, honey, why don't you come in and eat with us?"

"I'm not very hungry," I lied. "I'll get something later," I blurted and ran back up to my room.

I went to my desk and grabbed my shell, hidden behind a trio of accessories. The shell was small, barely two inches long and spiral-shaped. I ran my index finger down its side, feeling the bumpy ridges. I'd done this so much that the ridges were starting to smooth out and flatten.

No one knew about my shell, not even my dad, even though he was the one who'd found it on our trip to Florida when I was eight.

We had so much fun on that trip, my parents laughing with each other, and with me, in the waves, and I felt like everything was perfect, whereas just months before that, it had all seemed like it was falling apart. Dad had spotted the shell on the beach and pointed it out to me. He'd brushed off the sand and held it up in the sunlight, where it glowed a ghostly white. I told him it looked like a unicorn horn, and he said, yes, it had once belonged to the tiniest unicorn in the world.

Then he told me about narwhals, which were real, not like unicorns. A narwhal is like a unicorn of the sea. I liked that I thought it was cool to think about this totally weird animal out there in the ocean, living its life, doing its narwhal-like things with hardly anyone ever seeing it. It seemed impossible.

My mom wasn't a fan of my bringing home a bunch of shells, which she said would just get broken in the suitcase and leak sand everywhere, so I only kept this one, carrying it home in the pocket of my shorts, then tucking it behind the items on my desk, where it had been ever since.

I didn't think the shell had any magical powers, at least not like the kind that came from a genie's lamp, but I couldn't deny that when I skipped over its ridges with my thumb, I felt like everything was going to be all right, and that was its own kind of magic. I rubbed it one last time before putting it back. At some point, I fell asleep and dreamed of flying pigs.

Breakfast of Champions

I woke up in the middle of the night, 2:35 a.m., to be exact. I'd slept in my clothes. One of my legs was bent at an odd angle, and when I stretched, it felt like I was being poked by a million little pins.

I let my eyes adjust to the dark, then stepped into the hallway, where the little plastic nightlight cast its orange glow on the wall. I peeked into my parents' room. They were both asleep, and close to each other, Dad's arm thrown over Mom's shoulders. I paused a minute to look at them. It was nice seeing them so cuddly, even if they weren't actually aware of what they were doing.

In the spare bedroom, Tony was asleep on his stomach, wearing a blue plaid pajama top that looked like Dad's old one. Wrapped around the back of his neck was Mittens.

"*Psst*," I whispered. "*Psst*, Mittens, you *traitor*."

Had Mittens just climbed up there on her own? Or had Tony

put her around his neck like I did? How would he even know to do that? As I was standing there, wondering if I should grab Mittens or not, I remembered everything Dad had told me yesterday. I remembered the DNA test and realized that if Tony was my father's son, then he and I of course were bound to share some of the same traits. I just didn't want to think about that. And it's not like wearing a cat around your neck was some kind of inherited trait, like curly hair or brown eyes.

Tony stirred, and I quickly backed away from the room. I went down to the kitchen to pour myself a huge bowl of cereal, making up for the dinner I'd missed. From behind me came Mittens's "*Meowllll.*" She leapt up onto the counter.

A few minutes later, I heard footsteps, and then Tony appeared in the doorway, rubbing his eyes. Those were definitely my dad's old pajamas, buttoned wrong, just like my dad did sometimes. That wasn't an inherited trait, was it? Although it was fairly dark in the kitchen, there was the glow of the clock on the stove, and the streetlights outside. It was enough light for me to notice that Tony's nose, the dimple in his chin, his hair . . . they all belonged to my dad. Unmistakably.

I focused intently on my cereal. What do you say to a half-brother you didn't know you had until a few hours ago, when you meet in the dark kitchen at 3 a.m. while eating your Lucky Charms?

Tony broke the silence. "Hey," he said, in a voice that was softer than I expected.

"Hey," I answered.

He blinked a few times. Then he reached out to pet Mittens, who was trying to figure out a way to score some milk from my bowl.

"Your cat's pretty cool," he said. His voice, too, was like my dad's, only higher and softer. "I always wanted a cat, but my mom wouldn't get one."

"Why not?" I asked. "Is she allergic?"

"No. It's just that a cat's one more thing to take care of, you know?"

I nodded. My mom had said the same thing when we were deciding whether or not to take Mittens to the shelter or keep her after we found her eating out of that trash can. I wondered what Tony's mom was like, what she looked like, whether she let Tony stay up late watching R-rated movies. I wondered what it would be like to have a mom who was sick in that kind of way. The sickest my mom ever got was when she had the flu for a week.

The sound of my chewing echoed in my head. It sounded like I was munching on rocks instead of marshmallow moons.

"Can I have some of that? I'm still pretty hungry," Tony said.

"Oh, yeah, sure," I said. I guessed I should have offered, but you couldn't expect much from a person at three in the morning.

He looked around.

"Oh, the bowls are in there." I pointed to a cabinet. "Spoons are in the drawer by the stove."

"Thanks," Tony said.

He poured his cereal and milk, walked around the counter to where the stools were. There were three, of course, because there were three of us in this house, and four would have looked wrong, and wouldn't have fit anyway. I'd picked them out myself when Mom said the kitchen was looking "tired." They were steel, with a bright yellow enamel finish. Everyone loved them. Tony sat on the end, leaving an empty stool between us.

He ate with his head nearly touching his bowl, his spoon flying, drops of milk landing on the counter. I remembered Dad saying he had showed up to school hungry and not looking great.

Bircher Middle School, he'd said, which was on the other side of town. It was a bigger school than Long Branch, named after some dead guy whose farm used to stand in the spot where the school was built. But the name always made me think of the tree, of a birch, and that made our schools seem somehow connected—Bircher and Long Branch—though in reality, the schools weren't connected at all. I wasn't sure I knew anyone who went to Bircher, until now.

Tony was slurping his milk, stained pink from the artificially colored marshmallows. It was kind of gross, so I looked away. It was so weird to know I'd had a half-brother living on the other side of town this whole time. Could we have seen each other, and not even realized it? Been in line for popcorn next to each other at the theater? Waited for the diving board at the city pool?

He poured another bowl of Lucky Charms. Little did he know, this was a special treat. My mom usually bought Cheerios and Wheaties, which she called "The Breakfast of Champions," and other stuff with hardly any sugar. But once in a while, she caved. Tony would find that out soon enough, maybe. We might get lucky. Maybe while Tony was here, Mom would keep the sugar flowing.

I heard a car driving slowly down our street. It was too early for the newspaper delivery guy. I held my breath while it passed, thinking, hoping, actually, it might turn into our driveway, and someone would hop out to collect Tony, whisking him away into the night before my parents even woke up. But then I looked at Tony gulping his food and felt bad for even thinking it.

Mittens licked my bowl. I could hear her little tongue lapping the milk. It was a comforting sound. Everything was going to be all right, I told myself. This was only temporary. Once Tony's mom got better, he'd be on his way, and maybe we'd see each other for the holidays. I'd give him a nice sweater or a video game.

I played with a strand of my hair. No, that scenario seemed too easy. Nothing was ever that easy. Mittens pawed my spoon aside with a loud clank, which snapped my mind back to the present.

Oh my god! This boy is my brother! I still couldn't believe it.

I stood up quickly, and the metal stool teetered, but I caught it, pushed it carefully, quietly, under the counter.

"I should get back to bed," I said. "I've got a math test tomorrow."

"You mean today."

"What?"

Tony pointed at the clock.

"Oh, yeah, today. Well, then, I *really* should get back to bed."

"Yeah, me too," Tony said, but he didn't get up. Mittens had crawled into his lap, full of milk and loudly purring, and was doing the thing where she walks in a circle until she finds the perfect position to settle into.

She rubbed against Tony's chest, and I resisted my strong urge to snatch her away. Then Tony suddenly turned to me, and said, "By the way, I'm Tony."

He stuck out his hand.

I looked at it for a moment. Kids didn't exactly go around shaking hands very often in middle school, even seventh graders like Tony. What do you do when a half-brother you didn't know you had until a few hours ago offers his hand in a dark kitchen at 3:20 a.m. after you both ate two bowls of Lucky Charms?

I reached out and shook it.

- • - ✦ - • -

In the morning, my mom was in the kitchen making scrambled eggs like it was any normal day, instead of the day after our world had turned completely upside down.

"You must be starving," she said. "I'm making you a big breakfast."

Dad was nowhere to be seen. Tony was asleep and snoring; I'd heard him when I walked down the hall, even though his door was closed. No one in the family snored. Guess that was another thing I'd have to get used to temporarily.

I put my backpack by the door and sat on a stool. "I had some cereal in the middle of the night," I said. "I guess you didn't hear me get up."

"No, I didn't. I was so exhausted last night, I wouldn't have heard anything."

She put my eggs on a plate and started buttering my toast.

"Mom, I can do that," I said. Did she think I was a baby?

She came and sat next to me while I ate, watching me with that look adults get when they want to make sure a kid is okay, that the kid isn't about to break into a million pieces, but what parents don't realize is that the look, *the look itself*, can make a kid feel like breaking into a million pieces.

I couldn't help it; I started to cry. Then I started to choke because I had eggs in my mouth.

"Oh, honey," my mom said, pushing a glass of milk toward me. "Honey, I cannot imagine what you're feeling right now, how hard this is for you."

I drank the whole glass of milk. I thought about when I first saw Tony outside our house yesterday after school. Was it just yesterday? It seemed that time had both sped forward a hundred years and stopped entirely. My mom said she couldn't imagine how I was feeling. Was it so hard? *Confused, scared, angry*—just for starters.

"Can we talk about this?"

I picked some more at my eggs.

"Maggie, you can't keep this all bottled up. We talk about things in this family. You know that."

It was really hard not to laugh. "Where's Dad?" I asked.

"He went into work. He wants to see if he can get a few days off, use some personal time, or at least get some flex hours or something."

"Well, don't you think Dad should be part of our family talk?" I asked, feeling some sarcasm creep into my voice.

I imagined Dad trying to explain this to his boss. What was he going to say? For that matter, what was I going to say to

Rachel and Olive? They'd seen *him*, after all. They'd ask about the mysterious boy from yesterday. Should I lie? But how long could I keep that up?

"It's all very complicated," Mom said, almost as if she could read my mind.

A thin tendril of smoke curled up by the cabinets.

"Mom, the toast is burning," I said calmly. At that point, I didn't care if the whole house burned down.

"Oh my goodness." Mom jumped up, and in the commotion, I stuffed down my last bites of egg, threw on my backpack, and headed for the door.

"I don't want to be late," I said, though I was actually a few minutes early. I just had to get out of there, away from Mom's worried looks.

"Okay, Maggie, but I thought, if you wanted to stay home, I could call the school? Given all that's happened in the last day, I think it's perfectly justifiable."

"What's *he* doing today?" I nodded toward the stairs. Seemed like he should be part of any family discussions as well. And what about Grandma? What was she going to say about all of this? We might want to call her in. At least I knew she'd always take my side.

"Tony? He's staying home," Mom said. "On Monday, you two can go to school together. Today, he needs to catch up on some sleep. You have no idea what he's been through."

Well, maybe I didn't, but I really didn't need to keep being reminded of my ignorance. "I've got a math test," I said. "I need to go." I wasn't about to stay home all day and sit on the couch with Tony, sharing our feelings while my mom supervised, like we were on some weirdo playdate.

As I shut the door behind me, I heard Mom say, "Okay, then, have a good day!" But her sunshiny attitude sounded really fake.

-•- ✦ -•-

I walked down the sidewalk. Thankfully, my tears had dried. Did Mom say we'd go to school *together*? I kicked a pebble across the street where the neighbor's poodle was out front doing its business, squatting right there and pooping like it couldn't care less whether anyone was watching. Too bad I couldn't be so nonchalant about what people thought.

I hadn't even considered that Tony would be coming to *my* school, though I was surprised that I was already thinking of it as "mine" when I hadn't even been there long. It was hard enough moving up to the middle school without all this mess. Now I'd be the kid with the mystery brother whose mom was on drugs. Or the kid whose dad had cheated on her mom . . . I shoved the thought away. Of course, it was a new school for Tony, too. I was sure he'd much rather be back at Bircher with his friends.

When I arrived at to the bus stop, Olive was already there, waving at me. Rachel was still strolling up her street with a stack of books in her arms. Last week she'd decided that backpacks were kind of uncool. She waved at me, too, and soon, we were all standing there together in our usual spots waiting for the bus to turn the corner. The Santmyer brothers were a few feet away, wrestling with each other like they did every morning.

"Get off me!" Jared yelled.

Josh laughed and pinned his brother against the grass. Then Jared started laughing, too, and flipped Josh over and sat on his back, Josh's whole body flattened like roadkill.

As I watched the Josh and Jared show, the only thing going through my head was *Guess what? I have a brother, too.* That wasn't something I could just announce at the bus stop, but I had to tell my BFFs! They had to know.

Olive was scratching at something on her ankle. Rachel tapped her foot, craning her neck to look down the street for the bus. That was when I noticed her new boots. They were black suede, and I'd never seen them before. Rachel did buy a bunch of clothes before school started, but she'd shown me all of them.

"When did you get those boots?" I asked.

"Last night," Rachel said, shrugging.

"Ooooh, pretty!" Olive said, leaning down to get a closer look. "Where did you get them?"

"The Shoe Depot."

"Were they expensive?" Olive asked. "They look expensive." She was still bent over, and now she brushed her hand over Rachel's toe.

"Are they real suede? Because my mom said there's no way she'd buy me real suede because if it gets wet even once it's totally ruined and she's not going to go around buying me more than one pair of boots every year and in any case, I need boots that are warm." Olive stood up. "Are these warm?"

"I don't know," Rachel said. "I guess not. Not really."

"I thought you had to work with Katelyn on your group project last night," I said. Who cared what the boots were made of or what they cost?

I watched as Rachel's neck broke out in red splotches. The same thing happened whenever she had to stand up and give a presentation in class, or when she had to do a pull-up in gym while everyone watched. Rachel could not hide when she was embarrassed. Normally, I felt sorry for her because of that, but not today. Today I was mostly feeling sorry for myself.

"Oh, we got done early," she said and turned away.

Olive looked at me and shrugged. I could feel that little burning spot in my chest. Sometimes, it felt like there was a match inside me just sitting there totally innocent, until some kind of meanness scratched against it, lighting it. And then it burned.

We got on the bus and went to our assigned seats, Olive with me, Rachel four rows up with a girl named Kendra. The bus was mostly full. We were the last stop before school.

"That wasn't very nice of Rakell," Olive whispered.

I shook my head. "No big deal," I said. "Don't worry about it."

I glanced over at Olive, whose lip was quivering like she was going to cry. Going to *cry*—on my behalf! It certainly wasn't worth crying over, but it was still sweet of her.

Suddenly, I wanted to tell her about Tony. She was a loyal friend. She should be the first to know. "So, hey," I said casually, "do you remember that boy from yesterday?"

"The boy with the basketball? Of course. What was he doing at your house? Who is he?"

"Well, you are not going to believe this," I said. I kept my voice low. Then I slunk down in the seat and scooched closer to Olive, not that anyone else on the bus was even listening.

"He's my brother."

"What?" Olive shouted, and now a couple kids looked over.

"Shhh," I said. I looked up to where Rachel was sitting. She hadn't bothered to turn around, though she must have heard Olive shout. "Don't tell anybody about it, okay? Though I don't know how I'm going to keep it a secret . . . because he's starting school at Long Branch next week. Seventh grade."

"Wait a minute, wait a minute, wait a minute." Olive was flailing her hands around. "Back up. What are you saying? What are you *even* saying?"

I took a deep breath and repeated all I knew, everything, which admittedly wasn't much. "My dad had a kid with some other woman, before I was born, and she didn't want my dad to have anything to do with this kid, but now she's on drugs or something and couldn't take care of him, so he's supposed to live with us, temporarily."

"*Who's* on drugs?" Olive was so wide-eyed and pale, I thought she might faint.

"The kid's mom, I guess."

"Is he nice?"

"Who?"

"The kid," Olive said impatiently. "What's his name?"

"Anthony. Tony. I mean, geez Olive, don't get all cranky with me. I don't know if he's nice because I've barely spoken to him for more than five minutes, but he's in my house sleeping in the spare bedroom right as we speak and he snores and . . . and he stole Mittens!"

"He stole Mittens?" Olive exclaimed, drawing looks again from some kids.

"Well, not really stole, it's just, Mittens was sitting on his lap and sleeping on his bed."

"Oh, thank goodness." She put her hand to her heart. Then she stared out the bus window for a minute, though there was nothing much to see. Beauty parlor, coffee shop, dry cleaner, coffee shop. Everything was clean and neat. It looked pretty nice, our downtown. There were always potted flowers or, in the winter, holiday lights, hanging from the lampposts on the main streets. But the boring stuff was the same boring stuff as everywhere. If you've seen one Dunkin' Donuts, you've seen them all.

Olive looked back at me suddenly, then slapped her hands on her thighs as though she'd just had some great insight.

"Well, this is just about the most amazing thing I have personally ever heard," she said. "To think, you had a brother out there all this time, and now, now you're reunited! It truly is the most amazing thing. Here you are, this whole family, and Tony, just coming out of nowhere in the middle of the night to be with you, just tiptoeing into your life, to make it complete."

I noticed Olive's lip quivering again. She cried when she was happy, or sad. She cried a lot. Her reaction made me wonder whether I was looking at this situation the wrong way, but that thought only lasted a second.

"Tony didn't 'come out of nowhere in the middle of the night,'" I said. "He came in the daytime, remember? And he didn't 'tiptoe into my life.' He crashed around like an annoying boy with a basketball."

I stole a glance at Olive. Her face had hardened. She didn't say anything else. Olive always acted like everything was *fantabulous*, when it often wasn't. The bus pulled up to the school, its brakes squealing, like it didn't want to be there any more than I did.

Most School Spirit

What was 6-⁶⁄₁₀ times ⁸⁄₁₂? I clutched my pencil tightly and stared at the empty line, which was waiting for my answer. I couldn't remember how to do it. I hated fractions! I was okay in math in general, but why did we have to start with fractions? I kept waiting for it to click, but so far, no such luck. My dad always said when you learned a new concept, not just in math, but anything, that it had to bump around in your brain for a while, and then everything would just *click*, like a puzzle coming together, or a light bulb flicking on, or fingers snapping.

"Wow, Dad, too many similes," I had said to him. We'd been studying figurative language in English at the time, which I had no trouble understanding.

Part of my problem with the test was that I was obviously distracted, thinking about Tony hanging out in my house with Mom, and maybe Dad, too, if he'd gotten some time off work. Talk about a new concept bumping around in my brain. *Instant brother.*

Somehow, I'd kept the news to myself all day, only telling Olive. The next time I saw her was at lunch, when we met up at our usual table that we shared with Rachel and a few other kids from our language arts section. Today, though, Katelyn was there. She was at the end of the table, with her legs crossed and sticking into the aisle, so I could see her boots. Black suede, just like Rachel's.

They were laughing as Olive and I walked up, and for a minute, I got that burning feeling in my chest because I was worried they were laughing about me. But Rachel smiled and patted the spot on the bench next to her.

"How'd you do on the math test?" Olive asked everybody.

"My group didn't have a test today," Katelyn said through her perfectly glossed lips. She was "gifted" in math, and didn't like anyone to forget it.

"I think I bombed it," Rachel said. "I couldn't remember how to multiply fractions when there's a whole number."

"Me neither!" I exclaimed, grateful for one little thing Rachel and I could share.

"Oh, that's easy," Katelyn said, waving her hand. "You just convert the mixed number into an improper fraction, then you, you know, just do the rest."

Rachel and I both looked at her with confused faces.

"I'll show you later, Rakell," Katelyn said. I noticed she had turned her body as far away from me as possible. Turn an inch more and she'd fall right into the aisle.

"Oh, who cares," Rachel said. "I'm probably not going to need much math for the rest of my life! Why get upset about it?"

I stopped chewing my PB&J and glanced at her, remembering when she and I were younger and she wanted to be an astronaut, and I was in a veterinarian phase. Then she got interested in interior design with me. You needed math for design, a little at least, to figure out placement of things and stuff like that. And you sure as heck needed math to be an astronaut. Everybody knew that. But lately, Rachel didn't seem interested in much besides which boys in our class were cute.

"Well, all the kids I've talked to thought the test was really hard," Olive said, "and I studied for it. You did, too, Maggie, right?"

I was about to answer when Rachel said, "How could she study, with all that *chaos* at her place?" She turned her body so she faced me. Katelyn leaned in, grinning.

"What are you talking about?" I asked. I felt my face getting hot, like I was breaking out in hives, even though that was Rachel's thing, not mine.

At the table behind us, a couple boys were arguing, one loudly calling the other a dillweed, which was the new insult of the week. Last week, boys would start yelling "Yeet!" for no reason. First a boy on one side of the room would yell it, then someone on the other side ("Yeet! Yeet! Yeet!"), so the lunchroom supervisor never knew for sure who was doing it. Today we had the mean lunchroom lady, who, unfortunately, had been at my elementary school. Guess she got transferred here, so she could have a chance to terrorize some middle school kids as well.

She went walking quickly toward the corner where the shouting came from, her sandals slapping the linoleum floor. She always wore sandals and socks, even in the winter.

"I've had just about enough out of you boys!" she yelled. "How would you like to eat lunch with Mr. Villanueva?"

I watched her closely, rather than look at Rachel, whose eyes were burning a hole into the side of my skull. I could feel it.

"Were you not even going to tell me you have a brother?" she asked, drawing out every word. "After we've been friends for, like, forever?"

"Aren't you supposed to be the BFFs?" Katelyn said, snotty-like. "That's what you guys call your little club, right?"

I ignored Katelyn and shot a look at Olive, who had bent her head so low over her lunch tray that her bangs were nearly dipping into her applesauce. I'd deal with her later.

The lunchroom was getting noisier, while our table was this little island of quiet. I took a deep breath and turned toward Rachel. "I only just found out last night," I murmured. "Of course I was going to tell you—*privately*," I said, with a glance at Katelyn, who was stirring her pudding, which obviously didn't need stirring.

But when would that be? I thought. We were hardly ever alone anymore. We used to be alone a lot, before Olive moved to our neighborhood, not that I regretted having Olive around. I loved Olive, and Rachel. Friend threesomes were great, most of the time, though if you ever wanted to have a private conversation with one of the threesome, the other was bound to feel left out. Now I had a feeling that maybe Olive and Rachel had been having some private conversations of their own.

I said, "It's not exactly the kind of thing I can blurt out, like, 'Oh hey, I've got a brother I never knew!' I mean, it's crazy! I haven't even had twenty-four hours to get used to it myself."

"Rakell says he's super cute," Katelyn added, and I couldn't help rolling my eyes. Tony looked like my dad, so I couldn't think of him as cute. Was my dad cute? Who knows?

"We were having a private conversation," I shot back. Stupid Katelyn with her stupid lip gloss.

"Whatever you say to me, you can say to Katelyn," Rachel said. "We're all friends here."

I laughed. *Yeah, right.* "Fine," I said, "if we're friends, then maybe you could be there for me, instead of talking about the *chaos* in my house."

I was raising my voice. I had to. It had gotten so loud in the lunchroom, and kids were out of their seats. No one was supposed to get out of their seats unless they raised their hands and got permission. "We can't all have your perfect family, Rachel," I added, thinking of her Barbie-and-Ken parents.

Now it was Katelyn's turn to laugh. Rachel didn't say anything, but she turned her body toward the front of the room and started picking at the bun on her chicken patty. She looked more sad than mad.

Meanwhile, Olive put her hand on my arm and quietly shook her head at me.

"What?" I said to Olive, pulling my arm away.

"Don't," she whispered to me, but was looking at Rachel.

At that moment, the lunch lady yelled "QUIET LUNCH!" which was a rule Mr. Villanueva had come up with.

He was the school's new principal, and he had a lot of rules, which was fine by me. As I kept telling Olive and Rachel at our BFF meetings, without rules, things fall apart—in design, and everything, really. Anyway, when the lunchroom supervisors thought the noise level had gotten out of control, they'd declare Quiet Lunch, and we all had to eat in complete silence like we were in church or prison or something.

We all looked down at our plates. I was thankful for an excuse not to talk to anyone. I just wanted this day to be over. But then what? I'd go back home, which I didn't want either.

During quiet lunch, every little noise was amplified—the squeak of a plastic knife across Styrofoam, a cough, the dozen little snorts of people trying to stifle their laughter. The lunchroom supervisor looked this way and that, trying to figure out who was making each noise, but she couldn't keep up. It was like a game of whack-a-mole, which reminded me of a birthday party Rachel had a couple years ago at this indoor fun park place with ball pits and arcade games and roller skating. When I asked her last month if she was going to have a party there this year, she said birthday parties were "for babies."

Nothing on my lunch tray tasted good, not even the chocolate chip cookie I'd been so excited about. (They only served them one day a week.) Olive was nibbling at some fries. When had she even had the chance to tell Rachel? And why would she do it? I could hear Rachel taking deep breaths next to me, like she was either annoyed or trying to meditate or something. We used to do these "mindfulness breaks" at Jefferson Elementary where everyone was supposed to close their eyes and take deep breaths, but almost nobody actually did it, except the teachers.

Finally, the bell rang, and a big whoop went up as everyone scattered. I headed to science, Olive close behind.

"I didn't tell her," Olive said, tapping me on the shoulder. "I swear I didn't."

I spun around. "Who did then?"

Olive had a very guilty look on her face. "I didn't tell Rakell," she said quietly, "but . . ."

"*Olive.*"

"Well, I told Neesha in band because she sits next to me and I had to tell somebody or I was going to burst and you know Neesha is so quiet, she never says anything to anybody!"

"Olive!"

"I'm sorry, Maggie, I really am, but I mean, you can't keep it a secret for long anyway, right? You said yourself he was starting here on Monday."

Monday. Maybe I could slow down time somehow, just stay in this day forever.

-•- ✦ -•-

But I couldn't. Eighth period came, right on schedule, and all the sixth graders had to file into the gym. It was another of Mr. Villanueva's assemblies. He'd had an all-school assembly the first day, during which he told us he had a real soft spot for the sixth graders because we were new to the school, just like him. He said his name meant "new house" in Spanish.

I hadn't taken Spanish yet, but my grandma knew some. She took a class with Grandpa before their trip to Spain a few years ago. She'd even checked out some interior design magazines in Spanish, and we'd looked at them together. I learned words like coche postal (chaise), hueco (alcove), and estante (shelf). I tried to use some of the words with Grandma occasionally, but ever since Grandpa died, it just seemed to make her sad, so I stopped.

That first assembly was all about welcoming everybody, and some rah-rah-we're-going-to-have-a-great-year stuff, and then Mr. V went through a bunch of rules. Like I said, he loved those. But I had no idea what today's assembly was about.

We had to sit with our eighth period class, no running around the bleachers to find our friends. I sat next to a girl named Claire, who was pretty nice but always doodling pictures of horses in her notebook, so when she was called on, she never knew what the question was. Olive was a half dozen rows below me, and as soon as she was seated, she turned around and waved with a look that said *you forgive me, right?* I waved back with a look that said *yes.*

It was hard to stay mad at Olive, and in any case, she was right about Tony. He would be here soon, and I'd have to deal with it. I couldn't keep it a secret. I was learning that information traveled fast at Long Branch. Just an hour ago, someone told me a kid had spilled milk in the cafeteria and another kid slipped in it and busted his lip. I didn't need to know any of that, and yet here I was, knowing it. If news of a milk spill could spread that fast, imagine what these kids would do with information on Tony.

A few rows farther down and to the right, I could see Rachel. That messy bun on the top of her head was unmistakable. She'd once admitted it took her a long time to get just the right amount of messiness. I didn't understand why she'd take a half hour to make herself look like she'd just woken up.

Mr. Villanueva was standing in the middle of the floor with a microphone. He wore a dark suit every day, but switched out the ties. Today's was blue, with some little animal or something on it; I wasn't close enough to see it clearly. He raised his hand in the air, which was the signal for everybody to listen up.

All the kids quieted down pretty quickly, and Mr. V said, "I'd like to introduce our guests." He pointed toward a side door where a dog and a cop entered the gym. "For those of you new to Long Branch, this is an assembly we do every year, with a few changes each time. Maybe our older students think they don't need to hear it again, but let me tell you, you can always pick up something new." He cleared his throat. "Now, Police Officer Lutsky had an emergency at the last minute, so he couldn't be with us, but Officer Bell was kind enough to step in, along with his special friend, Daisy."

Daisy was a huge German shepherd who looked kind of cute, but scary at the same time. I liked dogs, but I wasn't insane about them, like a bunch of other girls who started going *awww* when the dog walked in. The officer made a series of motions with his hand, and Daisy sat, then lay down, then rolled over, but I noticed she was barely watching the officer. She was more interested in all of us kids in the bleachers, almost like she was trying to size up which kid would be tastiest.

Officer Bell said he was there to talk about drugs and how terrible they are. I wondered if there were kids in my school doing drugs. I mean, no one had ever offered me drugs, but that didn't mean anything. Maybe that's why they did this presentation in middle school. Catch us before that stuff starts. I couldn't help but think about Tony. Had he ever done them?

I felt my face getting kind of hot. I shifted in my spot on the hard wooden bleacher and looked at Claire, who was picking at her fingernail polish. I hated how things were sneaking up on me all of a sudden.

The officer told us Daisy "hated drugs." On cue, Daisy growled. A few kids in the front row leaned back into the legs of the kids behind them. I was glad to be a few rows up. The cop said the only way to never get addicted to drugs was to never start using them in the first place. Daisy stood on her hind legs and barked, like she was warning us.

The officer said you had to be "vicious" with people who offered you drugs, and Daisy growled even louder. I started feeling really nervous and sweaty, wondering how quickly I could make it to the hallway if Daisy started going psycho. How fast could German shepherds run? Meanwhile, down below, a boy had taken Rachel's scarf and was playing keep-away with it, and Rachel was laughing and not even trying to get it back.

"You need to just say no if someone offers you drugs." Officer Bell wanted us to yell it, so some kids did, but then he did that stupid thing grown-ups do where they pretend they "can't hear you," and he cupped his hand around his ear and made everybody yell louder. Some boys were really getting into it, standing up and screaming, "Noooooo!" while their faces got completely red, and their heads looked like they were going to explode. Honestly, it was embarrassing. I was glad Tony wasn't here to see all this. If it was as easy as saying no, his mom wouldn't be in the mess she's in. I mean, sorry Daisy, but I'm not buying it.

Next, the officer held up a cloth doll that had a piece of cardboard attached to it that read "DRUGS." He threw the doll to the other side of the gym. Then he let go of Daisy's leash, and she was a blur, on top of the thing in two seconds. She shook it until the stuffing was flying out. It was kind of horrifying to watch, but no one could look away. When she got tired of shaking it, Daisy went to a corner by a bunch of soccer nets and chewed the doll more daintily. Pretty soon, she had an arm torn off.

The officer stepped back up to the mic. "You might think you kids are too young to hear this talk, but statistics show that one in six sixth graders, *that's sixth graders, people,* has used a drug. That includes alcohol, kids, which is a drug, and don't let anyone tell you differently."

Some kids laughed and looked around at each other like they were trying to figure out who was that one in six. The cop asked if anyone had questions, and the school librarian, Mrs. Lloyd, came up to the bleachers holding a microphone in her right hand. With her left hand, she clutched at her knee with each step she took up the rickety wooden stairs. She gave the microphone to a boy on the other end of the gym whose hand was raised.

"Can you get addicted to markers? Smelling them, I mean?" he asked. A bunch of kids laughed, but he looked around with an expression that said, *What? I'm serious.*

Officer Bell held up his hand until everyone quieted down and said, "That's a real question kids, don't laugh. You can get a high from smelling things, like glue or markers or paints. It's called huffing, and—"

Mr. Villanueva took a few steps toward the center of the gym. His arms were crossed, and he didn't look especially happy with the substitute cop speaker. Daisy was still chewing in the corner. She had both arms off the doll now, and was working on a leg.

"Well, anyway," Officer Bell said, "just don't do that."

A girl in a green sweater raised her hand, and Mrs. Lloyd went over to give her the mic. I forgot her name, but she was in my social studies class and was one of those kids who raised their hands to talk just because they wanted to hear their own voice.

She said, "My mom showed me an old commercial on

YouTube about your brain being like a fried egg if you used drugs."

"Yeah, I remember that," the cop said. "Well, now, you kids don't want to fry your brains, do you?"

"I don't," the girl said and sat back down, smiling.

Mr. Villanueva came farther out and held up his index finger. Officer Bell looked at him and nodded. "Okay, one more question, kids."

A boy near Rachel raised his hand, and when Mrs. Lloyd gave him the mic, he wouldn't stand up until the cop said, "Stand up, son, so I can hear you better." The boy slowly stood, but looked down, his hair covering his eyes.

"What do you do if you see somebody who has, like, ODed or something?"

"That's a very good question. Well, the first thing to do in an overdose situation is to call nine-one-one. Can all of you say that?"

"Nine-one-one," a few kids mumbled, but everyone had really lost their energy at that point. Plus, the cop was treating us like babies. We'd known 911 since preschool.

The cop kept talking. "Once the police or ambulance gets there, we can use this spray. It's pretty amazing, actually. It's called Narcan, and it's this stuff that can totally revive a person who's overdosed. We just spray it into their nostrils. . . ." It sounded like the allergy stuff my mom squirted into her nose every morning.

"*Ewww*," some kids said. Probably the same kids who'd said, "*Awww*" when the dog came out. Did they know any actual words? I was suddenly so cranky and hot and hungry, and I wanted to go home, even if Tony was there. I didn't want to think about drugs or talk about drugs or watch a drug-sniffing dog tear a doll apart.

Claire leaned over and said to me, "My cousin works at the McDonald's on Broad Street, and she said someone overdosed right in the bathroom, and the cops used that stuff, and it was like the person just came back to life, like they came back from the dead or something."

I didn't say anything. This was just more information I didn't want or need. But it was crazy to think about. That McDonald's was only a few blocks from my house. I went there with my parents in the summer to get Oreo McFlurries. Had Tony's mom ever overdosed? What if Tony had seen it? My parents kept saying I had no idea what he'd been through, and of course they were right. And I didn't know if I could ask. How would I even start a conversation like that? It definitely seemed like the kind of thing Tony wouldn't want to talk about.

The cop was still going on about the Narcan stuff. "Everybody's stocking it now, gotta be prepared."

Mr. Villanueva quickly took the microphone. "Uh, thank you, Officer Bell," he said. "Everyone, let's thank the officer and Daisy."

While we all clapped, Daisy hopped up and followed Officer

Bell back out the side door. I noticed they'd left the doll, or what was left of it, in the corner. Kids started shifting around, getting ready to leave, but Mr. V held up his hand again.

"I have one more thing to share with you," he said, "something exciting."

Ooh! I just remembered, the decorating contest. He said he'd give us the details at the next assembly and *this was the next assembly!*

He said, "As you probably know, the middle school will have a Spirit Week this fall, the same week as the high school's Homecoming. We won't be having a dance here at the middle school, but we will have a pep rally and bonfire, and our boys will play football against the Rockets, same as the high school boys. The Centerville Rockets are a formidable opponent, and I should know. I used to teach there!"

Mr. V paused for a response from the crowd, but none of us really cared about his résumé. He cleared his throat. "Well, anyway, we'll all need to come together and show some school spirit!"

I knew the Long Branch Wildcats were supposed to be bitter enemies of the Centerville Rockets, but that was all pretty stupid as far as I was concerned, and so were pep rallies. I sang in the choir, and nobody had a pep rally for us. Nobody had a pep rally for Rachel's swim team or for the math club. *Get to the good stuff, Mr. V!*

He talked about Spirit Week theme days, like crazy sock day and school colors day, but he'd really lost his audience, all except me. Some kids had already stood up. Some were shoving each other along the bleachers, which started a wave of shoving that led to the kid on the end being pushed into the aisle. I tried as hard as I could to tune it all out.

Mr. V kept talking. "To get ready for the game, we also thought it would be fun to have a decorating contest, as I mentioned on the morning announcements. We're going to have teams compete to decorate different parts of the school, and you'll be allowed to vote for the winning team, who will get a trophy and a pizza party with their friends, and . . . "

The noise level had grown to a low roar. On the wall, the clock ticked forward, just three minutes until the last bell.

He put his hand up. "MAY I HAVE YOUR ATTEN-TION?" The microphone let out a squeal and a bunch of kids clapped their hands over their ears, but he got the desired effect. Everyone shut up.

"Thank you. Students, this is important. Everyone can be involved. We can have as many entries as we have rooms and hallways. Athletic teams, clubs, music groups, or just groups of friends—"

I felt a little fluttering in my chest. Yes, groups of friends. The BFFs! I went from feeling genuinely terrible, both physically and mentally, to the most excited I'd been in months! Olive turned around and looked up at me, beaming, and I gave her a huge thumbs-up, which she returned, and doubled. I looked over to Rachel, but she was still messing with that boy who had her scarf. Now he was pretending to give it back and then pulling it away at the last second.

Mr. V went on about how we lived in a democracy and it was important that we all recognized our obligation to vote and so on and so on. He was losing the crowd, and fast. Even me. I was already imagining how I could transform the hallways.

"THERE WILL BE PRIZES!" he yelled, drawing everyone's eyes back on him. "If we get one hundred percent voting participation, I will bring in a frozen yogurt truck, and the whole school will get free yogurt, with toppings! And in addition to the trophy and pizza party for the winning team, that team can designate someone to be Principal for a Day!"

Mr. V didn't say anything about the rules for the contest, which was surprising, and made me a little nervous. Rules made things so much easier. Grandma had taught me about design rules early on, about strengthening your foundation, considering your assets, not being afraid to mix textures, and probably most importantly, she taught me that in order to make a room look beautiful, you had to tear it apart first, then build it back up, bit by bit. Grandma always said, "Things are going to get worse before they get better." But I wasn't sure how much tearing apart I'd be allowed to do in the school.

The bell rang, and everyone forgot that we were supposed to exit in an orderly fashion. I tripped over a boy, but caught myself by grabbing onto the elbow of some girl, all of us moving like a clumsy stream of ants toward the doorway. For once in the past twenty-four hours, I wasn't thinking about Tony at all. I was thinking about how this contest could be the biggest break for the BFFs, how we could really make a name for ourselves at this school. My parents would be so excited for me, and Grandma would be so proud, and the BFFs would be right back on track, just like Grandma used to say while she looked at her garden: "Everything's coming up roses."

Before and After

I was still thinking about the decorating contest while I cleaned my room on Saturday, spraying some Lemon Pledge onto a scrap of one of Dad's old T-shirts, wiping it across the top of my bookshelf, then carefully rearranging the items I'd removed to do the dusting. There were three things: a framed photo of me and Olive and Rachel taken at the pool just after school got out last year (before all the Rakell business), my slightly wilted philodendron, and, lastly, my bronze winged pig. I liked it too much to leave it in the prop box.

I needed some space from Tony. He was spreading himself all over the house, either watching TV on the couch, or snacking in the kitchen (he was always snacking), or doing his homework in the dining room. He stayed out of my room, thankfully, because I had a lot of planning to do for the contest, and I didn't want anyone messing with my stuff.

I'd texted the BFFs after the assembly, and Olive had excitedly texted back, but Rachel hadn't yet. Any team that wanted to enter had to draw their location, the area they'd decorate, out of a hat. I hoped we'd get something really visible, like the school's main hallway.

I repositioned the three items on my bookshelf until they were just right. Then I started on my desk, carefully dusting around my shell; it never got dusty since I rubbed it so much.

"What smells in here?" Tony said, scaring the crud out of me. He was standing in my doorway, pinching his nose. "It smells like a grandma."

Okay, scratch that previous thought. Tony *used to* stay out of my room. "It's lemon," I said, and it didn't smell anything like my grandma, who smelled like her rose-scented perfume.

The lemon was covering up the new smell in our house, which I'd noticed right when I walked in the door yesterday. It wasn't bad, just different, like grass or mud. Must be from Tony; our house never had a smell before.

I held up the can. "You can use it when I'm done, if you want. I doubt anyone's dusted the spare bedroom in a long time."

Tony shrugged. "I didn't notice any dust in there," he said.

You wouldn't, I thought, but didn't say it. He was looking around at everything in my room. He was always just silently looking at everything. He had done it at dinner, too, sitting across from me, staring into the mirror behind my head and at the pictures on the walls, but not at any of us. Thankfully, my parents hadn't asked us to say "One Big Thing" that happened that day, which would have been, let's just say, *awkward*. I'd eaten silently, moving my chair closer to Dad so I could see any birds that came to the feeder without Tony's big head in my way.

I moved a stack of library books and swiped the dust rag across my desk. I thought if I kept working, Tony might leave my room, but he didn't. Meanwhile, I could see all the dust particles dancing in a shaft of sunlight from my window, just partying, like all my efforts to eradicate them were worthless.

"Bedroom dust is mostly dead skin cells, you know," I said. If he wasn't going to move, at least I could attempt a conversation. Better that than having him stare at me. "Your skin is shedding old cells all day long, and they just settle all over the furniture."

"Gross," he said.

I repositioned the stuff on my desk. "Well, I'm all done here," I declared. I held out the can and the rag to him, thinking he might want to do some cleaning in his room after all, but he looked away. Still didn't leave, though.

"So . . . speaking of grandmas," I said, "it's my grandma's birthday today. She's seventy-three." Wait. Was she *my* grandma? *Just* mine? Yes, yes, she was. She was my mom's mother, which meant I didn't have to share her with Tony. "We're going to pick her up in a bit and take her to an Italian restaurant that has these never-ending bowls of pasta," I said. *Mmmm,* my idea of heaven—all-you-can-eat pasta and breadsticks.

Oh no, I just realized, we'd had this dinner planned for weeks, but now with Tony here, maybe we'd have to stay home with him instead, or . . . he wouldn't come along, would he? I wasn't sure how I felt about that.

"I have to stay home and talk to my mom," Tony said. "On the phone," he added, because I must have given him a weird look.

"Your mom? Is she calling you from—?"

"From her rehab house, yeah. It's all arranged."

"Oh, okay, well, that's a bummer that you can't come," I said, secretly relieved. I wondered how she was going to call him. I hadn't seen him with a phone, and we didn't have a landline any-more. "Do you have a phone?" I asked.

"No, but she has Bob's . . . I mean, Dad's . . . number."

He said it like the word left a funny taste in his mouth, like he wasn't used to saying *Dad* with a capital *D.* It certainly didn't sound right. In Language Arts, we'd been reviewing when words like *dad* and *mom* and *grandma* needed to be capitalized. It was only when you were referring to a *specific* one. Tony's. Mine. Ours.

"You know, you could try calling him Robert," I suggested. "I mean, you're calling my mom Susan, right? That way it matches."

Tony shrugged, then brought his thumb to his mouth and started chewing on his nail.

"Anyway . . . Dad will be at the restaurant," I said.

"Yeah, no, he said he'd stay home, that you and your mom and grandma can have a girls' night."

A girls' night? We'd been planning this for weeks, the whole family with Grandma. "That wasn't the plan," I said.

Tony shrugged. "The thing is, Dad has to kind of listen in to the call, well, not really *listen*, but he has to be sitting next to me while I talk, so the calls have to be set up ahead of time. We can't rearrange it. She wouldn't like that."

"Who's 'she'?" I asked. "Your mom?"

"No, the social worker."

"Oh, is that who brought you here? The gray-haired lady?"

"Yeah, that was her. She's so annoying." Tony started laughing, like he'd remembered something. "She packed my duffel bag for me. She even packed my underwear!"

He laughed harder, and I couldn't help myself; I did, too.

"You can sit down if you want," I said. I pointed to the beanbag. "It's super comfy."

Tony yelped as he sunk into it. The beanbag was huge and white, and it looked like he was being swallowed by a giant marshmallow.

"Do you have a grandma?" I asked him.

"My mom's mom is still alive," he said, "but they sort of quit talking a while back. I haven't seen her since I was maybe five or something." He looked at me quizzically. "Are Robert's parents . . ."

"Oh, his parents both died. Before I was born," I said. "He has a brother out in California, but we never see him."

Tony brought his hand back to his mouth to chew on his thumbnail. I noticed the skin around it was red and jagged. I felt bad, all of a sudden realizing that I'd just told Tony his half-grandparents were dead. I wished Tony had more living relatives around him, more people looking out for him, though maybe I felt that way because he looked so small and helpless at the moment, being eaten by the beanbag and all.

I was surprised that I was already getting used to Tony being in my room. But I had homework to finish, so I sat down at my desk and opened my science book. I always liked to do homework on Saturdays, sometimes Friday nights, even. Otherwise, I couldn't enjoy my Sundays.

"Maggie!" Mom called up the stairs. "We need to get ready to go to Grandma's."

"Coming!" I yelled to Mom, and then said to Tony, "I guess I better go."

He struggled to get out of the beanbag, so I held out my hand to him.

"Thanks," he said. "Have fun at dinner." He followed me out of my room.

"Yeah, you, too," I said, stupidly. "I mean, have a good talk with your mom."

He gave a little wave, then disappeared into the spare bedroom. I started downstairs, then came back up, closed the door to my room, and went back down again to meet my mom.

In the car, Mom told me Grandma was getting more forgetful, and that she might have to look into an assisted living facility soon, but we weren't going to worry about that tonight. I didn't really know what my mom was talking about.

"Are we going to tell Grandma about Tony?" I asked.

"No!" Mom said quickly. "Not tonight. Okay? Let's just . . . have a nice evening."

-•- ✦ -•-

The restaurant was great. It was just like I remembered from Grandma's last birthday, and I ordered the same thing: never-ending penne pasta with marinara sauce. I ate two bowls

"Don't you want to be a little more adventurous?" Mom asked.

"Nope," I said, smiling with a mouthful of bread.

"She knows what she likes," Grandma said, and winked at me. "That's important."

I did miss Dad being there, though honestly, Grandma always acted a little more formal when Dad was around, so it was actually nice to have her so relaxed. Dad joked that Grandma acted that way because she'd always wanted Mom to marry her first serious boyfriend, but Mom said that wasn't true, so whatever. It wasn't so bad having a girls' night.

I talked a lot about the contest, and Grandma asked me a bunch of questions, like when would I find out which room or hallway we'd have (this week) and how was the voting being done (every student would have a chance to see the rooms and hallways and cast a vote, and Mr. V said he wanted 100 percent participation) and who would be helping me (Olive, and, hopefully, Rachel).

"Will you have any kind of theme?" Grandma asked. She hated when rooms were "matchy-matchy."

"I don't know. I guess it depends what room we have." I was still hoping for the main hallway because every kid in the school would see it, multiple times, so that was sure to help get us votes.

Grandma didn't eat much, just a salad, and I'd noticed Mom frown when she ordered. Grandma was already pretty skinny; she could have used some all-you-can-eat breadsticks. We did talk her into a big slice of chocolate cake, though, and Mom and I got one, too.

"As long as you don't tell them it's my birthday," Grandma whispered. "I don't want any ridiculous spectacle from the waiters."

So we kept it a secret, but before Grandma took her first bite, I squeezed her hand under the table and said, "Make a wish." She smiled and closed her eyes, then opened them and pretended to blow out an invisible candle. Then we all dug in, and for the rest of the night, I wondered what she'd wished for, but I knew she could never tell me because then it wouldn't come true.

-•- ✦ -•-

On the way home from the restaurant, after dropping off Grandma, I had an idea about decorating lockers. What if I did some kind of mural that was removable? I could use that peel-and-stick wallpaper. Grandma had decorated a dresser with that once, and it looked awesome. I decided to give her a quick call and ask her advice.

The phone rang for a while. Grandma didn't have a cell phone, and her landline didn't have an answering machine, so it was hard to catch her. Plus, she sometimes took her hearing aids out and didn't even realize the phone was ringing. I'd heard Mom get angry with her about that recently. She'd said, "How am I supposed to know you're okay when you don't pick up the phone?"

Eventually, Grandma answered.

"Grandma, I had so much fun tonight!" I said loudly, just in case she didn't have the hearing aids in.

"Who is this?" Her voice was thin and watery.

"It's Maggie, Grandma." She didn't say anything. "Your granddaughter?" Did she know more than one Maggie? "We just had dinner together!"

"My what?" came the weak voice. Was she joking?

I just stood there. What was I supposed to say now? "Um . . . I said, it's your granddaughter . . . Maggie."

"My granddaughter?" she replied, after a long pause.

I didn't know what to say. I made my way downstairs, my phone to my ear. I walked past the living room and saw my dad and Tony sitting on the couch, staring at Dad's cell phone on the coffee table as though they were expecting it to do a trick.

"Who is this?" Grandma said, and I quickly answered, "Just a moment, please."

Mom was in the kitchen. I handed her my phone. "It's Grandma, but she doesn't know who I am," I whispered. I looked at the clock. It was well past 8 p.m. I shouldn't have called. Mom had warned me about calling this late.

I started back up to my room, but I could hear Mom saying, "It's Susan, your daughter. No, Mom, that was Maggie, your granddaughter."

I pulled out my tablet and burrowed into my beanbag. My thirty minutes of screen time was already up for the day, but my parents weren't exactly keeping track lately. The other day, I was on Roblox for close to three hours before anyone even noticed. Now I played a cooking game, mindlessly slashing vegetables, sizzling meat, trying to think about anything except what had just happened. When Mom stepped into my room, I was surprised to see it was dark outside.

"Here's your phone," she said, handing it to me.

"Grandma didn't know who I was," I said softly. I still couldn't believe it. Just over an hour ago, we'd been having a great time.

"I know," Mom said, sighing. "I'm going to go back out there and check up on her this week, as soon as I can." Mom looked like she was mentally running through the week's calendar, and she wasn't liking what she saw. "And I need to take her to a doctor."

"Why?" I asked.

"Because I need to see what's going on, with the memory lapses. It might be—"

"Might be what?"

Mom leaned against my wall, looked at me closely. "Have you ever heard of something called Alzheimer's? It's a disease that causes changes in a person's brain—"

"I know what it is," I said. "Olive's grandpa had it." I remembered Olive saying her grandpa kept telling the same stories from when he was a little boy. And sometimes, he actually thought he *was* a little boy. Unfortunately, pretty soon after Olive found out about his disease . . . her grandpa died.

"Why am I just hearing this now?" I asked Mom, feeling my body tense. "Alzheimer's is serious! Why am I always the last to know anything?"

Mom put her hands on her hips. "Maggie, you don't need to get upset with me. *We* don't know anything either, not yet, anyway."

"But . . . is Grandma going to die?" She couldn't! Not now!

"You need to calm down and quit jumping to conclusions," Mom said sternly, which was no help at all. My brain didn't work that way. My brain was always going to run ahead to the next intersection and try to see if there was a semitruck coming around the corner. Mom added, "I told you not to call her so late."

"Oh, so this is my fault?" I said. "Are you seriously blaming me?"

"You know what, I don't want to talk about this right now," Mom said, holding up her hands. She left my room.

I sat at my desk, flicked on the lamp, and tried to finish my science worksheet, but I just couldn't concentrate. How could Grandma have Alzheimer's? She was so normal, except for just once in awhile, when she couldn't remember something, but that happened to everybody. Okay, maybe not everybody forgot they had a granddaughter, but still. She wasn't like other old people, the ones you didn't think had much time left in the world. I thought about her making a wish at the restaurant before she blew out her invisible candle. Did she wish to be well? Did she even realize she might not be?

It wasn't long before Dad came in. He leaned against my doorway.

"Hey, Mags," he said, "sorry we haven't been hanging out much. It's just that, well, obviously, we have a lot of crazy stuff going on right now."

He said that like the stuff we had going on could be anything, like he had a deadline at work, at the same time as I had a math test, at the same time as Mom had two new house listings. Like *regular* craziness, not what it actually was, which was on a whole other crazy scale.

He rocked on his feet a bit, looking around the room at everything except me, the same way Tony did.

"How are you, Mags?" he asked.

It was an impossible question to answer. If I told him I was freaked out, he'd try to reassure me that everything was going to be just fine, but if I said I was just fine, he'd suspect I was lying. I really couldn't win.

I shrugged.

He sat on the floor next to my desk, his back against my wall. "We're going to get through this," he said, "you and me, and mom, and Tony, too."

"And Tony's mom," I added. "Tony's mom will get through it, and then Tony will move back in with her." So maybe it was selfish of me to want Tony to move out, but wasn't it also nice to want Tony's mom to get better?

"Yes, of course, her, too," Dad said.

I hadn't meant to start crying, but it was late, Grandma didn't know who I was, and I felt like I didn't know who my dad was anymore, and, honestly, all of that meant I wasn't too sure about who I was either. I sniffled loudly, and Dad looked over, then got up and wrapped me in a hug, but instead of the hug making me feel better, I felt trapped.

It was my dad who had always picked me up off the playground when I'd skinned a knee, my dad who talked me through scenarios at school when I was caught up in whatever silly friend drama was going on. He'd always been so smart and wise. I'd always trusted him. But now . . . ?

I wriggled away, grabbed a tissue out of the box on my desk, and blew my nose.

"How was the phone call? With Tony's mom?" I asked.

"She never called." Dad drummed his fingers against his leg in an agitated way. "And Tony walked out of his counseling appointment today, even though the social worker's case plan requires him to get counseling."

"Dad," I said quietly. "If Tony wasn't here, I mean, if there was no Tony, ever, at all, would you even have told me, or Mom, about any of it, I mean, about Tony's mom?" I couldn't stand to think about it, but I had to know.

He kind of looked angry for a second, just a flash across his face, and I didn't know if the anger was at me, for asking these questions, or if he was just mad at himself.

"You're at a weird age, Mags," he said. "Mom and I are still trying to figure it out, what we can talk about with you, I mean, because you're kind of on this bubble, between being a kid and being a grown-up. Do you know what I mean?"

"I guess," I said. "What you're saying is I'm suddenly really hard to talk to."

"No, Maggie, that's not—"

"Yes, it is, and that's fine, and you know what? You're not easy to talk to either these days."

He just stood there and looked at me while I felt my tears starting up again. Had he said I was *on* a bubble? Well, I felt like I *was* the bubble, and I was ready to pop.

Dad wiped some tears off my cheek with his thumb. "Sometimes we don't tell people things because we're trying to protect them. Because we love them."

I took a couple ragged breaths. "Is that why you told Mom you didn't . . . want me? Because you wanted to protect me?"

That seemed so wrong. It couldn't have been to protect me, and it certainly couldn't have been because he loved me.

"What? Maggie, what are you talking about?"

I turned away from him, hiding my face. "In second grade," I said. "When you and Mom were going to get divorced, and I had to decide who I was going to live with, Mom said you didn't want me to live with you."

He took a very slow, deep breath. "You remember that?"

Of course I did. I would never forget it. Why do parents think kids forget everything? We might forget to brush our teeth, but we remembered the important things. And not just the hurtful moments. I remembered all our talks, how they said we had to stay close as a family, how we were like a stool, the three of us, all balancing each other out.

He let out a long sigh. "Your mom shouldn't have said that to you," he said flatly. "I only suggested that a girl would probably want to live with her mother, but we weren't even at that point, not by a long shot. That was premature, on her part, to imply we were separating. She was hurting, and she . . . well, we've worked that out now. A long time ago. You were only what, eight?"

"Seven," I said.

Outside, the streetlight flickered on, and Mittens crawled up on my beanbag. I picked her up and put her around my neck. A minute or two passed while we both listened to Mittens purring.

Finally, Dad said, "Tell me something good, Mags."

The only thing I could think of that was good right now was the contest, but he knew about that. I hadn't told him about the prizes, however.

"So, the winner of that design contest? At my school? She gets to be Principal for a Day," I said. I could suddenly see it so clearly, me in the principal's chair, feet up on the desk. I could tell other people what to do for a change. I'd be in charge.

Dad stood up and moved to the door. "Sounds fun, honey."

That was it? That was all he had to say? "There's also a trophy and a pizza party," I added.

"Well, isn't that wonderful? Time for bed, okay." He left my room but poked his head back in a minute later. "I assume a big kid like you doesn't need anyone tucking her in anymore," he said.

I gave him a half smile, then got into my pajamas, went to the bathroom and brushed my teeth, and bumped into Tony on my way out.

"Hey," I said. "Sorry about your mom, you know, not calling."

"Yeah, well, I better brush my teeth," he replied, and scooted past me.

Guess he didn't want to talk about it yet, or maybe ever. Back in my room, I kicked aside some *Better Homes and Gardens* that were littering my floor.

I hadn't thought about it much before now, but you know, nothing was ever as perfect as it looked in those magazines. The photographers spent hours staging a little area of a room to get the perfect photo, but we couldn't see what was just outside the frame. I mean, we never saw the cat's hairball on the chair around the corner, never heard the camera guy snap at the designer over some stupid thing, or find out the posh tablecloth was actually made by a kid who was forced to work in some factory on the other side of the world when she should be out playing in the sun.

And the families in these magazines . . . a husband and wife and two kids in matching polo shirts, a baby on the mom's hip. And everybody smiling, always smiling, like there was an extra-large ice-cream sundae waiting for them after the photographer was done. I thought of our own family photos on the wall in the hallway, everything so posed and perfect. All "before" photos. Or were they? Would I always think of our family as before and after Tony?

I sat in my beanbag and read some Edgar Allan Poe for an upcoming Language Arts assignment, but it started to freak me out, so I put the book away and crawled into my loft, where I found Mittens curled on one of my pillows. I carefully picked her up with one arm and climbed back down with the other. Then I snuck into Tony's room, where he was sprawled on his stomach and already snoring. I set Mittens down on the foot of his bed, petting her a minute while she got settled, and I went back to my room.

I missed the feel of my dad's hand smoothing the sheet down, missed the way the last smell in the room at night was his aftershave. Did I *need* someone to tuck me in? No. Did I *want* someone to? Yes.

I imagined Tony did, too.

The Focal Point

Monday morning, and my mom was driving fast. She was usually pretty careful, following the speed limits and everything. But today she was rolling through stop signs and hitting the gas too hard on green lights, which was giving me a stomachache.

Tony and I were both in the back. He had tried to sit in the passenger's seat, but Mom shook her head and said, "I'm not totally sure what the height and weight requirements are, Tony. I know Maggie doesn't quite weigh enough to sit in front yet."

"I always sat in front in my mom's car," he said.

"Yes, well, that may be true, but I just wouldn't feel comfortable, until I double-check the rules," she'd replied.

Tony had been frowning ever since. I knew how he felt. I was, like, only five pounds under the recommended weight for sitting in the front. I liked rules and all, but this was one case where I wished we could forget them.

His backpack was on the seat between us. It was red and had a big marker splotch on the front where it looked like someone, maybe him, had colored over another kid's name.

We could have taken the school bus, but Mom wouldn't hear of it. For some reason, she wanted to drop Tony off on his first day. She never did that with me, and I didn't know why she was being so overprotective. Maybe she just wanted to make sure he went inside and didn't make a break for it.

Honestly, though, this was better than riding the bus. No other kids to deal with. Fewer questions about my "new" brother. And since Tony was a grade ahead of me, I wouldn't see him at all once we got to school.

"So, Tony, your homeroom is with Mrs. Kauffman," my mom said. "I've already spoken with her. But you need to stop by the office at some point today to pick up some paperwork. Maggie can show you where everything is."

I felt my chest tighten up at the thought of being Tony's tour guide. I barely knew where everything was myself, and I'd never even been to the seventh grade wing. Tony didn't react. He was busy staring into space.

"Did you like your other school, Tony?" Mom asked. She probably just wanted to fill the silence, but I wished she'd focus on the road and quit looking at us in her rearview mirror.

"Sure," Tony said. "I mean, it was fine."

"Bircher Middle School, right?"

"Yup."

He started flipping the zipper back and forth on his bag.

"Do you miss your friends?" I asked. "At Bircher?"

He shrugged.

"You probably played basketball, right?" I had almost expected him to bring his ball to school, but he just had his backpack, and that seemed to be empty, except for the brown-bag lunch I saw my mom zip into it earlier.

"Yeah, I played, for a while," he said, "but I didn't have a way to get to practice, and you had to pay for a uniform, and the coaches wanted us to sell all these pizzas or else they said you weren't 'pulling your weight.' "

"What's that about pizzas?" Mom called back. Tony was mumbling. Even I was having trouble hearing him, and there was only a foot of space between us.

"Nothing," we both said at the same time.

"Jinx," we both said at the same time.

I thought I saw the start of a smile on Tony's face, but it quickly disappeared. "Did you have friends from the team over to your house or anything?" I asked.

I don't know why I was so worried about it, but it was the same feeling as when I'd asked Tony if he had grandparents. I imagined him being alone, and it made me feel sad. My mom and dad would probably let him have some of those friends over, if he wanted. I could make myself scarce, go to Olive's or something. As long as they stayed out of my room, it would be fine.

"My mom didn't really like me having people over," he said kind of gruffly.

"So you went to their houses?"

Mom turned into the car loop at school and found a place to pull over.

"No," he said, quickly exiting the car. "I don't know! Okay?"

"Have a great day!" Mom yelled to us, way too enthusiastically, especially considering that Tony was starting to lose it. It was kind of Mom's fault for playing Twenty Questions with him, when he clearly didn't feel like talking. But I guess I shouldn't have been asking him about his friends, either.

Mom had said I should show him around, but Tony was already through the doors before I even had a chance to get out of the car. I kind of missed Mr. Friendly Handshake from our middle-of-the-night cereal feast.

- • - ✦ - • -

I went to the office after morning announcements. I had a feeling Mr. V just wanted to prove Long Branch had as much school spirit as his old employer—now rival—Centerville, because he'd given another pep talk over the intercom about getting as many groups as possible to participate in the contest. Yet there were only five other team captains there to draw our locations.

One of them, unfortunately, was Katelyn, who was representing the cheerleading squad. All the groups were school clubs or sports teams, with way more kids than just our BFF threesome. We were the only friend group participating. But I wasn't worried. How many of them had studied design? How many of them had been paid, by real clients, to redo a room?

I pulled a slip of paper out of a basket held by Mrs. Abbott, the secretary. *Outer office*, it read.

"Oh no," I groaned, then slapped my hand over my mouth.

"Something wrong, Maggie?" Mrs. Abbott asked.

"No, everything's fine," I said. Was it? The outer office was the space I was standing in right now, the little lobby area where Mrs. Abbott sat. Behind her desk was a hallway that led to Mr. V's office, and some other administrators' offices. Hardly any students ever came through here unless they were in trouble.

Next, Katelyn reached her fingers into the basket. I noticed her nails were glossy and pink, just like her lips.

She opened up the slip of paper and waved it around triumphantly. *Main hallway.* One of the other team captains—the head of the math club—yelled, "Dangit!" but I didn't say anything, didn't want to give Katelyn the satisfaction of knowing I was disappointed.

But by the time study hall came around, I had altered my thinking. Olive helped.

"There's way more opportunities in the office than in the hallway, with a bunch of dumb old lockers," she said. We had a sub who was letting us talk quietly.

"Yeah, but I won't be able to try out my wallpaper mural idea."

"Come on, Maggie, you know that wouldn't have lasted anyway. Kids would have torn it down."

She was probably right. There were just tons of things to consider in a space like the outer office, but that also made the job more interesting. The BFFs loved a challenge.

Ideas and questions started popping into my head immediately. "Do you have your BFF notebook, Olive?" I asked.

"Of course," she said, pulling it out, along with her pink pen.

"I'm wondering if we want to decorate with books. Or if we need a rug. What kind of art?"

Olive scribbled.

I said, "We need to provide a cheerful place for visitors to the school."

"But we've got to show there's serious learning going on," Olive added.

I nodded, getting more excited by the minute. "And calming colors, definitely," I said. Nothing like calming colors when you're going to visit the principal.

Ten minutes into our discussion, a kid came in to tell us all the teams were allowed to check out their spaces so they could start planning. Olive and I jumped out of our seats and practically ran down the hall. I texted Rachel on the way.

When we got there, Mrs. Abbott offered us lemon drops from the bowl on her desk. They were wrapped in white paper and coated in powdered sugar that got on my fingers when I uncovered one. I licked the sugar off, popped the candy into my mouth. Sweet and sour at the same time, and absolutely delicious.

"How many are in your group?" Mrs. Abbott asked.

"Three," Olive said. She looked at me. "Has Rakell texted back yet?"

"Nope," I muttered. I knew I couldn't count on her much lately, but even thinking about the possibility of her not helping us set off a wave of panic. Winning this contest would require all three of us. And Katelyn was a team captain, which made me think, what if . . . oh, man . . . what if Rachel decided to work with Katelyn? Giving the enemy all our secrets and maybe even helping her win? Just the thought of it made me feel faint and wobbly, like a stool without a leg. I had to grab the edge of the desk.

"I can't wait to see what you girls come up with," Mrs. Abbott said. She had a purple pencil stuck behind her ear, which was sporting a gold earring in the shape of an owl. "So, do you need anything from me?" she asked.

"Well, it would be great if we could interview you," I said. Steady now, I pushed the lemon drop with my tongue so it nestled inside my cheek. Mrs. Abbott was the only one actually occupying the outer office, so she would be our primary client. "Rachel usually asks the questions, though."

Just then, the door opened, and I turned, hopeful, but it was only a teacher leading a boy, who, from his facial expression, seemed to be in deep trouble. Mrs. Abbott pointed to a chair sitting outside the hallway leading to Mr. Villanueva's office. The boy sat down, hard, which made the chair thump against the wall. His face looked so sour, it was like he was sucking on a hundred lemon drops.

I stepped back to the room's entrance, closed my eyes for a moment, then opened them quickly.

"What are you doing?" Mrs. Abbott asked.

"She's finding the focal point," Olive whispered, like it was a mysterious process that required silence.

"And there it is." I pointed to the goofy plastic flower on Mrs. Abbott's desk. It was wearing sunglasses, and dancing, and no one who came into the office could look at anything else.

"The flower?" Olive asked.

Mrs. Abbott reached out and patted it. "So happy, isn't he?" she said.

"Mmm-hmm," I replied, forcing a smile. I didn't want to spring it on her so soon, but that flower was a huge distraction. We'd have to get rid of it.

"Should we take some measurements?" Olive asked. "We don't need Rakell for that."

"Good idea, Olive." I asked Mrs. Abbott, "Do you have a tape measure?" I really should keep my mini tape measure in my backpack from now on, I thought. Never knew when I'd need it.

"No, but I've got a ruler." She handed it to me.

I moved the ruler across the floor from one wall to the other, calling out numbers for Olive to write down in her notebook. It really was not a very big room. And yet, it was a room that had to accomplish many different things. I felt my shoulders start to tense up just thinking about it. Then, out of the corner of my eye, I saw some movement in the rectangular window to the side of the outer office door.

It was Rachel, and she was smiling. I felt myself relax.

"Sorry I'm late," she said, breezing in, notebook in hand. "A kid told me I was excused to come down, but I got distracted, and then I forgot, until I saw your text." How could she forget about something that quickly?

"I hear you're going to interview me!" Mrs. Abbott said. She sounded actually excited.

"Sure, why not?" Rachel said. Too casually, I thought. She pulled a pen from her pocket and sat in the chair by Mrs. Abbott's desk.

"Okay, if you could vacation anywhere in the world, where would it be?" Rachel asked.

Rachel had asked this question of other clients, and every time she did, I thought of the beach in Florida, of how I had felt so loved and safe and how our family was perfect and nothing would ever change. My parents knew about Tony when we were on that trip, I realized. They knew, and didn't tell me. I wondered if I'd ever again think of the beach in quite the same way.

"Anywhere? Oh, Paris. Definitely," Mrs. Abbott said. She had a dreamy look in her eyes like she was already there.

"Awesome," Rachel said, writing it down. "Now, which words would you use to describe yourself? Casual and comfortable, or chic and stylish?"

"Goodness, I don't think anyone's ever called me chic. Or stylish. Oh, but I suppose my Paris answer might be misleading then. You might assume someone who answered Paris to be a stylish sort of person."

"There are no wrong answers," Rachel said cheerily, even though she knew there were answers that maybe weren't "wrong," but would make our job more difficult. When clients' tastes were all over the map, it was definitely more difficult. Rachel was a good interviewer; even when she was doing an impromptu interview like this, she never seemed judgmental.

Mrs. Abbott played with her gold owl necklace, which matched her earrings. She was wearing a thick yellow sweater that looked very soft.

Rachel was staring at that sweater. "Should we go with comfortable?" she asked.

Mrs. Abbott nodded.

Then, Rachel turned to me. "Do you happen to have the colors with you, Maggie?"

"I do," I said. I had stopped to get my design binder from my locker on our way to the office. Inside was a piece of cardboard with a bunch of paint color swatches glued to it, which the BFFs had put together months ago. I set the cardboard on Mrs. Abbott's desk.

"Okay," said Rachel. "Can you choose your top two favorite colors?"

When I redid my own room, I chose yellow and orange, which were adjacent on the color wheel, though colors that were opposites worked well, too.

Mrs. Abbott looked at the colored squares for what seemed like a long time. Just when her finger started heading toward one, she'd lift it back up. "No, wait, maybe not," she said. She took the pencil out from behind her ear and tapped on the cardboard. "I can only pick two?"

"Just close your eyes," Rachel suggested. Mrs. Abbott did as she was told. "Now," Rachel said, "imagine a clean, white sheet of paper from your printer. Nothing on it."

Mrs. Abbott's eyelids fluttered, but remained closed.

"Okay, now open your eyes and look!" Rachel said.

She did.

"Where did your eyes land?"

"Here," Mrs. Abbott said, pointing to a turquoise blue.

"And here." She pointed beneath it to a pale green. "Those two. Yes." She held up the card in front of her. "I really like both of those."

This was perfect. I had just reviewed an article at one of our BFF meetings about the calming properties of ocean colors. It was a wonderful choice for outside a principal's office. Everything currently in the space, from the battered chairs, to the torn poster above the bookshelf, to the books themselves that happened to be sitting out on a long table full of school newsletter pages waiting to be collated, were in bright shades of red and orange—vibrant, but potentially angry.

I noticed that the boy sitting in the chair waiting to see Mr. Villanueva had slid so far down in the seat that he seemed in danger of crashing right through the floor. If a secret trapdoor had opened, he wouldn't have looked back. Rachel noticed it too, and wiggled her eyebrows at me. I gave her a big smile. She'd done such a great job of helping Mrs. Abbott to focus.

Olive started making a quick sketch in her notebook of the room, showing where different items were currently located, while me and Rachel asked Mrs. Abbott some more questions— about how the space was used, how many people came through every day, what the traffic pattern was like, stuff like that. We only had a few more minutes until the bell rang, but we definitely had enough information to get started.

"Thank you so much, Mrs. Abbott," I said. "We so appreciate your—" But just then, the door opened, and in walked . . . Tony. I had a sudden panicky feeling. I glanced at Olive and Rachel, who were giving each other knowing looks. They must have recognized him from the other day.

He nodded at me. "Hey," he said as he went up to Mrs. Abbott's desk.

"Hey," I answered, so quietly I wasn't sure he heard me.

He said to Mrs. Abbott, "Um, excuse me, but my stepmom said I had to get some forms to bring home? I'm a new student? Anthony Miller?"

Everything was a question. I realized I was clutching my color chart so tightly, some of the squares had come off and fallen on the floor. Midnight Blue and Dusky Dawn. I picked them up and put them in my pocket.

"Oh yes, I've been expecting you. Your stepmom called earlier," Mrs. Abbott said. She looked up at us. "You girls better run off to class."

As soon as the door closed behind us, Rachel immediately started grilling me.

"That's your brother, isn't it? What's he like? Is he going out for basketball? What music does he listen to?"

"I barely know him," I said. "We haven't exactly been having heart-to-heart talks."

"I bet he's super nice," Olive said. "I could just tell by the polite way he talked to Mrs. Abbott."

"Yeah, he's *fantabulous,* all right," I said as I gathered my stuff. "Let's get to class."

Olive split off to go to art while Rachel and I continued walking together.

"I thought you said his name was Tony," Rachel said.

"Anthony, Tony, same thing," I replied.

Rachel stopped outside her classroom. "Did he tell you to call him Tony?" she asked.

"Um . . . I think so?" I didn't remember. Maybe it was Dad who told me. What did it matter?

Rachel shook her head. "You should call people what they want to be called, Maggie," she said and went into class, leaving me to wonder, *what did I do?* Then I realized, this was all about the Rakell thing. I didn't understand why she cared so much about being called something ever-so-slightly-different. Weren't there bigger things to worry about? Like a sibling who shows up out of nowhere, and whether your dad was going to love him more than you?

The bell rang, but I was still standing there, having that last, terrible thought, which I hadn't dared to think before, but which had probably been lodged somewhere in my brain ever since Tony arrived.

It's Only Temporary

I was hiding out in my room again, where I could make believe that nothing had changed. In my room, at least, nothing had. Olive was here, and we were putting together our "concept board" for the outer office, but Rachel hadn't shown up. I guess that was one thing that had changed, that I couldn't pretend away; Rachel wasn't with us.

It felt weird working without her. We all had our roles, and there were certain things Rachel always did, like cut out pieces of furniture and decorations from magazines to affix to our room sketches.

Little did I know, however, that Olive could draw all those things, and really well, too. We didn't need Rachel to cut out pictures. With her colored pencils, Olive drew a set of chairs and a bookshelf, complete with tiny titles on the spines of the books. Then she rubber-cemented them onto our poster board of ideas, along with scraps of fabric we liked, and the colored squares Mrs. Abbott had chosen.

The board was propped up on an old music stand I'd found at the BFFs' favorite thrift store, the Good Samaritan Thrift Shoppe. I'd spray-painted it silver to give it a little bling. My wand from a Harry Potter summer camp served as my pointer for presentations. Yesterday, I brought a few initial ideas to Mrs. Abbott, who thought everything was great. She was kind of like Olive in that way, generally seeing the positive side of things, though, right now, this morning, Olive wasn't her usual self. She seemed impatient and kind of snippy, especially when I wondered aloud whether Rachel was going to show or not.

"At least she could text to say she's not coming," I said.

Olive sighed. She was very slowly brushing rubber cement onto the back of a little desk to add to her sketch.

"Could you hurry up with that?" I said. "That stuff stinks."

"Open a window if it bothers you," she said sharply. She slapped the tiny desk drawing onto the board, the rubber cement oozing out from underneath it. The desk was crooked, so I tried to straighten it, but Olive knocked my hand away.

"You know, Maggie, it's not like you haven't smelled rubber cement before. I mean, what do you want me to do? Anything else you'd like to critique?" she said, her voice quivering. Olive's jaw was clenched, her eyes squinty. She turned away from me.

"Olive?"

She crossed her arms and squeezed, like she was hugging herself. "It's just that—oh, forget it. Never mind. Actually, no, you need to . . . you just . . . it's hard when you're so negative, about Rakell and everything."

Me? *I* was negative about *Rachel*? After she pretty much abandoned us? "Come on, Olive, she hasn't exactly been pulling her weight. I mean, we're a team, aren't we?"

"Yeah, we're supposed to be a team, but you never let me do any of the important stuff, and when you do, it's only because Rakell isn't here, and then you can't stop worrying about how we're going to do it without her, and, ugh! I hate this!" Olive fanned both hands in front of her face, like she was trying to quickly evaporate any tears that might seep out.

"Olive, hey, Olive, don't cry. It's just that, you know we're a threesome." I pointed to my bookshelf knickknacks. "You know the rule of threes."

She dropped her hands by her sides and choked back the tears that had started coming. "I swear sometimes you just *don't get it.*"

"*What* don't I get?"

"For one thing, Rakell isn't coming."

"How do you know?"

Olive hiccupped. "She texted me."

"What do you mean she texted you?" Why would Rachel text Olive and not me?

"I mean she sent me a text," Olive said softly while putting her notebooks and colored pencils into her backpack.

I felt confused and hurt and angry. "What did Rachel say?"

"I already told you, she said she's not coming."

Olive looked at me for a second, her eyes all red and puffy.

"I need to get going," she said, hoisting her backpack over her shoulder.

"Wait! Stay. Talk to me," I said. I blocked my doorway. "We're a team, Olive! If we're going to win this contest, we've got to be in it together, all of us. And we really need to win this contest."

She nudged me aside and walked into the hallway. "You keep saying that, Maggie, but really? I think, really? It's *you* who needs to win it." And then she left without even looking back at me.

-·- ✦ -·-

When Dad came in later to see what I was up to, I launched into an explanation of the work I was doing. When I was upset, sometimes I could distract myself if I just talked, a lot, preferably on a topic I knew a ton about. I couldn't stop thinking about what Olive had said, about how I was the one who needed to win this contest, and I didn't think it was fair. Didn't we all want to win? My dad had come up to ask if I was going to stay in my room all day, and instead of answering him, I thrust a piece of fabric into his hands, a swatch of acrylic with a bold yellow chevron pattern.

"I'm thinking of using this fabric to cover the chairs in the outer office," I said. "It's technically an outdoor fabric, so it can take a lot of wear."

He nodded appreciatively, running his hand over it. We were standing in front of my concept board. He leaned in, looking closely at it.

"What are these dotted lines?" he asked. "Is that where people walk?"

"Yes," I said, tracing the lines with my wand. "When guests enter the space, they'll come this way, to the secretary, Mrs. Abbott, or else continue down this way to the principal's office."

No longer would Mrs. Abbott have to bump her shins on the stupidly placed mini-fridge. My arrangement would provide a much better flow. No more shin bruises! Yes! Sometimes, it took a shake-up of the normal to find a new, better way. I couldn't help but think of Olive, and the fact that I hadn't even realized how good she was at drawing until Rachel flaked out.

"Okay, that makes sense," Dad said, "and what's this metal thing?"

"It's just a sample of a drawer pull I like, for a new filing cabinet." I pointed to a magazine photo of a white lacquer filing cabinet with bin-style pulls.

My dad shook his head. "Wow, Mags, seriously, I think you've thought of everything."

I smiled so big, my face hurt. "You have to say that. You're my dad."

"Now excuse me, I don't *have* to say anything."

He put an arm around me and squeezed me close, and I squeezed him back, smelling the gel that he used, unsuccessfully, to get his messy hair to behave. When he hugged me the other day, I'd felt trapped, but not now. Now I didn't want to let him go.

"Where do you get all these ideas from?" he murmured. "Must be from your mother because it certainly isn't from me."

I giggled, thinking about how Dad often came downstairs in the morning in pants and shirts that looked so terrible together, Mom would make him go back upstairs to change. Mom, meanwhile, used her realtor's eye to merchandise countless rooms in the homes she was selling, hiding the flaws, highlighting the attributes. But if I got my design know-how from Mom, it was because she got it from Grandma. Thinking of Grandma, and of our phone call, still gave me a lump in my throat.

Dad kept an arm around my shoulders as he asked me, "How are you doing? With all the changes around here?"

I didn't feel so huggy anymore; I ducked under his arm. "Fine," I said. I moved closer to my concept board, pretending to study it.

"You know, we have to be honest with each other," he said. "You can tell me anything, Mags."

Yeah, right, I thought. *Except that* you *don't tell me anything, and* you're *not honest. Not* telling somebody something is still a lie, just a different kind.

From the hall came the thump of a basketball. I often heard Tony before I saw him, I realized. On cue, he came strutting into my room wearing that blue hoodie again with frayed jeans. Dad tried to take a swipe at the ball, but Tony jerked it away, pretended to take a jump shot, then motioned to Dad, who took a few steps toward my loft, and held up his hand for Tony to pass to him.

"I've got moves that were invented before you were even born," Dad said.

"Way, way before I was born, old man." Tony laughed.

They said these lines like they'd said them before, like it was a little private joke. I stood in the corner of my room, feeling my hands forming into fists. Were they actually trash-talking each other? Like Dad did with his basketball buddies? I used to go to some of his games at the YMCA, and he'd ask if I wanted to shoot around at home, but I never did. So he quit asking.

"Please don't throw that ball in here," I said. They could break something. If they hit my concept board, they'd wreck it.

"Don't worry," Tony said, grinning, "it's only a problem if we miss, and we are not gonna miss." He held out his hands, wanting my dad to throw the ball back to him.

Dad glanced at me. "You know, we really shouldn't throw the ball in the house, Tony."

Tony's face fell. "Oh, okay. Well, are you ready to go?"

"Where are you going?" I asked.

"To the park," Dad said. "Some of the guys and their sons are coming. I thought Tony could meet some other kids."

"Oh."

"Do you want to come, Mags?" Dad asked, a note of hopefulness in his voice.

This was a chance, maybe, to do something fun with Dad again, but I saw Tony look away. I knew he didn't want me along. My dad probably didn't either. I finally understood what it meant to be a third wheel. Besides, he said *some of the guys and their sons.* Where did I fit into that statement? Nowhere.

"No, that's okay," I said quietly. "I should finish my board."

"You sure?" Dad asked.

"Yeah," I said. I smoothed my hands over my fabric sample, watching Tony gleefully run out of my room, spinning the ball on his fingertip, like he thought he was in the NBA.

-•- ✦ -•-

Mom was washing dishes. She liked to use super-hot water, so hot that the steam rose up around her like a smokescreen. She ran one of our yellow dishcloths around a frying pan. I didn't say anything, just took a towel out of the drawer and started to dry. Mom liked to get everything dried and put away rather than leave stuff out overnight. It always bothered her when people who were trying to sell their houses left dishes out. "Such an *easy* solution to that problem," she'd said on more than one occasion. Most problems weren't so simple to solve.

"You didn't want to play basketball with the boys?" she asked.

So they were "the boys" now, like a dynamic duo? I couldn't help but think . . . I mean, if Dad had really wanted a son, why didn't he and Mom have one of their own? I was twelve years old, almost thirteen. They'd had plenty of time.

"Well?" Mom asked. She turned and took a long look at me, then turned back to the sink to scrub at a spatula covered in bits of egg.

"No," I said.

We washed and dried quietly for a few minutes until Mom said, "Your father loves you so, so much, you know." How was it that my mom always knew what I was thinking? Even when I didn't want her to?

She shook the water from her hands and looked at me. "They have thirteen *years* to catch up on," she said.

"But this is just temporary," I sputtered. "Tony's going back to his mom, and then everything can get back to normal."

Mom let out a big breath, which parted the steam cloud in front of her. "We really don't know yet what's going to happen, sweetie. Tony's mom just got out of detox. She's got ninety days in the program house to try and get herself together. And that's not a lot of time." She ran some more water. "There's a lot to undo. No matter what, though . . . your father has met his son, and we can't take that back. We wouldn't want to."

My eyes started welling up, and I covered my face with the towel. I thought Tony would be back with his mom by Christmas, but what if . . . ? I felt especially bad because I knew that, despite what Mom said, I *did* want to take it back, take it all back. No Tony, none of this, just me and my parents on the beach finding the horn of the tiniest unicorn in the world.

I felt like a terrible person for thinking that.

The next thing I knew, Mom was hugging me, and although I still had my face covered with the towel, I could hear her crying, too, her voice husky and choked. "This is very hard for me, too, Maggie, you understand that, right? Even though I've known for a few years that Tony existed, and that there was a chance someday we'd meet him, well, I certainly didn't expect . . . I didn't expect it would be like this."

I pulled the towel away from my eyes, and we looked at each

other, and for some reason, the realization that we were both crying made me feel better, weirdly, like we were in this together. Without really meaning to, I felt myself smile, and that made her smile, and just as suddenly as we had started crying, we stopped.

"What do we do now?" I asked, wondering about the weeks, the months, the years ahead.

Mom shook her head like she didn't have an answer. She ran some cool water into the sink. The scalding stuff must have gotten the better of her, even with her tough hands. She said, "We finish the dishes."

-•- ✦ -•-

Back in my room, I was still feeling really cruddy about how Olive and I left things, and I knew I'd be worrying all night unless I apologized, so I texted her.

> *Hey, sorry things were weird at my house.*
> *Didn't mean to take the Rachel thing out*
> *on you. Sorry . . .*

She replied right away.

> *You've got a lot of stuff ur going through. Everybody does.*

> *Yeah. Hey. You are an awesome artist!*

> ☺ *awwww, thanks*

> *I know what would cheer us up!*

> *Shopppp-payyyyy!*

When Olive and I entered the Good Samaritan Thrift Shoppe the next day, Mildred, the owner, yelled, "Hello, my favorite thrifters!" from behind the counter, which made us laugh, as it always did. We loved the store, don't get me wrong, but a lot of the reason we loved it was Mildred, who was the cool grandma every middle schooler wished she had, every middle schooler but me, anyway. My grandma was already pretty cool, even without red cowboy boots like Mildred's. Her long, white hair was swinging as she came around the counter, pointing to her boots.

"Like 'em?" she asked. "Came in yesterday, and only cost me five dollars. Little big on me, but they'll do."

"They are fantabulous!" Olive said.

"They absolutely are," I added.

"Thank you," Mildred said and did a little curtsy. "Now, what can I help you girls with?"

"We're competing in a design contest at our school," Olive said. "And we have to decorate an outer office."

"An outer office?" Mildred asked, looking puzzled.

"It's basically a lobby," I explained. "The secretary sits there, and you have to go through it if you need to see the principal."

"Uh-oh, I hope you girls never have to see her," Mildred said.

"It's a him, and he's not so bad," I replied, though I saw Olive raise her eyebrows. She, along with most of the sixth-grade class, it seemed, was not a fan of Mr. Villanueva. They didn't like all his rules, even if that was kind of why I *did* like him. Still, I didn't want to ruin things with Olive just after patching everything up, so I didn't say anything more.

Mildred asked, "So, do you girls need any help from me, or do you just want to browse?"

"Browse," we both said. There was nothing more fun than browsing the Shoppe. We'd once asked Mildred why it was spelled that way, and she said it was meant to be fancy. We liked to pronounce it *shop-pay*. Rachel was best at it: "Ladies, let's go to the shop-pay," she'd say in this snooty accent.

I was still kind of miffed that Rachel had texted Olive to back out of our meeting. Why wouldn't Rachel text me? Was she afraid I'd get mad?

I had to be honest, though: I would have gotten mad.

"What about this one?" Olive asked. She held up a fluffy rug with blue and purple stripes.

"Do you think we should text Rachel? Tell her we're here?"

Olive frowned. "Well, we're already here. By the time she'd get here, we might be gone."

"Yeah, I guess . . ."

"So?" Olive shook the rug at me. "What about it?"

"That could work," I said, tilting my head and squinting at it. "But then we're kind of committing to purple as our primary accent color. How do we feel about that?" I knew how *I* felt about it, and it wasn't good.

"Purple's nice!" Mildred called from an aisle over.

"I don't know," Olive said. "I feel like it's going to make the room seem too cold, with all the blue and green. I think we need a brighter accent. Yellow, maybe."

"I agree," I said. Olive put the rug back on the shelf, and I breathed a sigh of relief. That purple would have been a seriously bad choice.

We walked up and down the aisles, trying on dopey sunglasses, picking up super-old electronics and wondering what they were used for.

We found an old phone on a cluttered shelf and moved it to a table so we could play around with it.

"There aren't any buttons," Olive said. "How do you dial the numbers?"

I looked at the plastic thing around the numbers. "I think you move this plastic thing around? But do we pick up the receiver thingy first?"

We started laughing, holding the receiver up to each others' ears, until Mildred came over and gave us a demonstration.

"Like this," Mildred said, and stuck a finger into the plastic thing over the number three and moved it around until it hit a metal thing. Then she repeated it nine more times with nine more numbers. "I just called my number."

"Are you kidding me? That took forever!" I said.

Mildred held up her hands. "Well, that's the way it was, girls." She winked. "Just think if they didn't answer. You'd have to start all over again."

In the next aisle, we found a funky yellow rack for sorting papers and some green and yellow baskets to match. Olive agreed with me that they'd be great on top of the existing bookshelf, which I planned to paint blue. My dad had already picked it up from school and brought it home to our garage.

Eventually, Mildred said she had to close up, and we'd better get walking home before dark. It ended up that the baskets and paper rack were the only things we bought.

"Who's going to paint the bookshelf?" Olive asked. "You and Rakell usually do that stuff." We were making plans as we walked, Olive writing in her mini notebook. There was a lot to do and there was . . . just the two of us. A part of me was starting to envy my competitors. They might not have the training, but at least they had more hands. I wasn't sure how we were going to get it all done.

"Yeah, don't remind me." Rachel and I had a system with furniture. We'd set up in my garage, put on some music, get out my dad's big tarp. I'd sand. Rachel would prime. We tag-teamed the next coats, one of us brushing while the other caught any drips. "Do you want to paint with me?" I asked Olive.

"You know I hate painting, unless it's decorative stuff," she said. "I can add a design to it when you're all done."

"Maybe a design to mimic whatever shape is on the rug we find."

"Yeah, that's what I was thinking," Olive said. She held up her hand, and I high-fived it.

We turned the last corner before my house, and I noticed a man and a boy walking a block ahead of us. I didn't recognize them in the fading light, but then the boy started dribbling a basketball, *thump thump*. Guess the father-son park thing was becoming a nightly event.

"Maybe you could ask Tony," Olive said, pointing.

I stopped walking and looked at her like she was crazy. "No way."

With my luck, not only would Tony be a basketball whiz, but he'd probably be great at painting, too. The decorating contest was my thing. With everything else changing so fast around me, I thought—no, I *knew*—that this was something I could control. I knew what I was doing. I was in charge. It was going to be amazing.

Maybe Olive wasn't so far off when she said I needed to win the contest.

Out of Sync

The following Sunday, Mom suggested I come with her to pick up Grandma and tour an assisted living facility. I wanted to see her, but I was worried. Would she call me by the wrong name? Would she even know who I was?

I dove into my disaster of a bedroom closet, tossing aside stuffed animals and hair ties and mateless socks until I found it, the birthday card Grandma had given me a year ago. It had a picture of a black-and-white kitten on the front, and Grandma had drawn an arrow pointing to it and written, "Looks like Mittens, doesn't it?" I grabbed a decorating book and took it, and the card, out to the car where Mom was waiting for me.

"Why do you have that card?" Mom asked.

"I'm going to show it to Grandma," I said, "in case she can't remember me. Maybe she'll remember Mittens, or remember sending the card, and that will help."

"Oh, honey, she'll remember you," Mom said. Then she added, "I'm sure," but that made her sound really unsure.

Mom pulled out of the driveway and started down our street. She was driving a lot more carefully, and slowly, than she had taking Tony to school the other day. Today, it seemed like she wasn't in any hurry. She said, "The phone thing, Maggie . . . well, you have to remember that was at night when she was tired, and she didn't have her hearing aids in. It was your voice she couldn't place. If she could have seen your beautiful face over the phone, she would have known you."

Mom turned and gave me a big smile, and I noticed her eyes were shiny. She sniffled a bit, then turned on the radio station that played all the music from when she was in high school. Normally, I'd groan and ask her to change it, but I didn't. I had a feeling this was going to be a long day, for everybody.

Grandma lived almost an hour away, but the assisted living facility my mom was interested in was on the edge of our town, which would make it easier for us to visit Grandma.

"I have some news, actually, Maggie, about Grandma," Mom said, and I could tell by her voice what was coming next. "Remember when we talked about Alzheimer's the other day?"

I drew in a quick breath. Obviously, I remembered. How could I forget? Mom didn't wait for me to answer.

"Well, the disease has different stages. Early on, a person

might just seem forgetful, like they can't always remember where they are or can't remember people's names."

Margie, I thought. I'd heard Grandma right after all.

"Or they might have trouble planning or organizing things, too."

"I can help Grandma organize! I'm great at that!" I said.

"Oh, baby, that is so sweet of you." We were stopped at a red light that was taking what seemed like an hour to turn green. Mom glanced back at me. "But I'm afraid it's beyond what you, or any of us, can help with."

I felt my hand tighten around the birthday card and had to force myself to relax. I didn't want to bend the card. It was the most recent thing I had with Grandma's handwriting—that big, curvy *M* for Mittens, for Maggie.

"Can't they cure it?"

"No, there isn't a cure for it, not yet. Doctors are working on it."

"They should work faster," I said quietly. "And besides, doctors can be wrong. It could just be old people stuff. Like, Dad forgets his keys all the time. He always comes back in the house to get his coat or his keys or briefcase, or whatever."

"This is different," Mom said. "And it's getting worse. The doctor thinks she's getting into the moderate, middle, stage of the disease, which means she's going to have trouble with her day-to-day activities. She might get more frustrated, more angry, for no reason—"

"How could she be in the middle stage when I'm just finding out about it? It doesn't make sense!"

"Maggie, please, I know it's hard to understand. There's a lot you haven't seen. Grandma has been having these kinds of lapses for a while now. It's just not something we've talked about with you."

I threw my head back against my seat. "You should have," I said, gritting my teeth. I stared out the window as we passed a big billboard for an insurance company that showed a flooded basement. *Call now, before it's too late!* it said. Yeah, right, I thought. My family seemed to have an unwritten rule that they'd only tell me things once they'd become disasters.

-•- ✦ -•-

"Maggie!" Grandma said and gave me a big hug.

I'd never been so glad to see her, or so glad to hear my name. She was wearing one of my favorite scarves, pink with all different types of birds on it. I tucked the cat card into the book I was bringing along since it didn't appear I would need it.

After she got situated in the passenger seat, Grandma pulled out a peanut butter sandwich from her purse. "In case I get hungry," she said, with a wink at me. Then she showed us her travel umbrella.

"Weatherman said there's a forty percent chance of rain later this afternoon," she said, waving it, then shoving it back into her large, black purse.

From the backseat, I heard her mutter, "And that idiot doctor says I'm forgetful." My mom cleared her throat but didn't respond. Then a song came on with a guy kind of yelling *Ahhh-haaahhhhhhaaaa*. Grandma reached out and turned the knob until it clicked off.

I heard Mom mutter, "Here we go."

"What did you say, Susan?"

"Nothing, Mom, never mind. Why don't you rest your eyes until we get there?"

"I don't need to rest my eyes. I just got up," Grandma said irritably, but she did settle back into her seat and stared out the window. After a few minutes, she pulled out her sandwich and ate it.

I tried to stay focused on my book, which was called *Color Me Happy*. It's about using color to create mood. Like, for example, a red dining room stimulates people's appetites. I'd already read the book several times, but it had great before-and-after pictures, which I loved staring at. I especially loved one of a boring, neutral den that was redone in blues and greens, the same colors Mrs. Abbott had chosen for the outer office redo. Plus, there were yellow accents, just like Olive and I had gotten at the Shoppe.

I was so caught up in the book that I didn't realize we were at the assisted living facility until Grandma made a *hmmf* sound in her throat, and I looked up to see we were turning into a winding driveway next to a pond with some very angry-looking swans. I wondered how they got them to stay there, or if the swans were just temporarily passing through on their way to somewhere else. Maybe the assisted living people had done something to their wings so they couldn't fly, and that was why they were so mad. Or maybe they were just lost.

We parked and walked up to the door of a newish brick building, Grandma hanging deliberately behind. Her mind might be slow sometimes, but her body usually wasn't. I hung back with her while Mom pressed a buzzer and spoke into a little box when a voice asked for her name. Then there was a loud buzz and a click, and we entered.

I was immediately struck by a strong smell, like the stuff Mom put on me when I got a cut or scrape before she covered it with a Band-Aid. The woman who met us in the lobby had curly blond hair and a red blazer and introduced herself as Jasmine, which prompted Grandma to let out another *hmmf*. I saw my mom try to take Grandma's hand, but Grandma swatted it away and reached down to take mine instead. She squeezed it, and I squeezed back.

Jasmine talked fast to my mom, but slowed down when addressing Grandma, who she called Mrs. Hanson. She spoke more loudly to Grandma, too, even though Grandma had no problem hearing, as long as her hearing aids were in.

"And here is the aviary, Mrs. Hanson," she said as she walked up to a huge glass case with a half-dozen birds flitting around some little trees.

They were very different from the types of birds I watched on the feeder outside our dining room window. These were brightly colored parakeets, in gorgeous green and blue. There were those colors again, in nature this time. Nature always knew what she was doing.

I put my face very close to the glass, catching the notice of a mostly green bird who cocked his head toward me, fixing me with a stare from one black eye that looked like a tiny marble. I wondered what he felt like, being trapped.

Mom asked Jasmine a bunch of questions about exercise programs, and what kind of food they served, and rules about visitors. For a moment, I thought about Tony, and what rules there might be for him visiting his mom. Was it even allowed? He hadn't seen her yet, as far as I knew, and she kept not calling him when she was supposed to.

"You and your daughter are welcome to stop in at any time during visiting hours," Jasmine said to Mom, pointing at me. "We highly encourage as much family interaction as possible. The fact that you live nearby will make things so much easier for you."

"Yes, that's exactly what we were thinking," Mom said, nodding. I wasn't sure who "we" was, me or Dad? From the look on Grandma's face, not much information had been shared with her either.

Jasmine turned down a hallway with a sign that said "Memory Lane," which opened into a kind of mall. It almost looked like a movie set, with fake storefronts that seemed old-timey, not my mom's old times, but Grandma's, maybe. There was a shoe repair shop, and a hat store, and a place selling "Ice Cream Sodas for 25 cents," but you couldn't go into any of the shops because they were all fake. That seemed sad to me, and also kind of mean. Being promised an ice cream soda for 25 cents and finding out the door wasn't really a door but just a painted rectangle with a knob that didn't turn? Mean.

There were a half-dozen old people sitting in this "Main Street," some on benches, others in wheelchairs. Jasmine called them "residents." One of the residents gave me a look that was kind of creepy, and the medicine-y smell was stronger here, which was starting to give me a headache.

Grandma looked like she had a headache, too. And why wouldn't she? This place was nothing like her home. It wasn't warm and cozy, and didn't have the right smell or the right things, like that box in her bedroom of Grandpa's clothes that she wouldn't donate even though Mom told her to. You've got to be in sync with your space, I knew. Everything in my own room, from the way my closet smelled to the way I draped my gray sweater over my chair, was totally me. I thought of Tony again, in our spare bedroom, living out of a duffel bag.

I pulled on Mom's arm. "Can we go now?" I whispered.

"No, Maggie, we still have a lot to see," Mom said, shaking off my hand.

"Maybe she'd like to see the birds again," Jasmine offered. She smiled sweetly at me, but I could see that was fake, too, just like Main Street.

"I've heard enough," Grandma suddenly said, making all three of us jump back. She hadn't made a peep the whole time. "We need to go, Susan," she said. "Maggie doesn't feel well."

I didn't know how Grandma knew that, but she was right.

"But I haven't even shown you the cafeteria," Jasmine exclaimed. She looked from Grandma to my mom and back again

"Seen one, you've seen 'em all," Grandma said. We turned and headed back toward the way we came in. Grandma led us.

- • - ✦ - • -

In the car, Grandma searched her purse for the sandwich she'd already eaten on the way to the assisted living facility. She must have forgotten. Was that a sign of Alzheimer's or just a normal, forgetful thing?

"I'm starving," she said, so Mom suggested we go to a drive-thru and grab something, but Grandma didn't want to.

"I don't want to eat that terrible food," she said. "The aide will fix me something at home."

My mom had hired a home health aide to look in on Grandma each day, to make sure she was taking her medicines and eating right. I guess I should have figured out things were getting worse when that happened, but I just thought it was because we lived too far away to check in on her as much as we should.

I saw the golden arches pass by my window and quietly sighed with disappointment. There went the McDonald's. The thought of some salty French fries had my mouth watering.

"I wish you had paid more attention on the tour, Mom," my mom said to Grandma, irritation in her voice. I wondered if Grandma could hear it as clearly as I could. "That facility comes highly recommended."

"By whom?" Grandma asked. "The zombies they have living there? Who knows how many drugs they're giving them. Just drug them, and keep them quiet, that's the ticket." She shifted in her seat, adjusted her giant purse on her lap. "Zombies," she growled again.

There might be a bunch of things happening to Grandma's brain, but it was pretty clear we were still on the same page, at least about the facility. That place felt creepy. I wondered if Mom

was overreacting about Grandma's forgetfulness. Sh
her normal self to me right now.

I watched the side of Grandma's face as she blankly ⌣
the windshield, but after a few minutes she closed her eyes and
fell asleep, and my mom turned on the radio, very softly, to a news
station that I completely ignored.

We ate lunch at Grandma's house, just some canned vegetable
soup Mom found in the pantry and toast with lots of butter.
Then Grandma wanted to take a nap, so she went upstairs to her
room. We didn't leave right away. Instead, we did a load of Grandma's laundry and checked the fridge for expired food.

I twisted the cap off a gallon of milk and sniffed. "Yuck! This
is bad, Mom." She poured it down the sink, and I left the room
while she ran the disposal for a long while to clear out the stench.

I set myself up at the coffee table in the living room, pulling
out the box of crayons and the paper Grandma still kept in the
drawer. I could hear Mom in the kitchen talking to the health
aide on the phone, asking if she could come earlier to "discuss
some things." When I heard Mom start crying, I ran to the doorway, but her back was to me, and she seemed to have choked back
the tears. She was talking details now, very businesslike, just like
she was on the phone with a client.

I sat back at the table with the crayons. I hardly drew anymore,
but as I made a picture of a lake, I found myself really enjoying

the way the crayon moved across the paper, the waxy smell. It wasn't a lake like the one at the assisted living facility with the angry swans. This one was huge and had smiling turtles on logs and lots of little yellow birds flying against a blue sky, where birds were supposed to be flying. Blues and yellows, calming and happy. I hung it on the fridge so Grandma could see it later.

-·- ✦ -·-

"Sit up here with me," Mom said when we got back into the car for the trip home.

"I thought that wasn't safe, sitting in the front," I said, "until I got a little bigger."

"I'm living dangerously," Mom said with a wink.

"Really?"

She nodded, patted the seat. "You're almost big enough anyway, and I could use the company."

She pointed to the radio. "You can pick the station."

Seriously? The front seat and my choice of music? I looked over at her, and she was smiling, but her eyes looked shiny again.

"It's okay," I said. "I like your music." Some of it was actually pretty good.

"Thanks, sweetie."

From the front seat, I took in that big old road like I never had before. I got comfy while Mom sang along softly to some song about buying a ticket to the world, whatever that means. When the song was over and the DJ came on, I said, "Grandma doesn't want to leave her home."

"I know," Mom said.

"Does she have to?"

"Yes," she said sadly.

"Oh," I said. It didn't seem like something that should be up to us.

We drove along in silence for a few minutes. Everything was different up here in the front, bigger. But Grandma's world was getting smaller. I couldn't really imagine leaving my house. It was the only one I'd ever lived in. I'd had friends over the years who had moved to other towns or to bigger houses in our town. I couldn't imagine being someplace else.

Then I thought about Tony, wondered what his old place was like. Were the walls white or different colors? What kinds of pictures did they have hanging up? Dad had mentioned that Tony and his mom lived in an apartment, so although our house wasn't anything fancy, I figured it was probably better than what he'd had before, though "better" was kind of a hard word to define.

He certainly hadn't brought much of his stuff along, but

maybe he didn't have much stuff to begin with. All I ever saw was his duffel bag full of clothes and his backpack. And of course, his basketball.

"What will you do with Grandma's house? Will you sell it?" I asked Mom.

I could easily imagine Mom sprucing up all the outdated rooms, making it look modern again. Of course Grandma loved to decorate, and she'd redone the house so that it was once very stylish, but she hadn't changed a thing in more than ten years, and even though that didn't seem like a super long time, trends changed a lot faster than that.

An idea came into my head so quick, I almost patted my hair to check for the light bulb. I could help fix it up! The house had "good bones," as Grandma liked to say about things that might be old but were still sturdy and wonderful. There was a little den that could be so cute if we painted the paneling. . . .

But then, I thought sadly, but then, it wouldn't be Grandma's anymore, would it? The "after" picture might be pretty, but it wouldn't be *her*.

"No, I wouldn't sell it," Mom said. "Not right away at least." "I'd like Grandma to be able to think she could go back to it someday, if the house was still there and still hers. That will keep her spirits up."

"*Will* she go back someday?" I asked.

"No," Mom whispered.

She was quiet the rest of the way home, not even humming along to the radio. There was a woman singing a song about a guy cheating on her. Was it that common? People lying to each other? Until recently, I'd had no idea.

I closed my eyes for a while, thinking about Jasmine at the facility. *The birds love it here*, she had said when she caught me with my face pressed up against the aviary's glass. *The food looks delicious*, Mom had said to Grandma when we'd walked past one of the employees carrying a tray with some kind of meat covered in watery gravy. *The assisted living facility is "only temporary."*

Is that what my mom was going to tell Grandma? *All lies*, I couldn't help but think.

"Mom?" I said as we passed the Welcome sign to our town. "Is Tony going home?"

"His mom is working hard." She paused. "I'm sure it's her greatest wish to have him back, as soon as possible."

Her greatest wish. "Wishing doesn't make it so." That was something Grandma liked to say.

- • - ✦ - • -

Later that night, I got a bad sore throat, and by Monday morning, I had a little fever, so Mom thought I should stay home.

"Try to get the place nice and clean after the gigantic party you have today," Dad said, popping his head into my room.

"Ha, ha, Dad," I said, heavy on the sarcasm, but honestly, I liked when he teased me. He was being his old, jokey-dad self, which helped me forget about everything that had happened. I wished he could stay home and make me chicken soup and read me Harry Potter, but he had to go to work. *"American Power,"* he said and flexed his bicep, but I could tell he'd rather stay home.

"Are you okay to stay home on your own?" Mom asked. She stood in my doorway biting her lip. "I have to go back out to Grandma's and help her pack."

Mom had spent a long time on the phone with Grandma after enlisting the help of the home health aide to talk some sense into her. Since my mom was an only child, the assisted living situation was all hers to deal with—one of the downsides of not having siblings that I'd never really thought about before. When I was in preschool and asked for a baby sister, my mom had gotten me a huge stuffed cat instead. I'd carried it around for a year. I used to rub its head, kind of like I rubbed my shell now.

Mom leaned over to kiss my forehead, and she let her lips linger. That was how she liked to check my temperature, which wasn't exactly scientific. "Hmmm, maybe ninety-nine-point-five, not too bad. I'm going to call you at lunch and have you check your temperature with the thermometer and see if you need more Tylenol, okay?" she said.

"Okay," I said, "but wait, Mom, I have a question."

"Shoot."

I saw both Tony and my dad rush past my doorway and down the stairs, probably late.

"What are we going to tell Grandma? About Tony, I mean? Are we going to keep him a secret?" If Tony always stayed home when we went to visit the assisted living facility, if we never, ever, slipped up and mentioned him, and if Grandma never came to our house . . . but I was really tired of secrets.

"We'll figure it out," Mom said, but she didn't seem so sure. We were flying by the seat of our pants on a lot of things lately. That wasn't like our family, and I hated it.

In a few minutes, I heard the door open and shut three times— Mom leaving for Grandma's, Dad for work, and Tony for the bus. My concept board was still on its stand in the corner of my room, and I started thinking about Olive and our argument. We'd had fun at the Shoppe, but I still worried whether things were okay between us. Maybe I'd send her, and Rachel, a text, to hammer out some contest stuff. I could make use of the good-bad-good sandwich.

> *Good morning, team! I'm really excited to*
> *talk about art for the outer office.*
> *Yeah, ART!*

BUT I'm sorry to say I caught something
at the assisted living place we visited
with my grandma and I have a fever. 🤢
But it would be great if we could meet
with Mrs. Abbott in case she has some
ideas or posters lying around. I have a
collection of great frames in my attic!

There. Good-bad-good, sort of.

After a few moments, I got a reply from Olive.

Oh no!! I hope you feel better soon.
Hope it's not cookie day at lunch 🍪.
I will get you one if it is.

Aw, thanks, Olive. Don't worry, I'll be
working on the contest from home. If I
feel better later, I can paint the bookcase
today.

That would be awesome!!! Also, I can
stop by and talk to Mrs. Abbott today!

🙏 *Thank you, Olive!*

I lay in bed with the phone for a few minutes, but didn't
get any more beeps. Had Rachel even seen my message? I

felt myself getting sleepy and lay my head back against my pillow. I sent one last text:

Have a good day!

There was no response. Olive was probably off the bus already and headed to class. I pictured Rachel looking at the texts and deciding whether or not to reply—and then not replying. It was better to imagine that she didn't get them at all. Mittens hopped up on my bed, happy to find a warm body on a weekday morning, and settled in for a nap, while I burrowed under the covers and quickly drifted back to sleep.

-•- ✦ -•-

I woke to the sound of the front door slamming and looked at my clock. 11 a.m. Why would Mom be back so early? Couldn't she trust me to take care of myself? My stomach growled. If she was going to stay home and baby me, at least maybe I could get her to make me some pancakes.

As I started to get out of bed, Tony came rushing up the stairs. He poked his head into my doorway.

"Oh, sorry," he said, "were you sleeping?"

"I *was*," I answered, "until I heard the door. I thought you were my mom." I pressed the back of my hand against my forehead. It didn't feel very hot anymore. "What are you doing here?"

"Walked home."

"Why?"

"This." Tony pointed to his T-shirt. It had a picture of a big smiling poodle with a pink bow in its fur and the words *Sexy B*tch Dog Grooming* underneath.

"Ohhhh," I said. "Did Mom see what you were wearing this morning?" There was no way she would have let him go to school in that. She wouldn't even let me wear shorts unless they went down to at least the middle of my thighs.

"I had my hoodie over it. But I got too hot."

"Why didn't you just cover it back up?"

"I tried that! But Mr. V was being a total jerk. He said he was going to call my mom, but he meant *your* mom because he can't call my mom. So, anyway, your mom didn't answer, and when he called my . . . dad . . . Robert . . . at his office, the secretary said he was at another branch today and tied up in a bunch of meetings."

Tony tossed his backpack into the corner and dropped into my white beanbag chair so hard, I was worried he'd bust the seams and I'd have Styrofoam pellets everywhere.

"Take it easy," I said.

"It's not like it's even a swear," Tony said, looking down at his shirt. "I mean, it's a female dog."

"Oh, *come on*, Tony."

"What? It is!"

"Yeah, I know it is, but, you know that shirt is the kind of thing adults would say is *inappropriate*," I said, in a high-pitched voice like the mean lunchroom lady. "Children! Would you like to have your lunch with Mr. Villanueva!!!" We both started laughing.

"You look like you're feeling better."

"It's just a cold," I said. "I'm sure I'll be back at school tomorrow. What about you? Are you supposed to change and go back, or what?"

"I'm not going back," he said, "not today."

I sat up straighter in my loft, propping the pillows behind my back. Mittens didn't like being jostled, so she skittered down the ladder and went to rub against Tony's legs.

"You should probably just call him *Dad* from now on," I said. "I mean, Robert sounds weird, and . . . obviously he is your dad, so . . ."

Tony's face lit up like I'd given him some big gift, which made me feel really cruddy for telling him to call our dad Robert in the first place. And then I remembered what Rachel had said, about calling people what they want to be called.

"That reminds me," I said. "Do you like being called Tony? Instead of Anthony, I mean?"

"Oh, yeah, definitely." He rolled his eyes. "Only my mom calls me Anthony, and only when I'm in trouble." I imagined Mr. V calling him that today.

"Can't you just change your shirt and go back and talk to Mr. Villanueva? Show him that you're not trying to cause trouble?"

"What's the point? He's already got me figured out," Tony said. He gave Mittens a scratch behind the ears, then crossed his arms.

I wondered if that was true. Did Mr. V have all the students figured out? Did he have me figured out? There were so many students, and he'd just started at the school, so he barely knew most of us. He clearly didn't know how to motivate teams to enter the decorating contest because he'd said on the announcements that he was disappointed in the "paucity" of entries, which I'd had to look up. It meant there weren't many, just the six groups. That was good for the BFFs, though—less competition.

But being sent home for a dress code violation was not a good way for Tony to start out at a new school.

"My mom could take you shopping," I said.

"Yeah, she mentioned something about that," Tony replied, "but I guess she's pretty busy with your grandma right now." He pulled Mittens into his lap, and she started purring immediately. "What's she like anyway?"

"Grandma? Oh, she's awesome," I said. "She always wants to hear what I'm doing, and she knows all about design things." An image appeared in my head from when we'd left her with the health aide after the assisted living trip, how I'd peeked into her room and saw her asleep, and she looked so, so tiny. "She's sick, though," I said. "She has Alzheimer's. She can't remember stuff very well, and it's going to get worse. She can't take care of herself."

Tony nodded.

"You don't have to worry about it, though," I said. "She'll be at the assisted living place, and you don't have to go there. It's not like she's *your* grandma."

Watching this sad look come across Tony's face, I realized I was being an idiot. It wasn't just my grandma he was thinking about; it was his mom. After all, she was sick, too. She couldn't take care of herself either, not right now anyway, and so she couldn't take care of him.

"Ummm, you know, if you wanted," I said, "I could take you to the Good Samaritan Thrift Shoppe, so you could pick out some clothes. I've got a month of allowance saved up, and stuff there is really cheap."

"That's where my mom got this!" Tony said, looking down at his dog shirt, and we both started laughing again.

"Looks like you were just there anyway," he said, pointing to the bag sitting on my desk.

"Oh yeah, my friend Olive and I went shopping while you and Dad were playing basketball." I felt a little leftover pang of jealousy about that, but brushed it aside and climbed down my ladder.

"What do you think of these?" I pulled out the yellow paper organizer and baskets. "We're doing the design contest for Spirit Week. Have you heard about that? We're decorating the outer office, that lobby where you came to see Mrs. Abbott the other day. That's why we were in there, to get measurements and stuff."

"Yeah, I heard some cheerleaders talking about the contest at lunch," he said. "It seems like it's mostly sixth graders who are into the whole contest thing. The seventh graders are more into the football game and pep rally."

"But you heard about the frozen yogurt truck, right?"

"Yeah, I mean, it's a bribe for voting."

I didn't like the sound of the word *bribe*. "No, it's just that Mr. V wants the whole school to get excited, so, you know, if everybody votes, he'll bring in the truck."

"But how is he going to be sure everyone votes?"

"I don't know, I mean, he knows how many kids there are, and he can count the votes."

Tony put his hands on his hips. "Do you really think he's going to go through all that trouble? And what about people who aren't at school that day?"

Tony was acting like he was way older than me, instead of just one year. He was deflating my excitement balloon so fast I could almost hear the air leaking out.

He must have noticed, because then he said, "Listen, I love frozen yogurt, and obviously I'll vote for you." He was looking around my room in that way he had, like he was silently memorizing everything. "Your room looks really nice," he said. "Put together, I mean, like everything is just where it's supposed to be, but I don't mean, like it's boring, but more like . . . if something was moved somewhere else, it wouldn't look right." He scratched his ankle. "Never mind, I don't know what I'm saying."

I stood there with my mouth hanging open. Did Tony understand . . . design? Is that why he was always looking so closely at things? I found myself having two competing thoughts: First, designing was my thing. I didn't need Tony barging into it. But, second, with Rachel's disappearance, and with all the work we had to do . . .

"I totally know what you mean," I said. "Thanks, Tony."

At the very least, maybe I could help Tony fix up the spare room where he was sleeping. Right now, it was just an old boring room with his clothes strewn all over the floor.

"What was your place like? Your apartment?" I asked.

"Oh, nothing special," he said. "I mean, it's not as nice as this place, not by a long shot, but my mom . . . she always used to try and fix it up, before she got sick." He looked at my yellow vase. "The landlord wouldn't let us paint or put any holes in the walls, so there wasn't a whole lot we could do, but she liked to go to garage sales and buy stuff, like old vases that she'd put flowers in, you know, just wildflowers we'd pick alongside the road. She'd put them in a vase in the dining room." He looked embarrassed suddenly. "I don't usually notice stuff like that."

"Of course you do," I insisted. He looked at me and raised an eyebrow. "Even if you don't consciously notice it, your subconscious is paying attention, always," I said. That was the whole plan behind the color scheme, the calming happiness combo of greens/blues/yellows.

Tony stood up. "I've got enough problems with my *conscious* self," he said. "I don't need to go digging for more trouble beneath that." He laughed a little and so did I.

"So . . . you're okay, with living here? I mean, you like it here?" For the first time, I really felt like, if Tony didn't like it, then it was mostly my fault, and I didn't want to be a bad host, or a bad person.

"Yeah," he said, looking around. "It's a nice place. Robert, I mean, Dad, is a nice guy. It's nice to play ball again."

"Is that it?" I asked. "He's your dad, I mean, he's not just some guy." I felt a bit offended, like I had to stick up for my dad, even though lately I'd been having some confusing thoughts about him.

"Well, yeah, but he is just some guy, right now. You can't just meet somebody and have some instant connection like you've known them all your life."

I was thinking of stories I'd heard of long-lost family members reuniting. "Sometimes that happens, though," I said.

"In the movies, maybe," Tony scoffed. He chewed his thumb. "I miss my mom," he said.

"Has she called you yet?" I asked, but was immediately sorry I did. Tony looked away.

"Yeah, she did, but it wasn't easy to talk to her, you know? She doesn't . . . sound like herself, and she's got someone, some person, who's in charge of the house, standing there listening, plus a bunch of people in line waiting for the phone, rushing her."

"Where is she?" I asked. This was a house? It sounded more like a prison.

"She's in a rehab house," he said. "At least it's not jail, though it sort of seems like it is," he added, reading my mind.

He looked like he was about ready to cry. "I've never been there. She doesn't want me there. She said some of the people are 'scary' and anyway, she'll be out before we know it. She's just got to work really hard and . . . not mess up."

Tony talked like he was the grown-up, like his mom was the kid. "It's real easy to mess up, that's the problem. You think you've got yourself cured, and then your brain plays tricks on you, pulls you right back." He shrugged. "That's what my mom says anyway."

"I guess being around my mom is pretty different," I said.

I saw a slight smile appear on Tony's face. "You can say that again. They're different as night and day."

"Is that good or bad?"

"It's just different."

I kicked my legs out from under my covers. I didn't feel like lying around in bed any longer. I didn't feel very sick. But Mom had already called in to the school, and Tony wasn't going back today. I looked at my clock. It was only 11:30.

"Hey," I said. I couldn't believe I was saying this. "Do you want to help me paint a bookcase?"

Watching Paint Dry

Tony was a pro with the primer. I admired the way he made clean, careful strokes with his paintbrush. Most kids would just make a mess of things. Come to think of it, most kids wouldn't even know what primer is.

We took turns dipping our brushes into the can. "Where'd you learn how to paint?" I asked.

"My mom's boyfriend."

For a second, my dad's face flashed into my head, but he couldn't have meant him. They'd just met. Then I had another thought. Had Tony's mom considered my dad to be her boyfriend once? What had Dad thought? Thinking about it felt really gross.

"Hey, watch what you're doing," Tony said.

A big white dollop of primer plopped from my brush onto the tarp.

"Oops!" I said. I was normally much more careful.

Tony went on. "She was dating this guy with a house painting business, and I worked for him in the summer."

"That must have been kind of fun," I said. I was picturing him out in the sunshine, building some arm muscles, daydreaming while he worked.

"Fun?" Tony said. "No. Not fun. Not unless you like to get up at the crack of dawn, and stand on a ladder in the boiling-hot sun while some hairy guy yells at you to work faster." He stopped, his brush hovering for a minute like he was remembering something. "You know, he didn't even pay me. He said me and my mom were costing him a 'load of money,' and I had to 'earn my keep.'"

"Is he . . . at your house?" I asked. "I mean, you know, while your mom is in the rehab place?"

Tony laughed. "No, that guy is long gone."

He carefully removed the shelves from the bookcase so he could paint behind them. I took them into the cool garage and got out my sandpaper. "Long gone," I heard him say again, and then he whistled, a low, descending note, like the sound when you lose all your lives in an arcade game.

The primer stuck better if you roughed up the wood first with sandpaper. I went over all the surfaces a few times, watching the little pile of dust accumulate. Out in the driveway, the sun beat down on Tony. I saw him catch a white drip off a corner of the bookcase with his brush. He wiped the bristles across the top of the can.

He'd taken off his troublemaking T-shirt, and I could see the tan lines on his arms. He had the same shape as my dad, though skinnier, too skinny. Dad said he hadn't been eating all that well at home, but he was sure eating here. Two servings at dinner, sometimes three, so maybe he'd fatten up a little bit.

"Why don't we move that into the garage, where it's cooler?"

"I'm almost done," he answered, "then we can eat lunch."

Oh yeah, lunch. I'd forgotten about that. I suddenly had a great idea. "I'll make us a picnic!" I said.

I wiped the sawdust off the shelves and primed them. It didn't take long. Primer didn't have to be perfect. When I finished, I went into the house to gather some food and a blanket, and when I came back out, Tony was washing up at the spigot.

While I spread the blanket in the shade, he ran in to put on a different shirt, a plain orange polo. I set out some apples and pears and PB&Js, plus the good, really chocolatey granola bars that my mom thought she was hiding in the upper cabinet. Tony sat down, and we ate, staring at the bookcase.

"Well," I said, biting into an apple, "there's nothing as exciting as this, is there? Watching paint dry, I mean."

Tony swallowed a big bite of his sandwich. "It's fine by me," he said. "Sometimes it's too *much* excitement you have to worry about." He took a sip from his water bottle. "You want to know what I like about living here? It's this, peace and quiet."

I nodded, not totally sure what he meant. Excitement was always a pretty good thing in my book. Neither of us said much after that. We just ate and listened to the birds tweeting and the neighbor's spaniel barking at the back door to be let in. A car cruised slowly by, and after ten minutes, another one. If Tony didn't like too much excitement, he was in the right place.

"We can probably start the blue paint later," I said. "If you want to keep helping, that is." I looked down at the blanket, hoping he'd say yes.

"Yeah, sure," he answered. "It's not like I have anything else to do." He stood up and brushed some crumbs off his jeans. Then he stretched his arms over his head, blocking out the sun for a second and sending stripes of shade across the blanket. "Here's the thing, though. I'm helping you with this painting thing, so I need you to help me with something, in return."

"What is it?" I asked. Homework? No, he was a year ahead of me, doing stuff I didn't understand.

"Come to McDonald's with me after school on Thursday," he said.

"What?" That wasn't exactly the excitement I was hoping for. "Why?"

"I'm meeting my mom there. McDonald's. On Broad Street."

"Your mom? But I thought she was—"

"Yeah, she is, but she gets to see me sometimes, as long as the social worker is there. They don't want me to visit her at the re-hab place, and she can't leave it by herself." Tony put his hands on his hips. "You know I don't like the social worker."

"I . . . know, but . . . I don't know, Tony," I said, shaking my head. It seemed like it would be really weird. "I don't even know your mom at all."

"You'll be my moral support," he said.

I didn't say anything.

"Come on, please?" He gave me a big smile. "I'll buy you a shake and some fries."

I was leaning toward going anyway. I'd been craving fast food since last weekend. Plus, I had seen Tony talking to Rachel recently by her locker. I didn't even know they knew each other, but maybe he was trying to help me out with the whole Rachel situation. If that was the case, I owed him another one.

But then I remembered something.

"This girl at school told me someone overdosed at that McDonald's."

"Yeah? So?" Tony replied. "People OD all over the friggin' place."

Do they? I plucked some dandelions within reach of the blan-ket, started braiding their stems. "Has your mom ever overdosed?" I asked quietly.

Tony looked away from me, and then said, real low, "Twice. That I know of."

He sighed. "She'd been on these pain pills after her car got rear-ended, and she hurt her neck. But then she just couldn't get off them, and she couldn't get a prescription for them anymore, so she switched to even worse stuff, and she started dating some sketchy guys. The first time it happened, her boyfriend found her and called the ambulance, and then he took off, and she never saw him again. Nice, huh? He was probably the one who gave her the drugs to begin with."

I put down my dandelion stems. "I'm so sorry," I said. I didn't know what else to say. How could anything I said make it better?

Tony sat back down on the blanket and took three of the stems I'd put in a pile. He started neatly braiding them. I gave him a funny look, which he noticed.

"My mom used to ask me to braid her hair sometimes. She said I was better at it than she was."

We both kept our heads down, working on our dandelions. I started weaving mine into a crown.

"I don't have all the details about the second time it happened," Tony said. "I couldn't get the social worker to tell me anything."

He tossed his braided stems into the grass and wrapped his arms around his knees. "So, are you coming, or not?" he asked, and I saw something in Tony's face that I hadn't seen before. He was usually so good at hiding it, but he was really hurting. He was scared. And who could blame him?

"Yes," I said, "I'll go." I set the crown I'd made on his head, and he laughed, then took it off and set it on the blanket. "But only if I get large fries." I bumped his shoulder, and he bumped mine back.

"Okay," he said, hopping up off the blanket like he'd gotten a jolt of energy. "Should we do the blue paint?"

He pointed toward the can sitting just inside the garage door, right next to his beloved basketball.

"Let's wait a little while longer, make sure the primer is all the way dry," I said. I hopped up, too. "How about we play some basketball? I mean, I don't know much, but maybe you can teach me?"

I remembered when Dad used to play ball with me. It was all fun and games when I was little, but sometime after I got to maybe third grade or so, he seemed to get frustrated that I wasn't improving. He'd tell me to "quit messing around." Third grade is when girls can join a league at the Y, and I think Dad assumed all along that I was going to join. But I'd known all along I never would. Weird how we could both be so sure.

Tony ran over and grabbed the ball and dribbled it back to where I was standing in the driveway in front of the hoop.

"Can you dribble?"

"A little," I said. He passed the ball to me, and I immediately bounced it off my foot. It had been a while since I'd done this.

Tony took it back. "Like this," he said. "Use your fingers, not your palm."

I tried again, and again. Tony was a patient teacher, and I was pretty surprised how much fun I was having. We moved on to my shooting form, laughing and goofing around, when Dad pulled up, home early from work.

I started to scoot out of the driveway, but Dad called out, "You're fine! I'll park out here!" He parked in the street and got out, then walked up the driveway toward us with his briefcase. "Looks like you're feeling better, Maggie," he said, and then to Tony, "How was school?"

Dad had that goofy look on his face that adults get when kids are cooperating nicely with each other without being told.

"School was fine," Tony said, nonchalantly, as though he'd forgotten all about getting sent home for a dress code violation.

I held out my hands for Tony to pass me the ball, and then I took a shot and in it went, *swoosh*, all net.

"Nice one, Maggie," Dad said.

He was so pleased with us that he must not have realized it was too early for Tony to be home from school. Although, it was too early for Dad to be home from work as well. I wasn't sure what was going on, but I noticed Dad's smile start to fade, his face clouding over. He crossed his arms.

"Listen, I'm glad I got here before Mom and Grandma did," he said.

"Grandma's coming here?" I asked. Mom was supposed to get her settled at the assisted living facility today. "Is she coming for dinner?"

"Well, yes, for dinner," Dad said, "but then . . ." He shifted his feet a bit, his pointy, shiny work shoes glinting in the sun. "She actually needs to stay here, at the house, just for a bit. The facility, you see, they messed up, said they had a room, but it wasn't in the memory unit, where Grandma needs to be, and Mom had her all packed and ready, and so, well, Mom's just going to keep an eye on her here for a bit, temporarily."

Temporarily. There was that word again. I glanced at Tony, who was frowning. But I was excited about the prospect of Grandma being in the house. We could cut out pictures from magazines, of designs we liked, like we used to. She could help with the contest. I tried not to get my hopes up, though. With Grandma's illness, I didn't know what to expect.

"Where is she going to sleep?" Tony asked.

My dad ran a hand through his hair, which made it look even crazier than it usually did. He stared a moment at Tony, who was standing there with the basketball tucked under his arm. All the happy sounds from a few moments ago—the bouncing of the ball on the pavement, our laughter—all of that was gone. Even the birds had put their tweeting on pause.

"Would you mind sleeping on the pullout sofa for a little bit?" Dad asked Tony. "We can't very well expect Grandma to crawl up into Maggie's loft, plus she'll want a private space, so the spare bedroom is really the best choice for her."

"The *spare* bedroom?" Tony said. He was squeezing the ball tightly between his hands like he thought if he pressed hard enough, he could pop it. I could see the muscles tensing on his arms.

Dad kept talking. "It was Susan's idea to bring her out here immediately, and I told her it didn't make sense until we had a final confirmation from the assisted living people, but she went ahead and—"

Just then, Tony screwed up his face into a grimace and whipped the ball, super hard, against the house. It made a loud sound, and there was a black mark where it had hit the siding before rolling away into the grass.

"Tony!" my dad called, but Tony was already running into the house. He slammed the door behind him.

I felt my anger bubbling up in my gut. Tony shouldn't have to sleep on the couch, though Grandma shouldn't either. There had to be a better solution, and weren't the grown-ups in charge of figuring that out?

"Why did you have to tell him to leave his room?" I said to Dad. "I could sleep on the couch, and ... and Tony could sleep in my loft." I wouldn't like it, not that the couch was so bad. It's just that I wouldn't really like anyone—especially a somewhat smelly boy—sleeping in my room. But Dad shouldn't have kicked him out of his space.

"He already had to leave his apartment," I said, my voice rising. "And he was just getting settled here, and now you go and change everything on him."

"I thought you'd be okay with Grandma staying here," he said, "you, more than anyone."

"Yeah, I don't mind Grandma being here," I said. "It's not about Grandma, Dad. It's about you messing everything up with Tony!"

I watched as my dad's face flipped through a whole catalog of emotions, and while I didn't necessarily want to stand there, waiting to see which one he landed on, I also couldn't stop myself. There were things inside me that I needed to say, new things, surprising things, and now that I'd started, I had to see it through.

"Did you ever even really try to reconnect with him?" I asked. "Did you really try, or did you just give up? Because maybe it would have been nice to have a brother all this time, you know? Maybe it wouldn't have been so bad!"

"Maggie, I don't really appreciate your tone," Dad said. "There are a lot of things that you do not understand—"

"Then explain them to me!" I shouted. I was so tired of not knowing things.

Just then, Mom's car turned into the driveway with Grandma in the passenger seat, wearing a blue scarf and a scowl.

Dad dropped his hands to his sides and let out a long exhale, like a ball with a slow leak. "Wonderful," he muttered.

Mom pulled the car up, a grim expression on her face that stretched her lips into a thin line. She got out and headed around to Grandma's side. "You look much better, honey," she turned and said to me while opening Grandma's door.

"Maggie wasn't feeling well this morning, so she stayed home from school," she explained to Grandma, who didn't reply.

"Hi, Grandma!" I waved to her as she slowly made her way out of the car, but she was looking, not at me, but dismissively at my dad, who gave her a deflated smile. She didn't answer me, and I felt some tears sting my eyes. Grandma stood in the driveway with her big black purse in front of her, and I wondered if she had packed a sandwich for the ride. I wondered whether she'd eaten it already.

-•- ✦ -•-

Nobody had dinner together. Dad said he had to catch up on some emails since he'd left work early, so he was eating at the desk in their bedroom. Tony and I ate quietly, and quickly, at the kitchen island, while Mom served up a plate for Grandma and took it to the spare room (Grandma's room? Tony's room? What were we going to call it?) on a tray I'd decorated with heart stickers when I was in kindergarten. I could hear words floating down the stairs, Mom trying to coax Grandma to eat, like Grandma was a stubborn toddler.

"Just try a bite," she was saying. "I made it just the way you like it."

But Grandma had her own agenda. "And do you know when a bed will open up, Susan? When someone *dies*, that's when. That whole place is filled with *ghosts*."

Ghosts made me think of scary movies, which I didn't like. When Olive and Rachel and I had slumber parties at Rachel's, we always watched scary movies because Rachel's parents never bothered coming down into her basement to see what we had on. Rachel loved them, and Olive sort of did, but she would mostly shriek, while I hid under a blanket.

I had never really thought of ghosts as real people, though, like people who had just died at the assisted living facility. I never thought of Grandpa as a ghost. Did Grandma? Did Grandma think about becoming a ghost herself? I shivered.

Later, Tony and I spread out on the sofa bed doing our homework, while Mom sat in a chair with a bunch of paperwork from the facility. Dad had made up the bed with the extra sheets and blankets earlier, while we were out of the room. It felt like I hadn't said a word to Tony since our picnic.

I whispered, "Have you talked to Dad, after the whole . . . thing from earlier?"

Mom glanced up, and Tony shook his head. I noticed his

duffel bag behind the chair, clothes spilling out like they'd been packed in a hurry.

Suddenly, Grandma entered the room, almost as quiet as a ghost, and stared at Tony. She turned to Mom, asking, "Who's this?"

Mom set her paperwork on the coffee table. "It's Tony, remember? I told you about him in the car," she said, and I wondered just how much she'd actually told her.

"Hmmf," Grandma said and went back upstairs before Tony or I could say a thing to her. Mom followed her. I had thought Grandma and I could look at some decorating magazines tonight, but it was too late, and she was too out of sorts. I could see I'd have to choose my moments carefully.

"Not too friendly, is she?" Tony asked me after they were out of earshot.

"Oh, but she is! She usually is. We used to talk about design things together, especially landscaping designs because she's always liked flowers." I wondered if she remembered that she liked flowers, that lilies were her favorite. "Tony, I wish you could have known her before. She's different now. My mom says she doesn't have a 'filter,' like, stuff comes out of her mouth without her thinking about it first."

"That stinks," he said.

"What? That she doesn't have a filter?"

"No, that she had to change." Tony looked back down at his notebook. "I hate that."

I scooted closer to him, looking over his shoulder. "What are you studying?" I asked.

"Science. I've got a test tomorrow."

"Do you want me to quiz you?"

"Nah, that's okay."

I filled in an answer on my math worksheet, but I couldn't concentrate. I kept thinking about the argument with Dad.

"Are you sure you want to sleep here, Tony?" I asked. "Because I'd totally let you use my loft, if you wanted."

He put down his notebook. "You would?" he asked.

"Yeah."

Tony paused for a bit, like he was considering the offer, but then he picked up his notebook again. "Thanks, but, it's okay. I don't want to make trouble."

"Make trouble? You're not making trouble. I'm offering; you're not making me. I told Dad it wasn't fair to make you move again." I stood up and re-tucked the corner of the sheet.

"Yeah, I heard you," Tony said quietly.

"You did?"

"The window was open. And you weren't exactly whispering."

"Oh." I felt kind of embarrassed all of a sudden.

He picked at some fuzz on the blanket. "It's not like I'd already gotten so attached to that bedroom that it's a big deal to leave it. I mean, I'm in a strange house, living with people I barely know. It doesn't really matter where I'm sleeping, does it?"

That kind of hurt. "Of course it matters." I turned slightly away, letting my hair cover my face. "We're not that strange."

"I didn't say you were strange! It's just the situation."

We didn't say anything for a minute, until I said quietly, "Did you hear the rest of what I said?" None of this had to be strange. It was our parents who made it that way.

"Yup, heard that, too." Tony smiled at me. "Guess I shouldn't have whipped the ball like that. I was just so angry."

I shrugged. "You had a right to be."

"Yeah, it's just that . . . it's pretty complicated. You know when you asked me about what I thought of Dad?"

I nodded.

"Well, like I said, I like him, but I didn't tell you everything. You have to understand, my whole life, my mom has been telling me my dad was kind of a jerk, that he was just some dude who was passing through town, that he wouldn't even remember her name. I mean . . ." Tony looked away from me. "Maybe he could have tried harder, but it's not like my mom was helping things."

"Dad told me you'd moved away, but then he saw your mom

in town a few years ago and tried to get in touch," I said. Things had changed so quickly. Just last month, I would have lost my mind to think of Dad having a kid with . . . not Mom. Now it was like it was normal. "I think he wanted to see you, but . . . it didn't work out." I didn't know what exactly happened when Dad saw Tony's mom, but something about it led to my mom finding out about everything, which led to them thinking about getting divorced, which led to Dad telling Mom I shouldn't live with him. . . . And all of that was just part of the "things you do not understand" that Dad kept mentioning.

"Like I said . . . ," Tony started.

"It's complicated," we both said together.

"Jinx," we said.

"Buy me a Coke," I said.

"What?"

"Buy me a Coke," I repeated. "Did they do that at Bircher? When two people jinx each other?"

"No," he said. "Does someone actually buy you a Coke?"

"No," I said.

"Uh, okay," Tony said.

He got the funniest expression on his face, and I busted out laughing, and pretty soon, we were both laughing so hard we almost started crying. Eventually, we settled down and went back to our work, but after just a few minutes, I yawned, which made Tony yawn, which made us both laugh again, but we didn't jinx each other. It was past my bedtime. I didn't know if my parents had given Tony a bedtime, but he looked pretty tired.

"Are you sure about sleeping here?" I asked.

"Yeah," he said. "I'm sure."

I gathered my homework and handed him his pillow, which had fallen down behind the couch.

"You know, I would have liked to have known, too, that I had a sister," Tony said. He swung the pillow at me and just barely missed. "But better late than never."

Some Perfect Family

The McDonald's wasn't very busy inside, though there was a long line of cars at the drive-thru that Tony and I had to carefully weave around. I couldn't remember ever being inside the restaurant. On the rare occasion my mom or dad took me there, we used the drive-thru just like almost everyone else.

We were a little bit early. Tony wanted to "scope the place out," he'd said, find a good spot. He'd practically run here, with me trying to keep up, and now he paced around nervously, eyeing the tables. He had plenty of choices since the only other people here were a trio of old men in a booth on the far side.

"I'm going to sit at this long table," he said. "It's one of the cleanest ones."

"Yeah, but it's right by the door, so you'll be distracted every time someone comes in or out," I said.

Don't get me started on room arrangements. Different

purposes call for different spaces. The outer office at school, for example, had many different purposes, which was part of what made it a real challenge to decorate. Here, the purpose was clear—a distraction-free lunch for Tony and his mom.

"Take the corner one," I suggested. "It's bigger, and there's lots of light."

I took off my coat and looked the place over. It was clear they had just redecorated, going for that seventies vibe that was so popular right now. Grandma was right: eventually, everything came back into style. There were live plants on top of a low wall, which separated a section of booths from tables. I could smell the dirt, so someone must have just watered them. I reached out and rubbed a leaf between my thumb and finger. There were so many realistic-looking fake plants these days, but these were the real deal.

"Okay, I'll sit at the corner one, and you can sit in this booth," Tony said, pointing to one just on the other side of the wall.

"Oh," I said, "you don't want me to sit with you?"

"I think I might need a few minutes with just her. Then I'll call you over."

"Okay," I said, heading to the booth. This was actually easier, less awkward.

"I think she's really going to like you," Tony added, and I smiled back at him.

He seemed really nervous, which was totally understandable. I felt nervous, too. I wasn't sure why. Did it really matter whether Tony's mom liked me? Maybe not, but I wanted her to anyway. I wondered what she looked like. Movies made it seem like people who used drugs looked really scary, but I didn't know if I believed that was true. I guessed I was about to find out.

I slipped into the booth and studied the space to keep my mind occupied while Tony paced around. The walls were orange, except for one accent wall that was green, and there were framed pictures of ocean scenes hanging on the walls. That seemed out of place for a Midwestern McDonald's but reminded me of our family trip to the beach. I'd been thinking about that trip a lot lately, about finding the shell with my dad. I'd been holding the shell a lot lately, too.

It was hard now to remember that trip without thinking about Tony, without wondering what it would have been like to have Tony along. It was hard to remember anything now without also remembering that, since second grade, Mom knew about Tony, and Dad had known much longer than that. So, like, when I had my fifth birthday party where I rode a pony, Dad knew Tony was out there, getting ready for his sixth birthday. When I lost my first tooth, did my dad wonder if Tony had lost his? Did the tooth fairy come to Tony's apartment?

I didn't know if I'd ever stop thinking stuff like that. About the before and after of my life. Before Tony and After Tony, like those pages in a design magazine.

The door facing the parking lot opened, and a gray-haired woman I recognized as Tony's social worker came in, followed by a thin lady with lots of freckles wearing a green turtleneck and jeans. Her black hair was pulled into a curly ponytail, and her face looked very pale, except for a thick slash of red lipstick.

The woman spotted Tony and went quickly toward him, pulling him into her for a rib-cracking hug. She was shorter than he was. She wasn't what I'd expected, though I'm not sure I had a clear picture of what I'd expected. I guess I wasn't expecting her to look so normal, as normal as my own mom, though they didn't look alike at all. My mom had long, blond hair, and was pretty curvy. My mom also wore a lot of makeup, or at least she did when she was going out to show houses. Tony's mom wore lipstick like she wasn't used to wearing it. The color wasn't right for her.

I don't know why I was comparing her to my mom, but that made me think about Dad, which made me think about his cheating, which made me feel . . . gross again. I wanted to hate this mousy little woman sitting across from Tony, to blame her for everything, but it was hard when I knew she was sick, and when I knew how much Tony loved her, and when I knew, no matter how much I loved my dad, that he'd messed up. "I missed you so much," I could hear her say, and then she murmured something else, close to Tony's ear, that I didn't catch. The social worker cleared her throat and gestured toward the corner table, where Tony had tossed his coat. They all took a seat.

I wished I'd sat farther away. I was suddenly very aware that I looked like an idiot sitting in the booth by myself with no food. I thought of the BFFs and wished we were all here together, laughing and eating Happy Meals, but when was the last time we were together, happy? I could barely remember.

I hadn't brought any money because Tony had said he'd treat me. I reached instinctively into my pocket for my phone so I'd have something to do, but remembered it was charging back home on the kitchen counter. The only thing I'd brought was my yellow striped umbrella because it was supposed to rain today. Grandma would be proud of my preparedness, I thought, and I wondered what she was doing at home right now. She was probably sleeping. She'd been doing an awful lot of that.

The three old guys were sipping large cups of coffee, their baseball caps lined up on their table like they didn't think it polite to wear them inside, even inside a McDonald's. They were staring, though, at Tony and his mom and the social worker, which wasn't polite at all. Then I realized I was staring at the old guys, which wasn't cool either, so I gazed down at the tabletop. It was orange with faint white shapes that looked like the amoebas we'd studied in science.

Tony's mom asked him what he wanted to eat. "I brought some money, so it's on me," she said as she led the way up to the counter.

When they returned to their table, they had trays loaded with Big Macs and fries and shakes. An apple pie teetered on the edge of Tony's tray, so close I could have grabbed it when he walked by. It was terrible to smell all that food and not eat any. My dad said they wafted the french fry smell through special vents into the neighborhood to make people hungry. I didn't know if that was true. It didn't seem legal.

As Tony passed me, he gave a little shrug and raised his eyebrows, like he was apologizing for not getting me anything. His mom was in front and didn't notice Tony looking at me, but the social worker did, and she gave me the skunk-eye.

I tried to make myself smaller, shrinking down into the booth. The social worker didn't sit with them, but she was at the table right next to theirs, where she played with her phone while she ate, pretending not to listen in. I was listening, too. I couldn't help it. When was Tony planning to call me over? I was wondering if he'd give me some cue. *And introducing . . . my half-sister!!!!* And I'd hop over to their table, waving and smiling, like a game-show contestant.

But that didn't happen, and the longer they talked, the more I wondered whether I should have come at all. My mom and dad had been on the fence about it. But Tony had said he needed "moral support," and after the way he blew up at Dad and threw the basketball against the house, I think they didn't want to argue with him.

I heard Tony's mom ask how school was going, and Tony said, "Good, real good," and as she asked him about each individual subject, he replied how he had aced this test or that quiz and gotten an A on this or that presentation. I would have wondered if he was exaggerating, but I'd heard Dad and Mom talking about checking in with Tony's teachers and saying that he was doing really well. I knew seventh graders had more homework than sixth graders, but still, he seemed to spend a lot of time on it, when he wasn't shooting hoops.

I'd gotten kind of used to doing my own homework to the accompaniment of the *thunk, thunk, clang* coming from the driveway. A few times this past week, I'd even taken a break and joined him. He never corrected my shooting form, like Dad used to. We also finished painting the bookshelf during our basketball breaks.

When I snuck a glance over the plants, over at their table, Tony was still going on and on about school and hanging out with Dad's basketball friends and their sons for pick-up games, but his mom didn't look so happy anymore. She clutched her coffee in both hands, her fingernails showing the remnants of some chipped red polish that matched her lips.

Finally, she interrupted him. "Well, *I'm* doing better, if you want to know," she said.

Tony kind of stuttered, "Y-yeah, I mean, you look better, so I figured—"

Outside, the rain was starting to come down. Little drops splashed against the restaurant window. I saw the wipers of the cars in the drive-thru line all switch on like they were synchronized. There was an uncomfortable silence coming from Tony and his mom. I tried to keep my eyes on my table.

"Sounds like everything's just going perfectly for you," Tony's mom said, kind of sarcastically. Tony was chewing his thumbnail and playing with his hamburger wrapper. "You've got the *perfect* dad and the *perfect* stepmom, but let me tell you something, your dad is not as *great* as he thinks he is."

"Then why did you send me to live with him?" Tony asked, his voice loud.

The old men were really staring now and looking back and forth at each other like they were watching some TV talk show. The social worker sighed, gathering up all her trash onto her tray.

That's when Tony's mom turned and pointed at me. "And who's this then? Your girlfriend, or your sister?"

I bolted. Right out into the rain. I didn't wait to hear what Tony said, didn't wait to see if his mom was going to lump me into the "perfect family" she thought Tony was part of. Some perfect family! What a joke.

I got my umbrella opened, but not before the rain pelted me a million times, stinging my face. A car honked at me as I dashed in front of the line of vehicles. I wanted to run home as fast as I could, but I didn't want to leave Tony, especially when he seemed so upset. I skipped a puddle and waited on the sidewalk, the rain thrumming against the fabric of my umbrella like it might break through.

"Hey!" he yelled. He came around the corner, running over to me. I could see his mom and the social worker leaving the McDonald's from the other door and hurrying to their car. So soon? His mom had already seen enough of him?

"You can share," I said, waving him toward me and my umbrella. There was water running off Tony's shaggy hair, making tracks down his face, and I noticed one of his shoelaces had come undone and trailed in a muddy line behind him.

"Thanks," he said.

We squeezed under the umbrella, both of us smelling strongly of french fries. We didn't fit very well. One of my sleeves was still getting soaked.

"Why did your mom say all that stuff? About our dad?" I asked.

Dad had royally screwed up, and I was mad at him, too, but it was kind of weird how, when an outsider said something against Dad, I wanted to protect him. He was still my family.

"I don't know." Tony bit his lip and looked out into the rain, as though the answer was there. "Who knows why she does anything."

"Doesn't she want you to be happy?" I heard my voice getting high and squeaky. "To have a house and food and a school you're doing good at? I mean, if she didn't want you to be with your dad, why didn't she just keep pretending he didn't exist?"

"I know! That's what I asked her! It's all so dumb."

The patter of raindrops suddenly turned to the ping of ice pellets. Tony tilted his head and yelled, "This sucks!" into the sky, and I didn't know if he was talking about his situation or the weather, or both.

We watched the little pellets hit the sidewalk and bounce. "Let's keep walking," I said, and we set off. I didn't know about Tony, but this McDonald's was now the last place I wanted to be.

After we'd gone half a block, I asked, "What did she say, when you asked her that?"

"She said she didn't have any other choice, that she didn't want me to live with a stranger, and then she started crying, and the social worker told me to give her a few days and we could talk on the phone, and then they left."

"Kind of ironic, though. I mean, you are living with strangers," I said, and laughed, trying to lighten the mood. "You said so yourself."

"That's not what she meant," he said, and I could tell he was bitter at her, not me. "And you know it. She meant living with people I wasn't related to, a foster family."

We stopped at a light, and Tony pressed the button for the walk signal. Then he pressed it again, press, press, press, harder and harder.

"Tony," I said. But he kept doing it, and then he kicked the pole.

"*Tony*," I said again. There were raindrops rolling down Tony's skin, but there was something just under his skin, too, something I couldn't see but could only feel.

Finally, he stopped and shoved his hands into his pockets, and we just waited, huddled under the umbrella, watching people drive by in their toasty-warm cars. The stickman flashed on, and we hurried across.

I felt something cold against my ankle and realized my pant legs were soaked. I looked at Tony's and saw his were, too. At least my umbrella was keeping the sleet off our heads.

"Come on," I said, striding more quickly toward home. The important thing was to keep moving.

Dirty Little Secret

In the morning, when I tugged back my curtain, I couldn't see any sign of the freaky ice storm. The sun was shining, and it looked like it would be a beautiful fall day. I heard Mittens purring, but the sound wasn't coming from the foot of my bed.

"What the—!"

Tony! He was sitting at my desk, wearing Mittens around his neck. He had on my dad's old blue plaid pajamas, as usual, the cuffs rolled up, and he was bent over his math workbook, scribbling with my favorite pencil, the one with the green and yellow hearts all over it.

I certainly didn't appreciate having my personal space invaded, especially so early in the morning. Couldn't a person expect to get a good night's sleep in her own room without being scared to death when she wakes up?

"What are you doing here?" I asked. Then I noticed the nest

of blankets and a pillow by my door, the same ones that had been on the sofa bed. "Why aren't you downstairs in your bed?" I asked.

"It's not a bed. It's a couch," he said.

"It's a sofa *bed*, if you want to be technical."

"Well, I don't want to be technical, and it's not very comfortable," he said, kind of snotty. He flipped his workbook closed. Then he whispered, with a glance toward the hall, "*My* bed is being occupied by *your* grandma."

"What is that supposed to mean?" I said. I mean, I knew what it literally meant, but I didn't like his tone. It was too early to be having an argument. I'd barely woken up. What was with Tony this morning?

"Maybe you should go shoot some hoops," I suggested.

I took my purple brush from the shelf attached to my loft and started tugging out the mess of tangles that piled up every night.

"No," Tony said, without looking up.

"Fine," I said, "suit yourself."

He just sat there at my desk, Mittens around his neck, looking up at me like he was waiting for me to come down from my loft and fight him or something, though it was hard for him to look tough with a cat around his neck.

My nose twitched. I noticed his duffel bag had somehow found its way into my room. That thing smelled like old socks.

"Why are you acting so cranky?" I said. "And why don't you fold your clothes and put them in a drawer?" I added.

"Oh, and where would I find this magical drawer?" he shot back. He stood up quickly, which made Mittens leap down.

"Mittens!" I called, but Tony scooped her up and held her like a baby in the crook of his arm.

"Don't you worry," he said to Mittens, in this syrupy voice, "I'll just keep carrying everything around with me, like a snail, carrying its house on its back." He started wadding up the blankets in one hand, still holding Mittens in his arm.

"She doesn't like that," I said, though she actually seemed to like it very much. She even had her tongue sticking out a little, which she only did when she was relaxed.

"Yes she does."

Ugh, he was so aggravating. Was this what it was like to have a sibling? One minute you were laughing together and the next, at each other's throats? Maybe he just didn't get a good night's sleep.

"I'm sorry you had to sleep downstairs, Tony, but remember, I said I'd sleep on the couch, so you could sleep in my loft." I set my brush down, though I knew there were still knots in the back of my head. "And you said no."

He didn't say anything, just put Mittens down, then scooped his stuff into one pile and tried to carry it out of my room, all at once. I heard Grandma call to my mom.

"Susan!"

"Oh great, now you woke Grandma," I said. She needed a peaceful night's sleep more than any of us. I tried again. "I *told* you I'd switch places, Tony."

"You can't switch places with me!" He walked out, hidden behind a mountain of clothes and blankets.

I didn't understand what his problem was. It wasn't my fault he didn't take me up on my offer. I knew he was probably still upset about what happened with his mom yesterday. I would be. But he didn't have to take it out on me. I had gone with him! I was trying to help!

I got down from my loft and noticed one of his socks sitting just inside my doorway. Must have fallen out of his pile. I got my plastic dinosaur-head-grabby-thing that I'd won at the fair, picked up the sock, and carried it to the hall, where I dropped it down the laundry chute. Then I went back into my room and closed the door tightly. I needed a lock.

I thought about how Olive's little brother wrecked all her stuff and Rachel's brothers teased her. At least in Rachel's family there were three kids, so if one sibling was being a pain, you could turn to the other one.

I thought of that decorating show where families switched spaces and decorated a room in each other's houses. Somebody always ended up crying, and I don't mean happy tears. I used to think Rachel's family was great because her parents had a lot of money, so she always had the latest cool things. But her dad was hardly ever around, and I wouldn't like that. And I wouldn't want to switch places with Olive's family because things always seemed a little out of control over there, which bugged me. Were there no families that got along?

I balled up my fists and could feel my own not-happy tears coming. I went to my desk to get my shell. But it wasn't there. I moved the pencil cup, the little box with my paper clips, and the other box with pushpins for my bulletin board. The shell wasn't behind them where it always was. I could feel my heart starting to flutter as I looked again behind everything. I looked in places where my shell had never been before.

And then I saw it, or what was left of it, on the floor under my chair.

It was in pieces.

"Nooooooo!" I wailed. "No, no, no."

I picked up the shards, which pricked my fingers with their sharp edges. There were four larger pieces and then tiny bits, just fragments really, smashed into the carpet. Not even the strongest glue in my craft box was going to fix this. And I felt like . . . like all the memories that were part of that shell were ground to dust, and all that was left was the white powder on my fingertips.

I put the big pieces into the trash. My nose was running. I reached for the box of tissues I usually kept on my desk, but it wasn't there. *Where was everything?* I always kept everything right in the place where it was supposed to be, always, so it would be there when I needed it. I looked around and noticed my plant had been moved, and some of my books were gone, because there was a space like a missing tooth in my bookshelf.

I sniffled and got another leftover whiff of Tony's bag.

Tony!

He had been sitting at my desk doing his homework when I woke up. He was holding one of my pencils, which he must have taken from the cup. Who knew if it was the first time, either? What if he'd come in here before, when I was off with Olive working on the contest, and snooped through my stuff?

I heard him come out of the bathroom, then tromp down the stairs. Then I heard Grandma say, "Susan, I'm hungry," and then, weirdly, "I'm Eleanor Hanson," which was in fact her name, but why she needed to say it like that, I had no idea. Perhaps that was part of the disease, like her brain was trying to grab everything it could and pin it in place.

I heard Mom running up the stairs, heard the jangling of dishes on the bed tray. I couldn't go in there and help, although I wanted to. Not right now.

I leaned against my door and took deep breaths. My clock said it was well past the time that I should have been up and dressed for school, but I couldn't do it. I just couldn't do anything right now. I opened my closet door, pushed away enough stuff so I could fit inside, and closed the door with a soft click.

Ironic how my parents called my closet my "dirty little secret" now that I knew all the secrets they'd been keeping. I thought of it more as my "cozy little space." I took a deep inhale of that bubblegum-mixed-with-lotion smell and made a mental note to someday look for those gum wrappers. I couldn't really see anything in the dark closet, but I didn't need to. I knew the stuffed animals were in the back left corner. I knew in the back right, there was a stack of Lego kits I'd gotten for presents when I was into that. I still had a half-finished *Millennium Falcon.* Dresses I hardly ever wore hung from a metal rod, brushing against the top of my head as I sat there cross-legged, listening to nothing but my own breathing.

I leaned against my pile of stuffed animals. My favorites were on my bed, but I had a lot. I rotated through them occasionally, trying to give them all a chance, even the ones I really didn't like anymore, like a musty old carrot I'd won at the fair. If I gave any of them away, even that gross carrot, I knew I'd worry about them ending up in that big bin at the Shoppe, forever and ever, getting squished on the bottom, where no customers would ever find them, and it made me sad to think they wouldn't have anybody to love them.

I took another deep breath. I was starting to feel, well, still bad, honestly, but more like someone had merely punched me in the stomach, instead of running over my foot with their car. I reached up to a hook on the closet wall and pulled off the knitted yellow blanket that a coworker of my mom's had made when I was born. It was meant for a crib, way too small to be of much use in keeping me warm anymore, but I still loved it. It was soft from a million washings.

I didn't remember when I'd quit carrying it around. Mom said I'd taken it to preschool but some other kids made fun of me. Maybe that was when I stopped. At some point, I moved it to the closet. Had I used the blanket in the same way I used my shell? I was so young when I used it, I couldn't remember.

And then it hit me: the shell. The shell wasn't just a reminder of good memories. It had also held all my bad thoughts, all the things I'd rubbed into it, like when I was worried about Rachel not wanting to be my friend anymore or about whether we could win the contest without her, or when I'd worry (huge worries!) about this new brother I never knew I had. Before that, I was fixated on that old, bad memory of Mom saying she and Dad were getting divorced, and I needed to decide who to live with.

I'd rubbed all of those thoughts into the shell, and now it was broken. But maybe, maybe, with those broken shards I'd thrown into the trash, I had also thrown out those bad thoughts.

I wasn't going to forget the walks on the beach, the good stuff. I didn't need the shell for that.

-•- ✦ -•-

I couldn't hear anything outside my closet. The double sound barrier from my closed closet door combined with the closed bedroom door meant I could stay quietly inside my little cocoon, wishing this day could rewind like a tape in one of those old cassette players Olive and I found at the Shoppe. I could go back to the beginning, start again.

I didn't hear Tony come into the room. The first sign of his presence was the click from the closet doorknob. I quickly reached out to grab hold of it, but felt it turning in my hands. I caught a glimpse of his blue hoodie in the sliver of daylight when the door opened a crack.

"Get out!" I yelled.

He was stronger. He jerked the door open.

"Calm down," he said. "Your mom told me to check on you. It's almost time to leave for school, and you haven't eaten anything."

I had three stuffed animals clutched to my chest, but I could feel my heart thumping right through them.

Tony gave my pajamas a disapproving look. "Are you sick or something?" he asked.

"Sick?" I said. "What I'm sick of is you butting into my room and messing with my stuff."

"I didn't mess with anything!"

"You broke my shell! My favorite shell, my favorite souvenir of *my* trip to the beach with *my* dad."

"What are you talking about? I didn't break anything."

I lunged out of my closet, which he wasn't expecting. But he jumped back before I could shove him, so I landed on the rug in front of my desk. Behind me, the Lego kits toppled, and one spilled out all its pieces onto the closet floor. I pointed to a few tiny bits of shell embedded in the carpeting.

"What's that?" Tony asked.

"It's my shell, what's left of it."

Tony held up his hands. "Well, I didn't do that. I've never even seen your shell." He looked closer at the mess. "Why was it on the floor?"

"It wasn't on the floor. It was on my desk."

"Well, I didn't see it, or touch it, and anyway, if it's that special, why didn't you put it away somewhere? Why would you have it where anybody could just accidentally knock it on the floor?"

"Because *anybody* doesn't use my desk, get it? JUST ME!" I jabbed my thumbs into my chest.

"Well," Tony sputtered, "you shouldn't accuse people without evidence, and you should take better care of your stuff, I mean, look at that closet." He pointed, and his lips curled up into a terrible smirk. "What a complete mess! I thought you were the queen of organization, the queen of decorating."

That did it. "You really think *I'm* a mess? Really?" When I became Principal for a Day, my first order of business would be transferring Tony back to Bircher. I kicked the Legos into the closet, slammed the door. "Have you looked in the mirror lately?"

We just stood there staring each other down. I would have shoved him out of my room, but he had a look on his face that told me he'd shove back.

Just then, Mom came in with a look on *her* face that said she was about ready to clunk our skulls together.

"I don't know what is going on in here, but I have got enough to deal with, and . . ." She looked at my pajamas. "Maggie. Get. Dressed," she said in a voice so calm and steady that it was totally scary. Even Tony looked taken aback. "Then, both of you. Get your things and get to that bus. Right now. Or so help me God, I will take you to school in tiny pieces."

Great, I thought. *I'll be just like my shell.*

- • - ✦ - • -

When I heard my door open a minute later, I yelled, "I'm coming!" and spun around, still pulling a shirt over my head. But it wasn't Tony, or Mom. It was Grandma.

"Are you okay, honey? I heard yelling."

"Oh, Grandma, yes. I'm fine. I just . . . I was having a little argument with Tony. Sorry if it bothered you."

Grandma had on her long flannel nightgown, but over it was her cream-colored silk robe, knotted at her waist. Her silver hair was out of its typical bun and hanging loose around her shoulders, and she looked beautiful, especially her bright green eyes, which, this morning, seemed completely clear.

"Tony?" she said. "The foreign exchange student?"

"Uh . . ." So this is how my parents were dealing with the Tony situation? Another lie?

"Go easy on him, Maggie," she said. "It can be hard to get used to a new place."

She took a few steps toward me and held out her arms for a hug, and I squeezed her tightly until she pulled back and held me by the shoulders. She brushed a strand of my hair out of my eyes.

"Don't you look beautiful today," she said.

I knew I looked a mess. It wasn't like I didn't have a mirror in my room. But leave it to Grandma to find the beauty in anyone or anything. Why couldn't she always be this way? Why couldn't Tony always be like he was when we had our picnic? Why did things ever have to change?

-•- ✦ -•-

I sat on the bus, chewing the health-food Pop-Tart Mom had pressed into my hand as I'd run out the door.

A girl named Sarah leaned over the seat in front of me. "Do we have band today?" she asked.

"I don't know. I'm not in band."

She screwed up her face. "You're not? I thought you played flute."

She popped her gum, and I looked at her blankly for a moment. "I think I would know if I played the flute," I told her.

"You don't have to be *mean*."

"Sorry," I mumbled, but she'd already leaned across the aisle to ask someone else. You'd think she might have noticed all the instrument cases clogging the aisle, where they were not supposed to be. I'd tripped over a trumpet case myself.

I rested my head against the window and could see Tony's head leaning the same way, three rows ahead of me. Talk about not noticing things. How could Tony not have noticed my shell? Especially after crunching it under his foot, or the chair wheels, or whatever happened?

The bus started pulling away from the curb, but Olive was still missing. She hadn't shown up at the bus stop. And Rachel's mom was driving her to school more and more lately, probably because she thought the bus wasn't Rakell-cool enough.

Suddenly, I caught a glimpse of blue out the window. Olive's coat. She was running alongside the bus, yelling, "Wait! Wait!"

The driver hit the brakes, and I jerked forward and bumped my head on the seat in front of me. I heard the screech of the heavy doors opening and looked up to see Olive coming down the aisle, wheezing and panting. She sank into the seat with me.

"Whew!" she said, "that was a close one. That would almost have been a catastrophe. The opposite of fantabulous! My mom had already left for work, so how would I have gotten to school? Plus, we have that quiz this morning, and if I don't do well, I'm totally toast. Oh, and hey—" She caught her breath and looked at me. "What's wrong with your brother?" she asked.

"Huh?" I said. It was still so weird to hear someone say that. "Tony?"

"Yeah, he's crying, so something's obviously wrong."

I stood up and tried to crane my neck to look over the seats.

"Sit down, Miss Owens," the bus driver called out.

I sat down and pressed my cheek against the window again. I could see Tony's head leaning against his window, just as before. From my position, it looked like he was taking a nap.

"Are you sure he's crying?" I asked Olive.

"Pretty sure," Olive said. "His eyes are all wet, and he was rubbing them. Unless he has allergies. There's a high pollen count today. I checked this morning. Does he have allergies?

"How would I know?"

"Well, he's your brother," Olive replied with a shrug. "Hey, are you going to eat that?" She pointed to the other half of my whole grain, no high-fructose-corn-syrup Pop-Tart, which was still in the package sitting on my lap. I handed it to her.

"Thanks," Olive said. "You know, my baby brother is allergic to peas, which I think is totally lucky for him because he never has to eat even one bite of them. Pollen, though, that would suck. I mean, hello, it's everywhere."

Olive sniffed at the Pop-Tart and made a face. "What is this?" she asked.

"Um, could we, maybe, not talk right now?" I said. I was not in the mood this morning, for Olive or Tony or tripping over trumpet cases. "I'm just kind of tired," I added. My head had started aching like crazy. I pressed my thumbs over my eyebrows to try and make it stop.

-·- ✦ -·-

I decided to go to the nurse's office before my first class. I couldn't afford to spend another day at home sick, not with the outer office waiting to be finished, but if I could just get some Tylenol or something, I'd be fine.

"What's up, hon? Not feeling well?" the nurse, Mrs. Sherman, asked.

I hadn't personally talked to Mrs. Sherman before, but she was introduced during an assembly and seemed really nice. Plus, I knew all the students loved her. I'd heard some of them faked an illness just to get out of class and hang out with her, though maybe that was just a rumor. I'd also heard Mr. V was going to give all the students a vacation day if everybody voted in the contest, but that was probably a rumor, too; it seemed too good to be true.

Mrs. Sherman had short, gray hair, which seemed grandma-ish, but she also had a nose ring, which did not. I sure couldn't picture my grandma with a nose ring. I was pretty sure she'd just stick to scarves as a fashion statement.

"I've got a bad headache," I said, rubbing my forehead.

"Have a seat," she said. She pointed to a green, cushioned table just inside another room. Like the principal's office, the nurse's office had its own divided space: one outer room with her desk and a filing cabinet, and another room with an exam table and tall supply cabinet. I expected it to smell like a doctor's office, but all it smelled like was coffee. There was a big mug of it on her desk.

"I'm going to get you a glass of water," Mrs. Sherman said.

She went bustling out of the room just as the phone rang, and I heard her talking to someone about flu shots. The call got increasingly tense, at least what I could hear of it. "It's only available that one day . . . well, I really can't . . . you don't need to use that language with me . . ."

I heard her hang up the phone, then she came back in and handed me a glass of water. "Sorry about that," she said. She pushed her hair off her forehead and let out an exasperated sigh. "Seems like everybody wants something from me today, and the day hasn't barely started yet."

"Sorry," I said.

"Oh, don't worry about it. Have you eaten breakfast?"

"Not much," I answered, remembering my half a Pop-Tart.

"Let me get you some crackers."

She opened the army-green metal cabinet on the wall and started shoving things around. I saw a roll of gauze and some of those ice packs you smack against something to make them cold. There were several pink bottles of Pepto-Bismol, but next to those, something caught my eye—a white box with red letters and a picture of a bottle shaped like the allergy spray my mom squirted up her nose on heavy pollen days like today. I'd seen her using it this morning. *NARCAN* was written on the box in all caps.

I pointed. "Have you ever used that?"

"That? Goodness no," Mrs. Sherman said, pulling out a basket full of packaged saltines. "Here they are." She handed me a pack and closed the cabinet. "Drink all that water," she said. "Lots of headaches are caused by dehydration, you know."

I nodded and nibbled a cracker. The other cracker in the pack was crunched to bits. All those little white cracker flakes in the bottom of the bag unfortunately reminded me again of my broken shell, and Tony. Just the thought of our argument made my head throb even more. I wished at that moment he *were* an exchange student. Then there would be a set date for his departure.

"Do you have any Tylenol?" I asked.

"Oh, no, I'm sorry," Mrs. Sherman said. She patted my knee. "I can't give you any medicine, hon, even over-the-counter stuff, not without a parent's written permission. Your parents would have to come down here and sign a form."

She leaned against the table and rolled her eyes. "I know, I know," she continued, though I hadn't said anything. "If they're going to come down here and fill out a form, they might as well give you some Tylenol themselves. Or take you home." She rested a warm hand on my shoulder. "Is there anything else I can help you with? Anything you want to talk about?"

Suddenly, all my anxieties and worries, every issue, big and small, that had been jamming up my brain at night while I tried to sleep, came rushing into that spot behind my eyes where the headache was. Maybe that was why it hurt. I opened my mouth, but didn't know where to start.

Mrs. Sherman tilted her head. "I'm not a psychologist or anything, but people have said I'm a good listener."

She looked at me with these big puppy-dog eyes, like she couldn't wait for me to spill my guts. It felt weird. I started noticing how uncomfortable I was on the hard table. The tag in my shirt was scratching the back of my neck, and I was way too warm. I felt myself shut down.

I took a big swig of water. "Thank you, but . . . I think this water is working already. I think I was just dehydrated."

"Whatever you say," she said and gave my knee another pat.

I could tell I'd disappointed her. It seemed clear she actually enjoyed talking with kids about their problems, and she could tell I had some problems to talk about. In fact, the only thing that looked more disappointed than her face was this room. The whole place was so industrial-looking, the walls a pea green that looked like the soup Olive's brother was allergic to. There was no art, just a poster on how to give the Heimlich maneuver.

Maybe when the Spirit Week contest was over, I'd give this place a redo, just for fun.

Why not? It wasn't so different from doing the outer office. This was just another outer office on a smaller scale. I couldn't get it done in time for the judging, and Mr. V probably wouldn't let us have two entries anyway, but maybe I could get started. Talk about school spirit! What was more spirited than going above and beyond the contest just to do something nice for a nice person?

"Have you thought about redecorating in here?" I asked, following Mrs. Sherman back to the main room.

She laughed loudly. "What, you don't like my artwork?" Besides the Heimlich poster, the only "art" was a diagram on an easel about how to properly blow your nose so you wouldn't spread germs.

She stopped laughing when she saw I wasn't. "Are you serious?"

"Absolutely," I said. "I'm working on the outer office where Mrs. Abbott sits for the Spirit Week contest, and this space has a lot in common with that one."

"Well, I . . ." Her face softened, and I could see her picturing what could be. We both were.

Just then, her phone rang, but before she picked it up, she said, "I'd love that, hon."

I got out just as a boy went in, clutching his stomach and looking very pale. I started down the hall toward my locker while taking my hand sanitizer out of my front backpack pocket. I gave myself a spritz. My head was feeling better already.

Call It Done

"I'm proud of you girls," Mrs. Abbott said. She was standing in front of her desk holding her bowl of lemon drops. I'd already eaten three, and so had Olive. Because it was Saturday, Mrs. Abbott was wearing jeans and a sweatshirt with a big, fat bird on it. During the school week, she wore a skirt and blouse. She looked even more comfortable (and even less chic) in her weekend clothes. She also looked very happy with us, with everything we'd done.

"You girls have sure made a difference in here," she said. "I think I'm really going to look forward to coming to the office!"

I smiled. There was nothing as great as knowing you'd made your client happy. And once I finished a design, I just wanted to get right to work on another one. I needed to tell Olive about redecorating Mrs. Sherman's office, and Rachel, too, *if* she ever wanted to hang out with us again.

"I hope all the students feel the same way you do!" I said.

They'd have the chance to look at the entries on Monday, before they voted. Olive and I had checked the other rooms when we'd arrived at the school this morning, and no one had set up yet.

"We have to tell people to vote for us!" Olive told her. "The cheerleaders were handing out flyers in study hall yesterday, telling people to vote for the main hallway. And this kid had a Blow Pop and said the math team had given it to him."

"Can they do that?" I asked.

Olive shrugged. "I guess?"

"So, you've got the cheerleading team and the math team. Who else?" Mrs. Abbott asked.

"There's the boys' basketball team," I said. "They got the hallway outside the gym, and student council has the car loop hallway, plus science club is in the science room, which was a lucky draw for them." I'd seen no plans from any of those groups. Had they even made a plan? Who knew what they were going to do? It was all one big question mark.

"You look worried," Olive said to me. "Don't be worried. Come on." She motioned me over to our beautiful blue bookcase. Tony had done a great job helping me paint it, and Olive had added a swirly white pattern along the sides that almost looked like the Milky Way and matched the swirls in a rug we'd found.

She handed Mrs. Abbott her phone. "Will you take our picture?"

"Absolutely!" she said. "Smile!"

"Now, one over here," Olive said and moved to the poster of Van Gogh's *The Starry Night* that Mrs. Abbott had found when Olive asked her if she had any posters. I'd put it in one of the many frames I had lying around, a silver one that looked expensive but wasn't. It was totally normal to take photos of our "afters"; I usually took them myself and put them in a portfolio to show future clients. But I wasn't usually *in* them. Still, this was fun.

"Wait," I said, "we can't forget the new filing system!"

I pulled open a drawer full of copies of blank forms, stuff like permission slips that got sent home to parents. I didn't have enough money to buy a new cabinet, but I'd completely reorganized and labeled everything because Mrs. Abbott said she never had time to get to that.

"Say cheese," Mrs. Abbott said as we posed by the cabinet.

"No, not cheese. Say BFFs!" Olive yelled.

"BFFs," I said, but my smile was weak. I'd texted Rachel to say we were setting up the room, my last-ditch effort to get her involved. As usual, she didn't respond.

"Rachel didn't happen to text you today, did she?" I asked Olive.

"Nope," Olive said, but I couldn't see her face. She moved back by Mrs. Abbott's desk and spread her arms wide. "It really is fantabulous!" she declared.

She was right. For once, Olive's mash-up of *fantastic* and *fabulous* worked. The room was too great for just one adjective. The rug we picked out, and the chairs we refinished, and the painted bookshelf, and the art, and the office supplies—they all looked wonderful. And that didn't even take into account the way we'd rearranged the space to give it better flow. No more banged shins on the mini refrigerator. Hooray! I was really, really pleased.

But I was still me, so I couldn't help worrying.

"The basketball team has a ton of kids," I said, biting my lip. All the other teams had way more members than just little old me and Olive. There were no rules about team size.

"Sure, they have *quantity*," Olive said, "but do they have *quality*? Have they been doing this as long as we have? Do they have our special brand of design know-how-ed-ness?"

I laughed. "Okay, okay, I see your point." Olive leaned close to Mrs. Abbott and took a selfie in front of the bowl of lemon drops.

"You girls crack me up," Mrs. Abbot said. She popped a drop into her mouth. "What do you say? Should we call it done?"

I backed up a bit, looked carefully at each area of the room. I walked over to the trio of items on top of the filing cabinet: the yellow paper sorter we'd bought at the Shoppe, a rectangular bas-ket, and a 3-D metal *L* for Long Branch. I moved the *L* slightly to the right while I thought about starting on Mrs. Sherman's office. Heck, maybe I could redesign Mr. V's office. Why not?

I stood back, looked again, and smiled. This was probably our best job yet.

"Done!" I declared.

-•- ✦ -•-

Olive's mom came to pick us up. Noah was asleep in his car seat, and Olive sat next to him with me on her other side.

"He's always falling asleep in the car," she whispered to me. "Sometimes my mom takes him for a drive when she can't get him to sleep any other way."

I wondered what it would be like to have a baby brother, cry-ing in the night, making a mess of everything. I used to think the worst part of having a baby sibling was that they'd break your stuff, but apparently breaking stuff was something some people never grew out of. I shook the thought from my head and instead looked out as all the familiar stores and houses went by my window.

I noticed the brightly painted doors on Elm, as though all the neighbors on the block had gotten together with a bunch of col-or swatches and decided to make something beautiful. I thought of the outer office and felt a little flutter in my chest that I realized must have been pride. We'd just done something huge, a major design project for our new school that would really help us make a name for ourselves. Maybe someday I'd be accepting a mega design award, and I'd point back to this very contest as the moment that started it all.

And we'd done it with just the two of us, although Rachel had helped in the beginning, and Tony had helped later on. Come to think of it, I guessed there were always three people involved, just not the same three. And of course, there was Grandma, who didn't do any hands-on work but always inspired me. Would she be there to see me get an award someday? I didn't want to think about that, either.

Olive leaned over as I got out of the car. "You did good," she whispered, careful not to wake Noah.

"*We* did good," I whispered back.

- • - ✦ - • -

Mom opened the front door before I got to it.

"Where were you?" she asked, looking confused. I noticed she was wearing the same striped top and sweatpants she'd had on yesterday.

"At school with Olive, remember? We were setting up the room? Dad took the bookcase over there yesterday."

"Oh . . . yes, yes, that's right." She stepped aside to let me in and pulled her limp, kind of greasy-looking hair back into a ponytail with an elastic she had around her wrist.

"How's Grandma?" I asked, because I had a feeling my mom's messy look had something to do with her. "Is she . . . okay?" *Okay* wasn't the right word, but I didn't have another one.

Mom said, "I was just on the phone with the assisted living facility about the room we're waiting for in the memory care unit. They still don't have one, but there's a room in another unit, and they could transfer her later, and I really think . . ."

She paused, and it seemed like she was figuring something out. Then she put an arm around me and squeezed me close. "I don't need to bother you with this stuff," she said. "We'll get through it, somehow."

I pushed away from her. "Why does she need to go anyway?" I asked. I had thought I wouldn't like it, having more people in our small house, but now the idea of Grandma going away made me anxious. And she was fine just yesterday.

Mom sighed. "Honey, you know why. Grandma's disease is getting worse. I know sometimes it doesn't seem like it—"

"You just want to get rid of her!" My voice had gotten so loud so quickly, and I surprised myself with how angry I felt.

Mom's jaw clenched, and she looked like she wanted to pick up the nearest fragile object and smash it. Luckily, the only things within reach were our fall coats. After a few deep breaths, she said, "I'm not even going to reply to that."

"Good!" I said. "Don't!"

I ran to my room, gathered up an armful of magazines, dumped them on my rug, and sat in the middle, flipping through pages, staring at the pictures, and stopping to read captions about things like apron sinks or pendant lights.

The thing about decorating magazines? The thing that made me feel calm when I looked at them? They offered solutions. It didn't matter how messy a "before" was, because an "after" was coming, and it would be awesome. Of course, it didn't happen by magic. There was a lot of work involved, a lot of time. It didn't happen in the seconds it took to turn a couple pages.

I felt myself slowly calming down. I shouldn't have said that to my mom, I knew that. But also, I didn't see why we couldn't give the current situation more of a chance. Mom and Dad were telling me I had to adapt to Tony being in the house, so why couldn't everyone adapt to Grandma?

I heard Grandma flip down the footrest on the recliner in the spare room, making its big clunking sound. She'd been sitting in the chair to work on a cross-stitch she'd started after she got here. She'd done cross-stitch for as long as I could remember.

Maybe she'd want to look through a magazine with me. I grabbed one and tiptoed to her doorway, peeking in. She smiled, and set her fabric down on her lap. The smile meant the coast was clear, that she was okay with visitors, that she remembered me.

"What are you up to today?" she said as I sat on the edge of the bed.

"Well, actually, I just got back from putting the final touches on that room I decorated at my school, for the contest."

"How wonderful!" Grandma exclaimed.

She remembered! "I can show you some pictures if you want, on my phone," I said.

"Okay," she said, "but maybe later, dear one. My eyes are tired." She looked down at the fabric and the yellow floss in her lap. "I should stop this for today."

She'd made a lot of progress on her cross-stitch since I'd last seen it. I wasn't sure what it was before, but now it was clearly a house, her house, the one Mom said she'd probably never live in again. Grandma had a big magnifying glass that hung on a string around her neck and helped her to better see the holes in the fabric, and she wasn't wearing a scarf, which made her neck look naked. The string from the magnifier had cut into her skin, leaving a red line right below the low bun in her hair.

I'd brought in a *Better Homes and Gardens* magazine because it was Grandma's favorite. At her house, there was a bookshelf in the basement filled with tons of them, all dusty and musty. She never seemed to recycle any. When we used to visit her and Grandpa on Sundays, I'd push over a stool to reach them, and I remembered, when I was really little, accidentally pulling down a whole shelf full and watching them cascade onto the tiled floor. I remembered being scared Grandma would yell at me for making a mess, but instead she sat down on the floor with me, picked one up, and said I could look at anything I wanted, as long as I showed her the pictures I liked most.

Grandma's favorites were the garden photos. I'd found one in a recent issue that I knew she'd like. I held out the page in front of her, and she took the magnifier from around her neck and put on her regular reading glasses.

"Look at all the goldfish," I said. There was a pond next to a little stone patio with an old iron table and chairs.

"Oh, now wouldn't it be nice to sit there in the morning with a cup of coffee?" She reached back and rubbed her neck where the red line was.

"I thought you hated coffee, Grandma," I said. She always said she didn't need it, that the birds were enough to wake her up.

"Oh?" she said, lost in thought for a moment. "Well, tea, then." She smiled.

Next to the pond was a bed of wildflowers, all different kinds, all growing every which way.

"It's so random," I said, "but it still looks nice."

"It only looks random," she said, pointing. "Look here, see how the color carries through. How there's purple here, here, and here." Grandma moved her finger across the page. "See how the shape of this flower is copied in the stone planter, and even in the finial on top of the gate."

I leaned closer to her, looking at where she was pointing. The back of her hand had brown spots, and I could see her veins poking up, but her nails were perfect because Mom had trimmed them for her and painted them a pale pink. The diamond in the center of her wedding band winked at me.

"Do you see?" she asked, and I smiled because I did. I did.

Tell Me Something

When we ate dinner these days, there were five of us at the table—Tony across from me, my parents across from each other, and Grandma at the end like she was in charge, like if it was Thanksgiving, she'd have to carve the turkey.

Tonight, Tony brought his basketball to dinner and was moving it around with his feet under the table, which made a noise like some small animals were in a battle under there for scraps of dropped food.

"No ball at the table, Tony," Mom said.

"It's under the table," he said, shrugging.

Mom gave Dad a sharp look, and Dad said, "No ball *under* the table, either."

"Fine," Tony said, like he didn't care one way or the other, but I could tell, he cared. He rolled the ball into the living room, where it sounded like it knocked over one of Mom's plants or something. Nobody moved, though. We all sat there looking at the enchilada casserole and the basket heaped with cornbread muffins. I wasn't so big on the casserole, but I loved the muffins.

"Could you please pass me the muffins, Grandma?" I asked.

"Certainly," she replied. She was wearing a blue-checked scarf, and had even put on some red lipstick before she came down for dinner, which made her eyes look unnaturally green. I felt pretty sloppy next to her, in my T-shirt and the brown sweatpants with the big, white primer stain on my butt.

I took a muffin and passed the basket to Tony, who took three.

Grandma pointed to the napkin by my fork. "Don't forget, Maggie," she said softly.

"Oops!"

I unfolded my napkin and put it on my lap. Maybe one of these nights, I'd remember before Grandma told me. Tony immediately grabbed his and did the same, and so did Dad, which kind of made me laugh. Mom already had hers in the Grandma-approved position. We only had paper napkins at our house, not linen ones, so it seemed a little silly to even bother, but "proper manners are proper manners," Grandma said.

We all ate pretty quietly after that; it was almost like Quiet Lunch at school, without the giggles and lunch lady threats. Mom tried to put a second scoop of casserole on Grandma's plate, but she held her hand out to block it and said, "No, thank you."

"I had a looooong meeting today," Dad said, breaking the silence. "So long, I thought you kids would be all grown up by the time I got home." Mom and I laughed, but Tony and Grandma didn't. Still, he persisted. "I thought Tony would be walking with a cane and have a white beard down to his belt buckle."

"We get it, Dad," I said, not unkindly. He was hitting a little too close to Grandma with the old people jokes. "It was a looooong, dummmb meeting."

"Hmmm," Dad said, buttering a muffin. "Not especially dumb, just long. Necessary, but too long. When you kids get older, you'll find that . . ."

"No, no, no," Mom cut in. "No lectures about office life. We want these kids to *want* to have jobs, Bob."

I smiled, but Tony didn't. He'd stuffed two muffins into his face already and was sliding his casserole around on his plate with his fork. I didn't blame him; there were too many chunky bits in it. But didn't he know that you couldn't let anyone see you sliding it around, if you wanted to make it look like you'd eaten some?

Dad fake-pouted at Mom. "Fine, then, what did you do at work today?"

"Well, you know, it's mostly been calls from home for a few days." She had a tight smile as she glanced over at Grandma. I didn't think Grandma noticed. She was picking at her casserole just like Tony was.

"Yes, yes, that's right," Dad said quickly, and we all went back to eating silently for a few seconds, but I could see the silence was killing him.

"So, then, Mags . . . ," he started, and I knew what was coming. "Tell me something good."

Dad had tried this last week, and Grandma and Tony both said "pass," which I didn't know was allowed.

"Mags?" Dad said. "Anyone?"

I looked around, waiting for someone to speak. Mom looked kind of sad and disappointed, at something besides the casserole, I figured. Tony and Grandma just sat there. Well, fine. I had something important to say.

"Okay, I'll go," I said. "I finished setting up the outer office for the contest yesterday, and it looks really great!" I glanced at Tony, who wasn't even pretending to eat anymore. "And Tony helped!" I continued. "That can be your something good, Tony, or your something big, or whatever."

"Is that true, Tony?" Dad asked.

"I don't know. I guess."

"Of course you did!" I said. I looked around at everyone. "Tony helped me paint the bookcase. He's really great at painting. I may make him my new permanent helper!" I felt like I was talking too loudly, or taking up too much space, or both. I was trying to fill the emptiness I felt in the room, and I could only fill it by making myself bigger.

"How about you, Mom?"

"Me? Oh, uh, let's see . . . I got my email inbox down to twenty. Does that count?"

"Hooray!" I said, holding up my milk for a glass clinking, but we didn't seem to do that anymore now that it was the five of us. Mom left me hanging.

"I finished my cross-stitch," Grandma said, smiling at me.

"Hooray!" I said again.

"That's great, Eleanor," Dad said. I noticed he'd been calling her Eleanor ever since she moved in. He used to call her Mom sometimes, but maybe now he was trying not to confuse her. "See, you can find something big in every day! Just a matter of how you look at things."

Tony cleared his throat. "I'm going to my . . . I mean, I'm going to the living room," he said. "I have homework." He pushed his chair away from the table, and Mom said, "Don't forget to clear your place." Usually, Mom made everyone stay at the table until we were all finished.

Tony grabbed his plate, but his fork tumbled off, clanging on the table. He just left it there and quickly slipped out of the room. I didn't know what was bugging him, but with Tony, I'd learned it was best to let him cool off a bit, have some space.

As me and Mom and Dad cleared the rest of the things, Grandma stayed where she was, watching the birds at the feeder. There were a couple blue jays at the moment, regular visitors, but

I knew she would say that just because they were common, didn't mean they weren't beautiful.

The three of us shifted around each other in the kitchen for fifteen minutes or so, loading the dishwasher and washing the pans. At any other time, we'd be having a family discussion, but Grandma was right there within earshot. I imagined this was how it was if you had little kids and couldn't talk about serious things until they went to bed. I imagined this was how it used to be for my parents, with me.

-·- ✦ -·-

Later that night, I decided to take my phone into Grandma's room and show her the pictures of the outer office and the before and after of the bookcase. I walked across the hall to where Grandma's door was half open. I knocked.

"Yes?" came her voice, reed-thin and quivering like one of those stalks in the pond outside the assisted living facility.

"Hey, Grandma," I said, peeking around the door. I held up my phone. "I thought I could show you the photos of the room I did."

Grandma stuck her needle, threaded with red floss, into her fabric and looked at me blankly. Weird—I was sure this was the same cross-stitch she'd been working on for weeks, but it looked a little different, almost like she'd taken some stitches out.

I was going to sit on the edge of the bed, but it hadn't been made yet. Honestly, it smelled kind of bad in the room, like maybe Grandma needed a bath. My mom had been helping her with that, which I knew wasn't easy.

I suddenly thought, maybe Grandma wasn't able to make her bed. Well, I could help. That was an easy thing for me to do. I went to the side of the bed and pulled up the sheet, and that was when I saw my tissue box on her nightstand, the one that was missing from my desk, and next to it, a little stack of my books, *Easy Holiday Crafts* on top. Oh, well, if she wanted to borrow some things, that wasn't a problem.

"What are you doing, girl?" Grandma asked.

Girl? I tried to ignore that. Sometimes Dad called me "his girl," so maybe that was what she meant.

"I'm making your bed for you," I said. "Just sit right there. You can work on your cross-stitch while I take care of it. Do you want me to find your magnifying glass for you? I'll take care of everything."

I pulled up the blanket, catching a whiff of something sour, which I also ignored, and fluffed the pillows, noticing the cases were getting a little threadbare. And don't get me started on the comforter. Blue and orange roses? The whole room desperately needed a makeover. Maybe I could get my hands on it before Tony moved back in. I stopped making the bed for a moment, a pillow in my hands, when I realized I was actually picturing Tony in here, in a space that was all his. I thought that was pretty cool, but at the same time, I hated to send Grandma away.

I put the pillows in place and picked my phone up off the nightstand. I scrolled to the before picture I took of the whole room, with Mrs. Abbott standing behind her desk.

"Just look at how cramped everything was," I said, holding the phone out to Grandma. "The secretary could hardly get around all the mismatched furniture."

"What on God's green earth are you talking about?" Grandma said. She sounded not just confused, but kind of angry.

I held the phone up closer to her. I knew she couldn't see very clearly, even with her glasses. Mom said she hadn't passed her last driving test, so they wouldn't renew her license. Another reason why she couldn't live alone.

"Remember? My design contest at school?" I asked, but I felt the urge to flee, like somewhere in the back of my brain, I must have known what was coming next.

"Who . . . are you?" Grandma asked.

"What . . . what do you mean?" I lowered my phone, felt the tears rushing to my eyes. "I'm Maggie," I said. "I'm your grand-daughter." She didn't respond. "You said we could look at my pictures later and . . . it's later . . . and so . . ."

Grandma shook her head, as if to knock loose the right memory, but it didn't work, and as Mom came into the room, Grandma was only able to say, "I'm sorry . . . I'm sorry" to both of us.

What is happening? She was fine at dinner! I ran to my own room, really crying now, and lay down on my bed, right on top of all the magazines, some of them sliding down the ladder to the floor and making a pile just like they used to in Grandma's basement. Would I ever go back there? Grandma wasn't going back, not like this, and that meant Mom would sell the house. I wanted to pack my bags and go live there myself and keep everything as it always was.

Of course it was just then that Tony poked his head in. "What's going on?" I waved him away. He had enough of his own problems. He didn't need to hear mine, plus, as he'd pointed out to me once, she wasn't *his* grandma.

I kept my head buried in my pillow until Dad came in and climbed up enough of my loft's ladder steps so he could reach out and smooth my hair with his hand. He said softly, "Mags?"

My pillow was soaked through, and my eyes hurt, and my head. "Grandma didn't know who I was," I said. Saying it out loud made it seem too real, truer than true.

"I know," he said. "If it makes you feel any better, she doesn't always know who I am either anymore. I'm sure she's hoping I'm just the dishwasher repairman."

He laughed a little, but I didn't. Sometimes, I wished he wouldn't joke about stuff that wasn't funny. I sat up and leaned against my wet pillow, feeling its chill on my back.

"Will she get any better?" I asked, already knowing the answer.

"Maybe sometimes." Dad sighed. "But it won't last long." He climbed back down and started busying himself with the magazines that had fallen on the floor. "You should try and enjoy the good times, whenever they happen. Pretty good rule for life in general, when you think about it." He put the magazines into neat stacks, even though he wasn't usually one for neatness.

"It could be worse," Dad continued. "She could be really upset about Tony, and making things hard for him, and for all of us." He looked up at me and whispered, "Mom actually did tell her he's an exchange student, just like I suggested. I'm not sure if she remembers that, though."

"She does," I said, "or at least she did, a few days ago. She mentioned it to me." A few tears leaked out, and I wiped them with the back of my hand.

Dad said, "Hey, don't worry. She'll probably remember you tomorrow. It goes back and forth."

"No," I said. "It's not that."

"What is it? Is it Tony?"

"Yeah, no, it's just, everything. I just miss the old us." I lay back down in my loft so I couldn't see Dad anymore. Unfortunately, sometimes, if you listen really hard, you can hear a person's sadness even when they aren't talking.

"I've made a lot of mistakes," Dad said eventually. "I'm

trying to make it up to you and Mom, and Tony, too. You have to believe me."

I sniffled. "I do." I did. "Tony told me his mom wasn't very helpful in bringing you guys together, so it wasn't all your fault."

"I can't put this on her," Dad said, but then he didn't say anything for a while. I started to wonder if he'd snuck out of my room, but I didn't want to sit up and look. Then he said softly, "There are a lot of things I would have done differently, and certainly if I'd known Tony's mom was sick ... but she wasn't when I knew her. Her car accident happened later ... and everything—"

"And maybe you wouldn't have messed up in the first place, with her I mean, if you had to do it over again ... ," I said.

"Sure, yes, but it's hard to think that now, isn't it, when, well, Tony's here, and ... he's a good kid."

I lay still, for what felt like a long time. Then I whispered, "Am I a good kid?"

"Aw, sweetheart, you're the absolute best." He knocked on my bed rail. "Look over here so I can see you." I turned toward him, pulling my covers up to my chin. "Mags, you're amazing," he said, and I smiled there in the dark.

I thought about what Dad was saying, about trying to enjoy the good times and holding onto memories, and I knew I wanted to remember this moment for as long as I could. But then I thought of my shell and all those beach memories, and I realized ... Grandma had my books and tissue box, which meant she had been in my room, which meant . . . Tony was probably telling the truth all along. Maybe he hadn't broken my shell. I'd been so angry at him, but, well, how could I be mad at Grandma?

"I forgot to tell you, my shell got broken," I said.

"Your shell? What shell?"

I'd never even told my dad about it. "The shell I brought back from the beach, the one you said came from the world's tiniest unicorn."

"From that trip to Florida? I didn't know you saved that. What happened to it?"

"It was on my desk, and then I found it broken on the floor. I'm not sure what happened."

Dad looked over at the desk. "Well, I'm sorry about that, Mags, but I bet you can get a new one," he said. "I'm sure the aquarium sells them, probably all different kinds."

"Yeah, it's just that, well, it's not really the same," I said. I knew I sounded babyish, but I didn't care. I leaned over my rail. "It reminded me of our trip and how much fun we had."

"Aw, Mags, none of those memories are going away," he said.

I wanted to agree with him. But now I knew: Memories didn't always last forever.

-•- ✦ -•-

I woke up in the middle of a beautiful dream where I was on a stage getting a trophy, and Grandma was standing in the front row of a filled auditorium, clapping and smiling at me. But when I went downstairs for breakfast, it was back to reality.

Mom and Dad were snapping at each other in the kitchen. Mom was complaining that she wasn't making any commissions on house sales because she was having to give her showings to other realtors. Dad was saying it was time Grandma went to the assisted living facility, even if they didn't have a room in the wing she wanted.

"Or she can go to one of the others," he said. "There's four of them in town!"

"The other ones don't have good ratings," Mom said. She was peanut-buttering a sandwich with so much force, the knife went right through the bread.

I tiptoed around them, grabbing a banana. They didn't even stop arguing when I entered the room like they usually did. Although, honestly, this level of arguing was new. It had been years since they'd really argued, that I knew of, anyway.

"It's not just my mom, Bob," Mom continued. "We have children to take care of, you know, TWO children, and everything seems to be falling on me, which is pretty ridiculous, considering."

"Considering what?" Dad replied. He jerked the coffeepot out from underneath the steady drip and accidentally sent his mug crashing to the floor.

"Oh, great," Mom said. "I guess I'll clean that up, too."

I hated this. I grabbed my backpack and said, "I'm leaving now! Bye!"

"What?" Mom said, looking at the clock on the stove. "It's too early. You'll be waiting at the bus stop forever."

"It's the contest today," I said. "Don't you remember?" *Only the most important thing in my life right now.* "I need to be there early."

"Dad will take you," she said.

"No, Olive's mom is picking us up," I said. "Don't worry about it."

They both looked relieved, like they were very happy not to worry about me, which just made me madder, especially after I'd had such a good talk with Dad last night. Olive's mom wasn't actually picking me up, but it wasn't like school was very far away. I'd just jog. Anything to get out of this house.

I ran about a half mile, then had to stop because I got a cramp in my side. I stood there, clutching my waist, wishing I hadn't eaten that banana so fast. In a minute, the cramp went away, and I started power-walking instead of jogging. I tried to pull up that warm feeling of pride I'd had on Saturday when Olive and I were admiring our work with Mrs. Abbott. I thought about asking Mrs. Sherman for a meeting so I could get a start on her room.

But no matter how much I tried to distract myself with those thoughts, I still felt nervous, knowing that a bunch of kids—including my competitors—would be looking at the office just hours from now. We'd done an incredible job. Would they see it? Would it be enough?

When I'd signed up the BFFs for the contest, I'd wanted everyone, especially Dad, and Grandma, to see that I could do something special. But maybe that was silly. Was Dad going to be super impressed if I won a middle school decorating contest? In any case, he'd already told me I was amazing. Was Rachel going to be impressed that we'd done it without her? Would my fellow students lift me up on their shoulders, like I'd seen them do in pictures of basketball championships? Did any of that matter?

I didn't know anymore. As the school came into sight, the only thing I was sure of was that I was late meeting Olive.

Best Foot Forward

"Oh, thank goodness!" Olive shouted when she saw me. She was standing outside the front doors of the school, handing out bookmarks. She'd texted me last night to say she was making something, but I had no idea what to expect.

She held one out. "What do you think?" It said VOTE on one side, and on the other side was our BFF logo, which was three different shoes in a triangle and the words *Best Foot Forward: Interior Design*. She'd printed them out on some heavy paper.

"Olive, wow! They look incredible."

She smiled, but quickly turned as some kids walked by us. "Vote for the office!" she shouted. "Vote BFF!"

"If we're last in their minds, they'll think of us first," she said to me, smiling even bigger.

"Huh?"

"If we're the only group promoting ourselves right before the voting, we'll be fresh in everyone's heads."

"Ahhh, I get it. Olive, you're—"

"A great bookmark maker?" She thrust a fistful at me. "I know, but get to work. We don't have much time before the bell."

I was going to say she was a genius, but that worked, too. We both held out bookmarks as students passed by. Some kids took them and stuffed them into their pockets or backpacks. Some were clearly trying not to make eye contact. Other kids took them, then threw them on the ground once they got a few steps away from us. A handful of bookmarks were scattered all around the trash can, and who knows how many were inside it. I tried to offer one to an eighth grade girl, but she just laughed and shook her head.

"Why don't you stand over there so we're spread out," Olive suggested. "And smile!"

I wasn't used to Olive being so pushy, but I dutifully moved to the other side of the walk and tried again. "Vote BFFs?" I said to the next person, and after a couple more, I'd managed to take the question mark out of my voice. "Vote BFFs!" I said, much louder now. Olive gave me a thumbs-up from across the sidewalk.

Most of the students weren't paying any attention to us, but a few said they'd vote for us, although they may have just said that to be nice. I didn't see any other teams outside, but then a couple teams had handed things out last Friday.

I noticed a guy from the basketball team running into the school with a big roll of white paper and a Ziploc full of markers. I couldn't keep myself from smirking. If that was the competition, we had nothing to worry about.

As we stood out there, frantically pressing bookmarks into every open hand, I really had to give Olive a lot of credit. She'd worked harder on this project than any of our others. I'd underestimated her—big-time. Maybe she'd just needed the opportunity to show her stuff, and with Rachel out of the picture, she'd had it.

Then bus number ten rolled up, our bus, and I saw Tony get off, followed by . . . speaking of Rachel. I thought she wasn't riding the bus anymore?

"Hi, Rakell!" I heard Olive yell. "We're going to do it! Vote BFFs!" Olive kept yelling manically, to no one in particular and everyone all at once. The bookmarks rained down from her hands like fall leaves from a tree as the last bus emptied out.

Tony walked up to me. "Good luck today," he said. "You know you've got my vote."

"Thanks, Tony."

"I'm looking forward to seeing our bookcase in action," he said with a big smile. It was good to see Tony smile.

"Oh, it looks great," I said. "You know, the award's yours, too, if we win." Every time I said that, I felt like I had to throw salt over my shoulder or something, like even mentioning the voting was jinxing it.

I glanced over at Rachel, who was crouched down by the trash can, carefully picking up each bookmark from the ground. *Oh, nice,* I thought, *I guess she wants to make sure they all go directly into the trash.*

"What do you get if you win?" Tony asked, snapping my attention back.

"Oh, uh, a trophy, and a pizza party." I thought about the Principal for a Day thing. We'd never worked out which one of us would do it, but Olive wouldn't want to anyway, would she?

"I'm more excited about the frozen yogurt truck," Tony said, "and especially about the day off."

"Yeah, do you think he'll really give everyone a day off?"

Tony shrugged. "Dunno, but I'll vote for you anyway." He started toward Rachel. "Well, save me a piece of pepperoni!" he called over his shoulder.

Rachel held the stack of discarded bookmarks out to Tony. Then the two of them distributed them, *actually gave them out,* to kids by the door.

She was helping me? I could hardly believe it!

And then Tony stuck the rest of the bookmarks into his coat pocket and reached out and took Rachel's hand, and they walked like that, hand in hand, into the school.

I remembered seeing Tony talking to Rachel at her locker, remembered thinking he might be trying to patch things up between us. Was that true? Or was he really just trying to be her boyfriend? And did Olive know about any of this and not tell me, like she didn't tell me Rachel was texting her about our meetings?

When the bell rang a moment later, Olive was at my side, snapping her fingers in front of me. "Earth to Maggie," she said. "You look like you've seen a ghost." Not a ghost, I thought, but I did see something I definitely didn't expect and, to be honest, it was a little scary. Olive grabbed my arm, and we ran into the school.

-•- ✦ -•-

I was in a fog the whole day. I had a pop quiz in science on the solar system and couldn't remember Mars. I walked right into the boys' bathroom and had to back out, covering my eyes and yelling, "Sorry!" I even wrote the wrong year on one of my papers, like I was trying to go back in time.

Everyone around me was wearing green and brown, because today's "theme" for Spirit Week was School Colors. I was wearing my favorite blue sweater and jeans because I felt good in them, and I wanted to feel good on judging day. Besides, I would never wear the school colors, not those particular shades of green and brown together, ever. They were a hideous combination.

During study hall, when it was time to peruse all the rooms before casting our votes, I was so nervous, I thought I'd be sick. When we got to the office, Olive said, "Come on," but I couldn't do it.

"You go ahead," I said. "I'll stay out here."

"Are you sure? Don't you want to hear what people think?"

"No," I said. That was exactly what I was afraid to hear. I sat on the floor and leaned up against some lockers.

When Olive came back out the door with a bunch of kids, she was smiling really big.

"It was so great, Maggie!" she said. She shifted a lemon-drop-shaped lump to her other cheek. "Everyone loved it! Although . . . some kids asked where the dancing sunflower was. Remember when you had Mrs. Abbott put that away in her desk because it detracted from the new focal point?" Of course I remembered. How could they ever notice the seating area if they were looking at that goofy sunflower?

"So, they really liked it?" I asked, and we went back and forth like that for a minute, me pressing Olive for more, and Olive sharing all the praise. She held out her hand to reveal two wrapped lemon drops. "From Mrs. Abbott," Olive said. "She said to tell you good luck, even though we don't need it."

As I went around visiting the other rooms, a lemon drop poking from both my cheeks, I started to feel better and better. The gym hallway? Well, the boy I saw that morning with the roll of paper and markers must have been their entire decorating team. The only thing they'd done was tape paper to the walls with messages scribbled on it like "Go Long Branch!" Preschoolers could have done a better job.

Olive poked me when we walked by it. "This is not fantabulous," she whispered, and we giggled.

"Yup," I whispered back. "Amateur hour."

The music room was better. The math team had decorated it, and they had a theme, which helped, although it wasn't exactly an original idea. Cardboard music notes hung from the ceiling, and along the back wall they'd cut a music staff out of construction paper and written the football players' names inside the notes. Sure, they'd put glitter on them, but as Grandma always said, you couldn't put lipstick on a pig. It was so juvenile. I mean, you didn't see any glitter in *House Beautiful*.

I'd already seen the science room during class. It also had glittery objects hanging from the ceiling; in this case, planets. And the student council—the student council itself!—wasn't even finished with their area, which was the hallway that led to the pick-up loop. When we went to check it out, we found a sixth-grade boy desperately painting a papier-mâché thing that sort of, if you squinted, looked like our school's wildcat mascot.

That left the main hallway, the cheerleaders' hallway, which we'd walked through several times that day. I'd already gotten an eyeful of the hot mess of green and brown crepe paper. It was *everywhere*. If the colors looked bad in small doses, well . . .

They'd looped the paper from the ceiling, twisted it above the lockers, wrapped it around poles. There were signs, too, in the same clashing colors, with sayings that all made the same point, that Long Branch was supposed to crush Centerville in the football game, although the words were written in bubble font, which made the threats of domination seem way less serious. The signs were all over the wall, and some were even duct-taped to the floor.

"This hallway is giving me a headache," I said to Olive.

"Yeah, same," Olive said. "What's that you always say, about the eyes getting tired?"

"The eye needs a place to rest," I said. "You're exactly right. It's negative space, white space. If there's too much stuff, your eyes don't know where to focus, and it just gets overwhelming. It's why your bookmarks look so awesome, Olive. They have just the right balance."

Olive and I leaned against the lockers while the other kids were jumping from sign to sign like they were playing hopscotch. A piece of crepe paper came loose from the ceiling and landed right on my shoulder. Olive pointed, rolling her eyes.

"Typical," I said, laughing. I was feeling so pleased. I didn't want to jinx anything, but . . . I flicked the paper off and watched it float the rest of the way to the ground.

Katelyn was there, pointing out the posters on the floor to a group of kids. She was wearing her cheerleader uniform, and her lips were even shinier and pinker than usual. Clearly she'd just reapplied her gloss. She pointed. "See here, how it says to 'Stomp Out the Rockets,' and the sign is on the floor. Get it?"

"Yeah, cool," the kids said.

Now I rolled my eyes. What was next? Backflips?

Olive was listening to Katelyn's sales pitch. "Well, I guess that's *kind of* creative," Olive said, but I glared at her, and she didn't say anything else.

-•- ✦ -•-

At the end of the day, just before the dismissal bell, Mr. Villanueva's voice came over the speaker. I was beginning to wonder if he'd ever announce the winners.

"I have the results of our Spirit Week Decorating Contest!" he announced. *Nothing like waiting until the last minute, Mr. V.*

He started going on and on: "... congratulate all the teams ... examples of school spirit ... hard work ..."

Oh, get to the point!

"In sixth place ..."

Great, he's going backward.

"Is the basketball team for their decoration of the gym hallway."

I felt my body relax, just a bit. Of course the basketball team got last place. They had put in zero effort. It was only fair.

"In fifth place is the student council...."

That stupid papier-mâché wildcat. You can't put all your effort into one piece. It would be like buying a killer couch and sticking it in an empty living room. I mean, nice couch, but where are you going to set your popcorn on movie night?

"Science club takes fourth place. . . ." Now, that was a bit of a surprise. I thought they might take second. The planets were actually really cool, much better than the music notes. . . .

And then the bell rang, and everyone scattered out to the lockers. The bells were automated, so it was Mr. V's fault for being long-winded, but it was still a bummer, like when someone sneezed during an important line at a movie.

I strained to listen as I stood clutching my combination lock. I couldn't make my fingers work. I wasn't even sure I could remember the combination.

Mr. Villanueva said, "With their super musical decorations, the math team comes in third place."

I felt my breath whoosh out of me in one long exhale. That only left the BFFs and the terrible, no-good, crepe paper disaster. My head was spinning. I rested it against my still unopened locker.

There were kids all around me, slamming their locker doors, stuffing books into backpacks, not even listening. *How could they not be listening?* But even in all the chaos, it was like it was just me and Mr. Villanueva's voice floating out of the speaker in a corner of the hallway. I couldn't see or hear anything else. Nothing else mattered. I remembered Tony teaching me to shoot free throws. *It's just you and the hoop,* he'd say. *You and the hoop.*

Kids were running out to the buses. If I missed my bus, so what? I'd walk home. I'd run! I'd run through the door and announce the awesome news to my parents, and my dad would twirl me around and tell me again how amazing I was, and they would promise to never fight again. I'd run to Grandma's room, and she'd call me by my name and say how proud she was of me.

I'd treat Olive, and Tony, and Rakell, yes, even R*akell*, to hot fudge sundaes because we were all in this together and it was so silly to fight over petty little things. How could I ever have thought about sending Tony back to Bircher? How could I have been so angry at Rakell? Who had time for that?

Not me. I had things to do, big things, now that the BFFs were going to be on the map. Now that Maggie Owens had officially arrived. I was imagining where I'd put the trophy, thinking of how I should start writing my acceptance speech, thinking of colors for Mrs. Sherman's office, for Tony's room. I was tasting that cheesy, ooey, gooey pizza. I was waiting for Mr. Villanueva to say the magic words.

Crepe Paper Disaster

It was Katelyn's scream that I'd remember most, that shrieking "OH MY GOD!" that would ring in my ears far longer than Mr. Villanueva's flat, calm voice saying, "And in second place . . . is the BFFs, which means the Long Branch cheerleading squad takes the prize. Congratulations to all the teams."

It felt like Katelyn's voice was reverberating up and down the tiled hallways, but it might have just been echoing in my head.

Mr. Villanueva continued, "And because everyone in attendance today cast a vote, stay tuned for information on that frozen yogurt truck!"

All the kids in the hall started cheering at that, which made it so much worse, and then it was like I dove underwater. All I could hear was the pounding of the surf above me. I'd felt the same way when Dad first told me about Tony, first told me I had a brother.

My breathing was amped up, my heart in my throat, which was a saying I'd never really understood until that moment. All around me, the hallway was filled with kids, dashing to get their stuff and run for the exits, then to the buses, or to a waiting car, or just to the freedom of the rest of the world, outside this school, where their own two legs would carry them home.

My legs felt stiff and awkward, like they belonged to someone else. And I was not going home. Not yet. My eyes narrowed to take in just the few feet ahead of me, enough of a sight line to keep walking, but not enough to keep from clipping people left and right with my elbows.

"Ouch!"

"Hey!"

"Watch it!"

I looked for someone, anyone, for some friendly face, but I suddenly felt very alone. Rachel preferred Katelyn and Olive and, now, Tony; and Olive preferred Rachel; and Tony preferred Rachel, and nobody liked me and I wasn't a designer and I couldn't win anything and and and . . .

Up ahead, I saw Katelyn and her crew, hugging and jumping around and acting like complete idiots.

Then I saw something else, and I zeroed in on it. One end of a crepe paper loop was already on the ground. All I had to do was reach up, pinch it, and yank it the rest of the way. Crepe paper was so delicate and so . . . so useless. It wouldn't even stand up to most five-year-olds' birthday parties, so who could expect it to survive in a majorly busy hallway with hundreds of kids passing through every hour of the day?

Only someone who had done zero planning. Only someone who would do the bare minimum, buying a couple rolls of crepe in the school's colors, scribbling on a few squares of cardboard, and calling it design. Honestly, something this ugly deserved to be torn down. I was only putting this hallway out of its misery.

I worked quietly at first, even pausing for a second to consider that maybe I was being a poor sport. I also realized I might get in trouble. Who cared?

Just then, Katelyn looked over, and her eyes were huge with surprise and anger. How dare she be angry? She, who'd spent a maximum of two hours on this project I'd been working on for WEEKS. That did it. I flew into a rampage—clutching, tearing, stomping until every little bit I could reach was in shreds on the ground. I stopped only when Katelyn's friend Brittany put me in a headlock.

Bent over, trying to struggle free, I saw Olive out of the corner of my eye. She had a disappointed look that I didn't see on her very often which made it hit me even harder.

"Oh, Maggie," she said. "What have you done?"

Next to her was Mr. Villanueva. He looked taller somehow, but that might have just been because I was bent over. He had his hands on his hips and wore his *very displeased* expression, the same one he gave to the kids who'd started a food fight in the cafeteria a couple weeks ago. *But I wasn't one of those kids! I wasn't a troublemaker!*

Mr. V motioned for me to follow him, and Brittany let me go. There wasn't a sound in the hallway, except for the *shoosh shoosh shoosh*-ing of the crepe paper disaster as I waded through it, my footsteps in line right behind his, all the kids standing back to let us through. It sounded like we were walking through fallen leaves.

What had happened with the voting? How could anyone choose this hodgepodge of tacky junk over a tasteful design?

I tapped Mr. V's arm. "Did the students see the reorganization of all the files?" I asked. "You couldn't even find anything in there before!"

We were almost back to his office now. "Did they get to see how everything is *functioning*, before they voted?"

Mr. V sighed. "Save it for my office, Miss Owens."

I turned around to exchange a nervous glance with Olive, but she was slowly walking the other way.

-•- ✦ -•-

The worst part was that I had to walk right through my losing design on my way to Mr. V's office. I tried not to look, but I couldn't NOT see that beautiful fabric I'd used to recover the seats of those chairs. That staple gun had left my hand sore for days! I kept thinking how impressed Dad had been with my concept board, kept thinking of how much fun it had been with Tony, painting the bookshelf.

The color scheme had come from all three of the BFFs, though that interview with Mrs. Abbott seemed like ages ago. And all of it, the whole room, couldn't have been put together without the lessons I'd learned from Grandma. I caught the eye of Mrs. Abbott, who gave me a sad little smile, which made me start to cry.

When we reached his office, and Mr. Villanueva noticed my tears, his expression softened, but only for a moment. He told me to have a seat. The chair across from his desk had wooden arms and an upholstered back in a gray, scratchy fabric. It might be vintage in another ten years, but right now, it was just ugly. His own chair was tall and leather and on coasters. Everything else was just boring desk and bookcases, all in a cherry finish that tried to look expensive, but wasn't. I wondered if I should offer to redo his office, too. Maybe that would get me out of trouble.

"There's no need to cry," he said.

I looked around for a tissue but didn't see any. Where were all the tissues when I needed them lately?

He sat down in his big chair and leaned forward. "We all make mistakes. It's what we learn from them that's important."

I nodded and sat there for a minute, just kind of waiting for him to talk. I had no idea what was supposed to happen in these situations; I didn't have any experience with it. Maybe he was waiting for me to tell him what I'd learned, and I guess I was waiting for him to tell me.

One thing I knew was that I'd hurt a bunch of girls on the cheerleading squad, even though I'd only meant to hurt Katelyn. Seeing their faces as I walked through them on my march to the office? Yeah, I wouldn't be forgetting that. *Nor will I forget that headlock*, I thought, as I rubbed my neck. I imagined Katelyn sitting in front of me, in Mr. V's chair as Principal for a Day, and shuddered.

"Do you have anything you want to say? In your defense?" he asked.

I didn't know where to start. *I'm under a lot of stress because I have a new brother I didn't know about, which means people I love weren't telling me the truth and I don't know who to trust, and my grandma had to come live with us, and she doesn't know who I am half the time, and my best friend has kind of deserted me but also, she's maybe dating my brother, and the only thing that was going to make everything right, the only thing, was me winning this contest.*

But I didn't say any of that. What I said was "It's not fair."

I immediately wished I could take it back because I'd been on this earth long enough to know adults hated it when kids said that. They usually said some dumb thing back, like, "*Life's* not fair."

I tried again. "I worked really hard. I thought everyone would like it. Did you . . . like it?"

"Of course I did, and Mrs. Abbott is very pleased," he said, "but, Maggie, we didn't vote. Remember?"

"I'm going to redo the nurses, office, too. Did Mrs. Sherman tell you that?"

"No, she didn't. That's very nice of you." Mr. V took out a big red binder from a desk drawer. "It doesn't affect any of this, however."

He flipped through the pages. "Here we go," he said. He turned the binder so it faced me and pointed to a paragraph. "You'll notice item number four under Behaviors Leading to Suspension. Willful destruction of school property."

"But I . . . I didn't destroy any school property!" Destroying school property sounded like spray-painting graffiti on the bricks or hurling a rock through a window. And did he say . . . suspension?

"You most certainly did destroy school property," he said. "As soon as those decorations were affixed, they became school property." He closed the binder and leaned back in his chair. "Let me ask you this, Maggie. If the math team came in here and took a chainsaw to the bookcase you painted, how would you feel?"

I knew this was no laughing matter, but I couldn't help smirking. The idea was just too, too crazy.

"You have a one-day suspension." He looked at the clock. "The buses have left, but I need to call your parents anyway, so hopefully one of them can come get you."

"Suspension?" I said.

I was starting to feel really sick to my stomach. That lavender scent diffuser that I put in the outer office, for its calming effects, was way too strong, and the whole place smelled like chemical flowers.

"But I didn't do anything that bad!" I said. "It's not like I started a food fight!" Those were the only other kids I knew of who'd gotten suspended this year.

He looked at me closely, some kindness creeping into his face, and so I asked, "Can you make an exception?"

"I'm sorry, no," he said. "Stay home. Read a book. It's only a day."

He'd swiveled his chair and was looking out his window, tapping his pencil on his desk. "You know, my wife gets all those decorating magazines. They're all over our coffee table." He waved his hand and turned back to me. "You did a good job on the office, Maggie, and we like it a lot, but, you know, you misjudged your classmates." He shrugged. "They were expecting school colors and all that."

"That's not design," I said.

"No, it's not," he said, kind of sharply but not meanly. I was taken aback. "It's a decorating contest. No one said *interior design*,

Maggie. I think you wanted this contest to be something it never was."

Then it hit me, slowly, that maybe, just perhaps, the student body at Long Branch Middle School might not be as up to date on current interior design trends as I was. I sat there for a minute, rubbing my forehead and wondering if he could be right, then realizing he probably was. How could I have been so dumb? The first rule of design was to know your clients. I had thought all along that Mrs. Abbott was my client, but it was really the students. They were the ones voting.

"Crepe paper," I muttered. "They wanted crepe paper."

"Guess so," Mr. V said. "As my wife says when she's watching all those HGTV shows, 'There's no accounting for taste.'"

"Everybody still gets a day off, right? For voting?"

He laughed softly. "I heard that rumor, too. It's preposterous, of course. The academic calendar is set years in advance by the school board. I can't go around giving days off for no good reason."

That burned. No good reason? He turned to his computer screen, where he'd pulled up my emergency contact information. "Should I call your mom or your dad?"

"Mom," I said, without even hesitating. You'd think I'd want the good cop, not the bad cop, but I didn't want to disappoint my dad, not after I'd fantasized about how proud of me he was going to be when I won.

"Can I head home?" I asked. I didn't want to hear any of this phone conversation.

"I thought you rode the bus?"

"I walk sometimes," I said.

"Okay," he said, "you can go," and he turned his back as I left, hurrying out through the outer office with my head down. If I had to see Mrs. Abbott again, or our bookshelf or rug—any of it—I'd probably throw up.

--- ✦ ---

When I got outside, I was surprised to find Tony standing by the flagpole. All the buses were long gone. There were a few kids messing around, but Tony was just sitting by himself, like he was waiting for me. Or, on second thought, maybe he was waiting for Rachel.

"Hey," he said, cutting across the grass. "I'll walk with you."

"Why aren't you walking with *Rakell?*" I asked. I walked faster, but he matched my step.

"She took the bus. Anyway, I wanted to talk to you about that, before you find out on your own. See, Rakell and I are kind of—"

"Going out," I said. "I know. I saw you holding her hand."

It didn't mean anything. All it meant was that they declared they liked each other and held hands in the hallways, big deal.

Of course Rachel would be the first of the BFFs to go out with someone. It didn't surprise me a bit.

"Oh, okay," he said. He looked relieved that I already knew. "Well, what happened was, one of her older brothers was playing basketball with me and Dad, and she started hanging out, and we started talking, and . . . I just think she's cool, that's all, which I mean, you already know. She's your best friend."

I stopped walking. "*Was.*"

"*Is,*" he said. "As far as she's concerned, at least. She's just going through a lot right now."

"We all are," I said.

"Yeah, I know, but she's going through a lot of stuff that you don't know about, with her parents."

"Again," I said. "Who isn't?"

Tony blurted, "They're getting a divorce, Maggie."

"What? What are you talking about?"

Of all the parents I knew, Rachel's were the perfect ones, the ones who never dressed like slobs, even if they were just in the car pick-up loop. They got season tickets to the symphony, which I'd never even been to; the only concerts I saw were the free ones at the bandshell in the park. And they always spoke very carefully, e-nun-ci-a-ting everything. I imagined Rachel hearing the divorce talk, getting the question about which parent she wanted to live with. What would that conversation sound like in her family?

"Are you sure?" I asked.

"Yeah, I'm sure. I mean, Rakell is sure. They told her."

"But maybe they'll change their minds. Sometimes parents say that, and then nothing happens. Sometimes they even tell their kids to decide who to live with, and still change their minds."

Tony gave me an odd look. "I think it's pretty definite. Her dad already moved out."

I couldn't believe she hadn't told me. Had she told Olive? Had she told *Katelyn*? I'd be jealous if she had, but also, hearing that this was going on with Rachel made me think of her a little differently. I knew how hard it was to carry something like this around.

My phone dinged, and I had this crazy hope that it would be Rachel, but it was Olive.

Hey, you okay?

"Who is it?" Tony asked.

"Olive," I said. "I'll . . . text her back later." I remembered her face as I'd waded through the crepe paper. Remembered how I'd let her down.

Tony stopped walking and took his backpack off, set it on the sidewalk.

"What are you doing?" I put my phone back into my pocket.

"This thing is so freakin' heavy. Why do they give us so much homework?"

"I don't know," I said. "Do you want to switch bags? Mine's

pretty light." Sixth graders didn't get nearly as much homework as the seventh graders. The teachers probably didn't want to scare us right out of middle school.

"And why don't they give us enough time at the end of the day to put stuff in our lockers?" Tony continued. "Half the time I have to bring every freakin' book home with me because I don't have time to put things in my locker and still catch the bus."

Tony plopped down on the sidewalk like the wind had been knocked out of him.

I just stood there for a minute, not sure what to do. His moods were changing faster than I could keep up with lately.

"Is this really about your homework?" I asked. "Or is something else bugging you?"

He hugged his knees to his chest and looked up at me. "My mom hasn't been calling," he said. "She's supposed to call, and she doesn't, and I just . . . I feel like something's wrong, and like, I don't know what to do about it."

He gave his backpack a shove. My mom had bought him a new one. It was plain blue, but at least it was in good shape, unlike his ratty old red thing, though it wouldn't stay in good shape if he kept shoving it around. She got him some new clothes, too, so he wasn't being called down to the office for dress code violations anymore. Ha! Turns out I was the one getting called to the office these days.

"I guess I'm just pretty distracted," he said. "You know, I really don't care too much about measuring temperatures in Kelvins. I've got more important things to worry about."

"Who's Calvin?"

Tony laughed a little. "Never mind, you'll find out next year." He stood back up. "Hey, I'm really sorry about the contest," he said. "These kids don't know anything." He held up his finger. "Oh yeah—hold on a minute."

He turned and bent back over his bag, opening a small pocket and pulling out a little plastic container full of tiny colored shells, which he held out to me. There were pinks and blues and yellows and greens, each one no bigger than a thumbnail, and all different. There was even one that looked like a tiny unicorn.

"Dad took me to the aquarium gift shop," Tony said. "There's a lot in here." He gently shook the box. "So, if one gets broken, accidentally, by some totally awesome guy, it won't matter so much, and you'll forgive him right away."

"Oh, Tony." I felt the crush of guilt and appreciation all at once. "I . . . I meant to tell you, it wasn't you, I'm almost sure of it. I found some things from my room in Grandma's room, so she must have been in there when we were at school." I watched as Tony's face went from confused to totally relieved. "I'm sorry I blamed you."

He smiled. "Oh, good, I mean, not that your grandma broke it, but I'm glad it wasn't me."

He handed me the box. "Thank you," I said. "I mean it, Tony. This is really nice of you."

I gave him an awkward little hug, then put the box into my backpack, careful to nestle it between a pair of gloves so I wouldn't have any more smashed shells. "I can look through all these tomorrow," I said, "while I'm at home serving my suspension."

"No way! He suspended you? Just for tearing down some junky decorations that were half falling down anyway?"

"You heard?" I said. "Word travels fast around here."

"Yeah, yeah, Rakell told me," he said. He zipped up his pack and put it on. "Katelyn was being really crazy about it, but Rakell stood up for you. She told Katelyn it would have fallen down by tomorrow anyway, and she won the contest, so why was she even complaining?"

"Rakell said that?" It was the first time I'd said her new name out loud in a normal, not sarcastic, way. It didn't sound so weird. Hearing Tony and Olive say it so much, well, I'd kind of been getting used to it. Plus, I'd been thinking about what she'd said, about calling people what they want to be called. It didn't really matter if it made me uncomfortable or not. It was her name.

"Yeah, I told you she was cool."

I punched his shoulder. "Um, yeah, *I* know that. *You* just got here, remember?"

He laughed. "True, true," he said. We started walking, and he got quiet again.

"Is there anything we can do, about your mom?" I asked.

I wanted to help him. I'd had my head so deep into the contest, I hadn't realized how lucky I was. My parents were still together. They were healthy. They were there for me, even though they totally messed up sometimes. But other people, like Tony, like Rakell, weren't so lucky.

"I don't know," he said. "I don't know what we can do."

He didn't say anything until we got to the corner nearest our house, and then he got this mischievous look on his face and yelled, "Race you home!" and took off running, and it felt so normal, running after him, like Tony had been here forever, and this was just an old game of ours.

Try Your Best

I didn't know why we were in a hurry to get home. I went slowly up the walk, knowing that Mom would have talked to Mr. Villanueva. I was hoping I could sneak in and disappear into my room, hold off the lecture for a while.

But Mom was right there in the kitchen when I walked in, next to Tony, who'd beaten me by a mile. "Both of you are here," she said. "Good."

I was expecting Mom to tell me how my suspension would go on my "permanent record," and wondered whether Dad would come to my aid and say something like, *Now, Susie, let's not be too hard on her.* But this wasn't like coming home a half hour late from Rachel's, I mean, Rakell's, or eating a bunch of junk food right before dinner. I'd never done something this serious.

Mom was wearing her purple sweatpants that doubled as pajamas, holding a basket of Grandma's folded laundry on her hip. I hadn't seen her in her usual work skirts and blouses in weeks. Bits of hair had fallen out of her ponytail and lay flat against her cheeks.

But what Mom said wasn't what I'd expected. "I need you two to entertain Grandma," she told us. She pointed her chin toward the living room, then leaned in close to me and Tony, adding, "She is not happy about moving to the assisted living facility tomorrow. I'm hoping you can distract her while I finish packing her things."

Entertain her? Distract her? She wasn't a toddler, or a puppy. Could Mr. Villanueva have forgotten to call? It seemed like days ago that I had been in his office, but it hadn't even been an hour. I was certainly happy Mom wasn't yelling at me, but also, I was just a little bit put out that she hadn't even asked about the contest results. Obviously, she had a few other things on her mind, but it still kind of hurt.

Tony and I did as we were told. As Mom went upstairs, we walked into the living room and found Grandma next to the fireplace, picking things up from the mantle—a brass candlestick, a framed postcard of a bird, a bowl of fake lemons—and looking underneath.

What was Grandma looking for? A price tag?

Tony looked over at me, raised his eyebrows, and sat carefully down on the couch. I shrugged and took the recliner. How exactly were we supposed to "entertain" Grandma? We were way too old to put on a song-and-dance number. Couldn't I just talk to her, like always? I guessed some days, that just wasn't possible anymore.

She finished examining the items on the mantle, put them all back in the wrong places, which was not like her at all, then looked curiously at Tony.

"I'm Eleanor Hanson," she said. "You're the exchange student, Anthony, correct?"

Tony didn't answer right away, and I worried he was going to lose it again.

"Well," she said, "is that correct, or isn't it? Speak!"

"Yes, yes, ma'am," he said nervously. He didn't seem angry with her at all. He actually seemed a little scared.

Grandma went to the couch, still clutching one of the plastic lemons. She sat down slowly and turned her body toward Tony. Then she tilted her head and squinted, like she was trying to bring him into better focus. "Where are you from?" she asked.

Tony's eyes went big. He brought his thumbnail to his mouth and started chewing.

"Europe!" I cried. I hoped she didn't want more specifics. Our dad was mostly German. I had no idea where Tony's mom's ancestors came from.

Thankfully, Grandma didn't ask. "I went to Spain once, with my husband," she said. She leaned back on the couch cushions and got a faraway look in her eyes like she was recreating that trip.

Then she said to Tony, "It must be hard, leaving your home. You probably have a beautiful home." She looked down and gave the lemon in her hand a confused stare.

"It is hard leaving home," Tony said thoughtfully. He held out his own hand and motioned for the lemon. "Here, I can put that back for you," he said.

But instead of handing him the fake fruit, my grandma put her other hand on top of Tony's, and squeezed. She closed her eyes and took a couple deep breaths. Tony glanced at me, then closed his own eyes and did the same. I managed to close one of mine, but I kept the other one slightly open. I didn't want to let Grandma out of my sight. We must have looked odd, all of us breathing deeply and sitting like statues on the couch.

"I miss him," Grandma said, her eyes still closed.

I felt myself tearing up. I missed Grandpa, too, but to be honest, I'd never been very close to him. I was so much closer to Grandma. And that's who I missed, in this moment. Even though she was right here.

She was still Grandma . . . but she wasn't. I was starting to realize that, even though we might have some okay moments, times when Grandma seemed like her old self, they wouldn't last, and things would never be completely the way they used to be. She was the person who understood me better than anyone else, and she was disappearing. I squeezed both my eyes tightly shut, trying to keep the tears from spilling out.

"I really miss him," Grandma said again.

"I know," Tony told her. "So do I." There were tears in the corners of his eyes as he said it, and I knew he didn't mean that he missed my grandpa. Obviously. I knew he missed his mom. He missed his home.

A few days ago, I'd complained to Tony about my mom being on my case to get all my laundry folded and put away, and he had said he'd give anything right now to have his mom on his case again about something so normal, just like old times, before she got sick.

Grandma opened her eyes. She sat up straight, patted Tony's hand. "No use getting upset, Anthony," she said. "Your house is waiting for you. It will be there, with all your loved ones, when you get back. My house, however . . ."

She didn't finish her sentence. Instead, she got up, leaving the lemon to wobble and roll off the couch cushion. She walked up the stairs to her room, and I watched her, taking in every little detail I could—the swish of her skirt against the backs of her legs, the way her hand curled around the bannister, the light coming in through the pane of glass next to the front door and bouncing off her silver hair.

I turned back to Tony, who had crossed his arms over his face. I could tell he was crying. I got up and put the lemon back in its bowl and busied myself with the mantle, putting things where they were supposed to be. A place for everything, and everything in its place. That was another of Grandma's famous sayings. If only it was that easy.

When Grandma left tomorrow, Tony would move back into his own room, if that's what we were going to call it. Tony's room? It sounded a lot better than "the spare room." He'd at least have a bit of space to himself, which was so important. And Grandma would have her own room at the assisted living place, and I would miss her, but I'd visit all the time. I could help her decorate it. Our house had felt so small since Tony and then Grandma arrived, but at least I'd always had my own room, with a door I could close. I knew I was lucky.

I patted Tony's back. He wasn't sobbing or anything; he was a silent crier, but I saw a wet drop leaking out of one eye from underneath his crossed arms. I kept my hand on his shoulder and, before I could think it through, I was somehow saying, "I'm glad you're here."

-•- ✦ -•-

The "talk" didn't come until I was getting ready for bed. My dad poked his head into the bathroom while I was brushing my teeth.

"So," he said. "About this suspension."

Starting right off, huh? Not even going to give me any warning. I brushed up and down, and around and around, again and again. I'd never brushed my teeth so thoroughly. I could hear Mom downstairs loading the dishwasher.

But pretty soon my mouth got super frothy, so I spit, then swished some water around, spit again. Dad was still standing there, patiently waiting, or else he just hadn't planned out what he was going to say.

"Isn't it Mom's job to yell at me?" I asked.

"She thought I could handle this one," he said and smiled sheepishly. "And nobody's yelling."

I rinsed out my toothbrush, stuck it in my cup, and put them back in the cabinet. "Look, I'm really sorry," I said in a rush. "I was a poor sport, I get that, and I shouldn't have done it, and I know it was wrong, and it's just that I worked so hard, and I was really, really upset."

He held up his hands. "I know, I know," he said. "I'm not mad at you, Mags, believe it or not. I mean, you certainly did not make the best choices, but we've all been under a lot of pressure around here." He leaned against the doorway. "I look at it this way—if anything was going to be wrecked, I'm glad it was just some paper decorations."

I felt my body relax, the muscles in my shoulders unknotting. He was letting me off easy. This was *incredible*. Mom would not have been so kind. She at least would have taken my phone away or something. But I still wasn't sure I was completely off the hook.

"I promise I'll never do anything like that again," I said solemnly.

Dad nodded, then said, "Just try your best." He opened his arms and pulled me in for a hug. His cheek was scratchy, like he hadn't shaved in a couple days. "That's all we can ask for."

He pulled back and looked at me, holding my shoulders. "There's something I wanted to talk to you about," he said. "You know that Tony is supposed to be going to a counselor, but he walked out of his first session . . . and I was thinking, maybe it would help if we all went, as a family. We'd be supporting Tony, but also, I think it could do us all some good."

"Ummm," I said, and Dad cut in.

"You know, a lot of people go to counseling. Your mom and I went years ago, when we were having some troubles."

I wondered if a counselor had convinced them to stay to-gether. If that was the case, I owed her or him a thank-you. How bad could it be? It was just talking to someone, right?

"Sure, Dad, I'd go."

I heard someone on the stairs. Tony.

"Oh, sorry," he said. "I was just going to brush my teeth."

He was in his pajamas, probably had the sofa bed all pulled out, ready for his last lonely night in the living room. I wondered how long he'd been listening to Dad and me.

"It's fine, Tony," Dad said. "We're done in here."

I went to my room, and Dad followed. "Are you going to be okay at home tomorrow?" he asked. "With me at work and Mom getting Grandma settled at the facility?"

"I'll be fine," I said. "I've got a social studies report to finish."

"Okay, then," he said. "Mom or I will call and check on you. Good night."

He'd gotten to the door when I said, "Dad, could you . . . could you . . . tuck me in?"

"Sure," he said. He sounded surprised, but happy, too.

He climbed up my ladder and leaned over the bed to pull the comforter up to my chin, and I felt that wonderful warmth and heaviness spreading all over me, pulling my eyelids closed. We'd try as best as we could. That was the only promise worth making.

- - - ✦ - - -

When I heard someone whisper, "*Maggie, Maggie,*" I thought at first it was a dream. But there was Tony. He was standing next to my loft, calling up to me, and though he looked a bit ghostlike thanks to the moonlight coming from my window, he was definitely real.

"I can't sleep," he said. "It's too quiet downstairs."

I sat up and rubbed my eyes. Mittens was purring at my feet, and I heard Grandma snoring in the other room. Somehow I'd gotten used to it, and it didn't even bother me anymore, kind of like how I'd stopped noticing all the new smells in the house.

"You can sleep next to Grandma," I joked groggily. "It's not too quiet in there."

I could just make out Tony's smile from where he stood at the bottom of my ladder. He chewed his nail.

"You're going to chew that thing right off, you know," I said. "I'm surprised you haven't already."

He looked down at his thumb like he was seeing it for the first time and wiped his hand on his pajama pants.

"Are you okay?" I asked. "I know Grandma kind of . . . upset you earlier. Are you still thinking about that?"

"Yeah," he said. "I mean, no, not really." He walked over to my window, pulled the curtains back and looked out. I couldn't imagine there would be much to see on the street after dark except a person or two getting one last dog walk in, or some raccoons looking to dig through any trash cans that weren't covered.

"I'm thinking about my mom," he said. "She actually called earlier. It was a super short conversation. You probably didn't even hear it."

"No, I didn't, but that's good, right, that you got to talk to her?" Tony had been so upset after school that she wasn't calling. "That's progress, isn't it?"

"Yeah, it is. It's just that . . . she doesn't like it there."

"Of course she doesn't," I said. "That's why she's going to get better and get out."

He kept looking out my window, which was starting to bug me, like there was a monster out there or something. I wasn't typically afraid of things like that, except in the movies, but it was weird.

"What are you looking at?" I asked.

"Nothing," Tony answered. He sat on my beanbag chair, and I leaned over my bed rail. He'd left the curtain open so the room was brighter now. I could see his bare feet. His toenails were too long and kind of gross-looking. I wondered if his mom used to cut his nails. My mom still cut mine.

"Will you visit her again? At McDonalds or something?" I asked. If he wanted me to go with him again, for moral support, I would. I just hoped the visit would turn out better than the last time.

"We have a meeting set up in a couple weeks," he said.

I could tell by his expression that it wasn't nearly soon enough for him. Mittens had climbed down from my loft, and Tony petted her. She started up her purr motor.

"Dad told me how important it is that she really stays committed to her program," he said. "That's why I really hate it when she does stuff like miss calls, because I figure she's messing up other stuff, too."

Suddenly, he gave my beanbag a punch, and I worried, not for the first time, he'd send Styrofoam pellets everywhere. "I hate this," he said, too loud for a whisper.

"Shhh," I said. "Do you want Mom and Dad in here? Or Grandma?"

"Who cares?"

He put his head down in his hands so I couldn't see his face anymore. I didn't know what to do. Should I climb down and give him a hug? Should I go get Dad? I was still so out of it. I'd been having a dream where I was chasing Mittens down a dark alley, and it really got my heart thumping. Here in the present, everything was still and calm. But I knew there were shadows in the dark downstairs, and Tony was sleeping down there all alone.

"Hey, Tony?" I said. "If you want to stay in here tonight, that's fine. I mean, it's just for the night because tomorrow you'll have your own room again."

He looked up, his eyes bright with excitement.

"Really?"

"Yeah, well, you'll have to sleep on the floor, but if you bring all the blankets in and stuff . . ."

"That's fine, that's fine. I'll be right back!"

I vaguely remembered him mumbling good night from his nest of blankets, but I was already back in my dream, only this time I'd found Mittens, and she was purring as I scratched her in just that perfect spot under her chin.

One More Thing

When I woke up, Tony was gone. His pillow and blankets were folded and stacked against the wall. I hadn't set my alarm since I didn't need to go to school, and I'd *really* slept in. It was almost 10 a.m. already. The house was quiet, which meant Mom and Grandma had probably already left. I was sad I didn't get to say goodbye to Grandma, but I knew I'd be visiting her soon.

It was probably for the best that I'd slept in. Dad had told me yesterday that I might want to stay out of sight this morning. He said Mom didn't want to have to lie to Grandma about my suspension. "We really don't need one more thing to deal with," Mom had told him. "Not one more thing."

It wasn't so bad having the day to myself; I had plenty of things to do. I needed to finish my social studies report—that was first on the list—but I needed to do some thinking, too. I felt like I should reach out to Rakell now that I knew about her parents, but I wasn't sure how, and I wanted to check in with Olive.

After a couple bowls of Lucky Charms, I was in the living room on the couch with my books spread out on the cushions, looking for some facts about the Revolutionary War. Then, all of a sudden, Tony burst through the door, threw his backpack and coat on a chair, and sat on the couch, putting his head in his hands just like no time had passed since our beanbag conference last night.

"What's wrong?" I asked. "Are you sick?" He looked like he was about to throw up.

"That's what I told the nurse," he said.

"Doesn't a parent have to get you if you're sick? Wait . . . *are* you sick, or not?" He was all sweaty and out of breath. "Did you run all the way home?"

"Yeah. I told the nurse my mom had texted and was waiting outside, and then I just left. It's no big deal; I'm used to getting around on my own. My mom and I didn't have a car for a while. Anyway, that doesn't matter." He waved his hands in the air like this conversation was wasting his time and leaned toward me with this super intense look on his face.

"Something happened to my mom," he said.

"What do you mean?" I closed my book. My report was clearly going to have to wait. "What happened?"

"Well, she texted Rakell," Tony continued and explained, "I gave her Rakell's cell number, just in case."

"Are you supposed to do that?" I remembered him saying his mom wasn't supposed to call him directly, and this seemed like a sneaky way of getting around that. Maybe that was why he'd given her Rakell's number instead of mine, in case my parents were looking at my phone.

"That doesn't matter," he repeated, his voice rising. "Listen! This is an emergency." He sprang up and started pacing the room. "She told Rakell to tell me she left the rehab house, that she couldn't stand it anymore, so she left!"

"Can she do that?"

Tony tugged at his hair and looked at me like I was the dumbest person alive. "Of course she can't do that! She's got to be there at least ninety days. She's got to . . ." He sat down and crossed his arms over his eyes like the outside world would cease to exist as long as he couldn't see it. "She's got to get her life together!"

He put his arms back down. He wasn't crying, and I was glad to see that, but he looked scared. Tony hardly ever looked scared, except for that one time when Grandma was questioning him. Angry, yes, especially lately. Sad, unfortunately, yes, he always looked a little sad. But not scared, not even when he had first come to the house. Even then, he'd just stood on the front stoop doing basketball tricks, calm and cool.

He stood up abruptly. "We have to do something."

"What do you mean?" I said. "Like call the police?"

Tony gave me a withering stare. "The last thing we'd do is call the cops," he said.

I felt myself shrink. How should I know what to do? I didn't have the first idea how to deal with Tony's mom. The worst thing my mom ever did was wash a red sock with my new white leggings.

"Well, what, then?" I asked.

"She went home," Tony said. "She didn't say it. I just know it. She kept saying the last time we talked that she missed our house, even though it's just a tiny, crappy apartment. It was ours, you know?" He put his hands on his hips. "I think she misses having something that's hers."

I thought of Tony sleeping on the couch I was sitting on now. I was glad he'd be back in the bedroom tonight, even though it meant Grandma would be across town.

"But how can you be sure that's where she went?"

"Because she's my mom," he said. "Because I know how she thinks."

He didn't look as scared anymore. He looked focused and sure, like he had a plan.

He picked up his coat from the chair and put it back on. "I'm going to find her," he said. "I'm going home, and then . . . I'll figure something out. I'll talk her into going back."

He walked into the kitchen, and I followed him. The look on his face told me there was nothing I could do to change his mind. I'd just have to watch him go. Maybe I could call Dad and tell him what happened? He'd know what to do.

Tony paused at the kitchen door, then turned around. "You coming?" he asked.

"*Me?*"

"Well, I wasn't talking to Mittens," he replied. She'd gotten up from her bed when she heard Tony come home and, as usual, was rubbing against his legs.

"I . . . I don't know if we should leave the house," I said. I suddenly felt panicky. This whole thing, this whole situation, seemed like something no one would want to be involved with. It was getting really serious, really fast. Part of me was thinking this was something that Tony and his mom needed to figure out with each other, as a family. That I should stay out of it.

"We'll be back before anyone even gets home. They won't even know."

If I were a person who chewed my thumbnail, I'd definitely do it now. Tony looked at me across the kitchen island. He ran his hand through his hair, which reminded me of our dad, who did the same thing in the same way.

And I realized in that moment that if this was a family problem, I had to help. I was Tony's family, too. In fact, we were better than family. We were friends.

I took my coat off its hook. "How far is it?" I asked.

Tony was all smiles now. "Too far to walk," he said. "We'll have to take the bus. There's a stop near school."

I quickly packed my backpack—granola bars, a couple bottled waters, a pack of gum, and a notepad and pencil, in case I got a great design idea, which seemed unlikely, but you never knew. And my phone, of course. Tony stood there watching, growing increasingly impatient, but too bad. I liked to be prepared.

-•- ✦ -•-

"Have you ever ridden a bus before?" I asked Tony. We were nearing the school. I had a five-dollar bill in my pocket, left over from my latest trip to the Good Samaritan Thrift Shoppe. I didn't know how much it cost to ride the bus.

"Of course," Tony said, "tons of times. Haven't you?"

I searched my brain. I'd taken school buses forever, but the long, white city buses? I didn't think I'd ever been on one of those. I'd seen them downtown, and seen people waiting in those plexiglass boxes for the bus to come. I'd even stood in one of those boxes once, when my mom and I got caught in a rainstorm without an umbrella. But when the rain stopped, we walked to the parking garage and got in our car.

"Not that I remember," I said. "How much does it cost?"

"Don't worry," Tony answered. "I've got a card."

I didn't know if he meant a credit card, or like a card the teachers wore on lanyards to get them into rooms at school. I figured it wasn't the time to ask too many questions, which was too bad, because I had plenty. What were we going to do when we got there? What if his mom wasn't even there? Would we get back before anyone noticed we were gone? Tony seemed to know what he was doing, but it felt weird, not being in control myself.

We were almost directly across the street from the school now, and of course Tony chose this moment to stop and tie his shoe.

"Don't stop here," I hissed. "Someone might see you."

"So what?"

"So, you're supposed to be sick," I said.

"And you"—Tony took his time double knotting his laces — "are supposed to be suspended." He sounded so much like my dad when he said that, stern, but still kind of joking. It was easy to forget sometimes that he was only a year older than me.

He stood up and turned toward the school, cupped his hands, and yelled, "It's Maggie Owens, everybody! Total rebel!"

"Cut it out!" I said. I punched his arm.

"Ow!"

"I mean it, Tony!"

"I was just teasing you, just trying to lighten the mood, take my mind off things for a tiny second. Don't worry, I won't let anybody know about your bad-girl behavior." He wiggled his fingers at me. "Wouldn't want you to start sliding, one bad move after another . . ." He trailed off, and I didn't think we were talking about me anymore.

"What's your mom going to do?" I said quietly. "She can't just quit trying to get better. She wouldn't do that, would she?"

"She doesn't *want* to do what she does," he said. "She can't help it."

Tony zipped his jacket all the way up. The air had a real bite to it this morning. "I just need to see her," he said. "She listens to me, sometimes. If she's thinking clearly, at least."

"What do you mean?" Tony gave me a look. "Yeah, yeah," I said and let out a nervous sigh.

I was about to ask Tony more about his mom when I noticed someone exiting the school from the side door by the gym. The kid who came out the door left it propped open with his backpack, which was totally against the rules but definitely helpful at the moment. I had an idea, but I had to act fast. I'd thought when we left the house that I was prepared, that I'd brought everything I needed for this little adventure, but I wasn't, I hadn't.

"I need to run into the school for a minute," I announced to

Tony. "I forgot my social studies notes, and I have a report due tomorrow."

"What?" Tony said. "No, absolutely not." He shook his head. "What if we miss the bus?"

I ignored him, running toward the school. "I'll just be a second," I called over my shoulder.

Thankfully, the gym was empty, and I raced across it, turned down one hallway, and then another, noticing a girl from my math class coming out of the bathroom. She gave me an odd look, but I just put my head down and kept walking. I headed straight for Mrs. Sherman's office and stood outside it, wondering what to do next. I could hear her talking to someone.

Just then, a sixth-grade boy whose name I didn't know came out to his locker. "Hey, you," I whispered loudly.

"Huh?" He gave me a confused look.

"Can you do me a favor?" I asked. I dug my five dollar bill out of my front pocket, and the boy suddenly grew interested.

"What do you want?" he asked.

"Can you ..." What *did* I want? I hadn't thought this through. I just needed to get into that office. "Can you create some sort of distraction out here, like, pretend to be sick or something?"

"Why?"

"I need her to come out." I pointed toward the nurse's office and held out the money.

He snatched it and immediately started making gagging noises.

"Not here," I whispered, waving my hand, "down there, farther away."

He jogged down the hallway, to the place where the next hallway crossed. I tucked myself into an alcove and waited. He started yelling, "Ugh! I don't feel so good! Mrs. Sherman!"

His acting was pathetic, but it had the desired effect. She came running.

My heart pounding, I slipped into her office. *I shouldn't be doing this, I shouldn't be doing this.* But Olive and I had a meeting set up with Mrs. Sherman tomorrow, to interview her for her room redo. I'd just find a way to slip it back into the cabinet then. Grandma always said sometimes you needed to break the rules. Of course, she was talking about design, like mixing silver and copper, but still.

It only took a moment. The supply cabinet was unlocked just as before. The Narcan box was right where it had been. I grabbed it, slipped it into my backpack, and was out the door.

- • - ✦ - • -

My backpack felt heavy on my lap. Tony sat next to me. There were only a few other people on the bus, a mother with a toddler (who kept turning around to smile at us), a couple of older women, and a college-aged boy wearing headphones. I didn't know what song he was listening to, but I could hear the bass thumping.

Tony had swiped us both on with his bus card, but he was a quarter short. The bus driver said not to worry and let us on anyway, and we went about halfway to the back and settled into the big blue seats. My hands were still sweating from my little mission inside the school.

The little boy had opened a plastic bag full of Cheerios and was happily popping them into his mouth.

Tony asked me, "You got any food in there?" He reached for the zipper of my backpack.

"No!" I said, pulling it away from him. "I mean, yes, I've got food. But let me get it for you."

I didn't want Tony to know about the Narcan. I was afraid he'd think I didn't trust his mom and get mad at me. Better I keep it to myself.

I handed him one of the granola bars.

"Thanks," he said, taking it. "Don't you want one?"

"No, not right now."

My stomach was jumping; there was no way I could eat. I was wondering how we were going to get back home, with Tony out of money on his bus card. Add that question to my already big list. He finished his granola bar and started shifting around in his seat, crossing and uncrossing his arms, glancing out the window.

"Less than ten minutes," he said.

One of the older women pulled a cord, and the bus came to a stop by the curb. The mom and her son got off, too, and the little boy waved at us, and I waved back. Tony didn't notice.

Just then, I felt a buzz in my pocket and pulled out my phone. *Rachel*, it said. My heart skipped. It had been a long time since I'd seen her name pop up on my text messages. It also felt like a long time since she'd been "Rachel."

Is Tony with you? the message read.

I wrote back, *Yes.*

What's happening?

We're on a bus, going to his old house.

What?????

He thinks his mom might be there.

Maggie, I don't like this.

What could I do, he was going anyway.

I couldn't let him go alone.

There was a long pause. I stared at my phone, waiting. She must be at lunch. We weren't supposed to have phones out during class.

"Is it Rakell?" Tony asked.

"Yes," I said. "She's worried about you."

Tony got a slight smile on his face and tried to look at my

phone. "Tell her everything's going to be okay," he said.

"I will. I did." I scooted closer to the window, turning the phone away from him. I wasn't going to tell her that. How did I know everything was going to be okay? The phone dinged.

Be careful, Rakell's text read, then, *You're a good friend.*

He's my brother. Of course I'm going to help him.

Yeah, but I mean, you're a good friend to other people, too.

My fingers hovered over the screen. Finally, I typed:

Hey, you know . . . Tony told me about your parents.

I waited a minute. Would she be mad that I knew?

I'm really sorry, Rakell.

My phone autocorrected to Rachel, but I changed it back.

Yeah, I was going to tell you but . . . you always seemed to think my parents were perfect.

She was right about that. Her parents always acted perfectly. I guessed the way people felt and the way they looked didn't always match up. Maybe it barely ever matched up. I wrote:

Can we hang out sometime? Soon?

I wanted to say that I understood, at least a little bit, wanted to tell her about when my parents were fighting, but I didn't. Maybe I would, probably I would, soon, but not in a text.

I could go to her house, and we could have a long talk on her bed covered with the pillows we'd bought when we did her room redo. There was one that looked like cheetah fur, one with a winking emoji. One said LOL in blue sequins that you could brush with your hand and make change to silver, and there were two or three more solid-colored ones. I remembered Rakell's mom asking how a person could possibly need so many pillows and then Rakell looked at me and held up the LOL pillow, and we both fell off the bed laughing.

Sure, Rakell texted.

🙈 *I'm going to apologize to the cheerleaders and Katelyn, too. As soon as I get back to school.*

Don't worry about Katelyn. She was totally saying stuff about our office design behind my back. The cheerleaders could use a design 101 class.

We should teach it!!!!!!!!!!!!

LOL! Yes!!!!!!!!!!!!!!!!!! Call me when you get home?

👍

I put the phone back into my pocket. Nothing was perfect

yet, far from it, but it was a start. I was reminded of this one famous painting in a book at Grandma's. She had lots of art books in addition to design ones, which is why I knew Michelangelo wasn't just a Ninja Turtle. I was thinking of his painting, of God and Adam stretching their arms out to touch fingers. Rakell and I were reaching out to each other again.

Just then, Tony leaned over me to pull the cord by our window. I guessed we were there. But where were we?

Breaking and Entering

"Here we are," Tony said.

We'd speed-walked the two blocks from the bus stop, Tony for once walking even faster than me. We'd gone past a couple fast-food places and a store selling cigarettes that had bars on the windows. Down the street, the stores turned into apartment buildings and small houses, some with plastic toys in the yards.

Tony's duplex was an old, wood-sided two-story house with a blue sheet hanging in the front window as a curtain. Three steps led to the front door, and a rickety staircase climbed along one side of the house and up to another door on the second floor.

"Do you have a key?" I asked.

"No," he said, very matter-of-factly.

"Wait, no?" This seemed like important information, information we should have had before we began this little journey. "Then how are we supposed to get in?"

Tony stood by the front window, trying to look into the house, but the sheet was blocking his view. He started poking around in some weeds growing next to the concrete steps. "Sometimes she hides a spare key under a rock," he said vaguely.

I didn't know how he'd find a key in that jungle of weeds. Some of them were up to my knees. But I tried to help, spreading the plants apart, feeling around on the ground. Then I stopped.

"Tony, if your mom is here, wouldn't she answer the door? If she sees it's you?"

Tony was on his hands and knees in the weeds, but now he hopped up the three steps and knocked. It didn't seem like he knocked that hard, but the street was deserted and the door was thin, and the sound really carried. Tony jiggled the doorknob, and again I thought we were doing this all backward. Check the doorknob *first*. But it was locked. He knocked again, but no one came.

"Let's check the windows," he said and ran to the side of the house with the staircase.

"Tony, I really don't think she's home," I said. "I'm sorry, but . . ."

He completely ignored me. He pressed his hands on the window, trying to slide it up, but it didn't work. It must have been locked. Then he made his way around the house, doing the same thing to all the windows. I followed him, watching his movements become quicker and more erratic with each failed attempt.

Eventually, he'd worked his way through all of them and we were left standing next to an iron door, a bit bigger than my backpack, cut into the siding, a few feet up from the ground.

"What's that?" I asked.

"A coal chute," Tony said. "I told you this house was old."

"You heat your house with *coal*?" I asked. The only place I'd seen that was in very old books.

"Of course we don't. But the old houses still have these chutes." He shrugged. "The landlord never bothered to seal it up."

Tony stood there and looked at me, really studying me, starting with my toes and going all the way up to the top of my head. Then he looked back at the coal door.

"Oh no," I said, backing away from him. "No way." I pulled out my phone and handed it to Tony. "Try calling her. Tell her you're here, and find out where she is."

"She won't have her phone," he said, but he took my phone anyway and pressed the numbers. The phone rang and rang, but no one picked up. "I told you," he said, handing it back. "She must have borrowed a phone to text Rakell. They don't let her have a phone in the rehab place."

Tony sat down in the grass and dead leaves. He cupped his elbow and brought his thumbnail up to his mouth. We were both shivering. The wind had picked up. A plastic bag was twirling around in the street and landed in a spindly tree, where it hung on for dear life by its handles.

"I bet she's in there and taking a nap," he said, "or a bath. She listens to music when she takes a bath, so she wouldn't hear us. And if she's sleeping, she wouldn't hear us then either, because she's a really sound sleeper. She wasn't sleeping well at that place. She told me."

Tony's eyes filled up with tears, and he tried to wipe them away with a twist of his knuckles. I took a deep breath. I knew what he wanted me to do, but wasn't I in enough trouble already? I wished the BFFs were here, though I already knew what they'd say. Olive would screw up her face and say it was too dangerous, and Rakell would say *go for it*. Or maybe not. They were both surprising me lately.

There was a small handle on the coal door. I lifted it, finding it was heavier than I thought it would be. I peered into the darkness.

"Where does this go?" I asked Tony.

He jumped up and grabbed the handle from me. "To the basement," he said, "where the furnace and washer and dryer and stuff are." He looked at me with a hopeful expression. "I'd go in, but I tried once to sneak out of the house when I got in a fight with my mom's boyfriend, and I almost got stuck. Plus, I'm way bigger now."

I took a step back. "Isn't this breaking and entering?" Did I really need to add that to the vandalism already on my permanent record? *Not to mention stealing*, I thought, as I looked at my backpack.

"You're not breaking anything, just entering," he said. He had fresh tears on his face. "Please, Maggie."

-•- ✦ -•-

I stuffed my backpack in first and heard it land with a quiet *thunk*. I could see it there on the basement floor, which didn't seem too far down. I could jump it. It would be no different than jumping off our front stoop.

Getting through the door wasn't very difficult, but I had to go feet first, backward. I scratched my stomach as I slid over the metal, but it didn't hurt too bad. There was a little wriggling for my shoulders, but then I slid and fell a couple of feet.

I landed right on my butt, on the cold concrete floor. I stood up and rubbed it, let my eyes adjust to the dark.

"Are you okay?" Tony called through the rectangular patch of light.

"Yeah, I'm fine," I called back. I knew my butt would be sore later, and my stomach stung from the scrape, but there wasn't any blood. I had dirt all over my clothes—ages-old coal dust, I guessed. I tried to brush some of it off.

Tony yelled, "Go upstairs and unlock the front door."

I picked up my backpack and skirted a pile of laundry on the floor by the washing machine. There were some old baseball bats in the corner and cans and cans of paint lined up and stacked on top of each other. A pegboard hung on the wall with a bunch of paintbrushes and other tools hanging from it, and I wondered if it all belonged to the boyfriend who'd made Tony help with his business. Was that the same guy Tony had tried to get away from through the coal door? At least Tony had a real father now, one who not only shared his DNA but who acted like a dad.

Just then, the furnace let out a series of bumps and groans that scared me, and I sped right out of the creepy, dusty basement, sprinting up the stairs into a kitchen.

"Hello?" I called. "Mrs. Miller?" I didn't know if that was Tony's mom's last name. Lots of kids at our school had last names that were different from their parents'.

The kitchen was tiny but clean, except for a few dishes in the sink. There was a little table in front of a window facing a square patch of backyard grass surrounded by a chain-link fence, and two chairs pulled up to the table. I could picture Tony and his mom there, having breakfast.

On the table was a white milk-glass vase, the kind that went for fifty cents at the Shoppe, and there were a couple dead wildflowers in it, their fallen petals crisp and fanning out around the base. I remembered Tony saying his mom used to try and make the place pretty even though they didn't have much money for decorations and things.

I heard a pounding at the front door. Tony! I'd forgotten to let him in.

I walked out of the kitchen, through a little dining room filled with nothing except a half-dozen boxes, and into the living room, where . . . where I saw her.

- • - ✦ - • -

"Mrs. Miller? Mrs. Miller!" *Oh God, please, please don't be . . . please.*

I slapped her face like I'd seen in the movies. "Mrs. Miller!" I yelled into her ear. Her lips looked completely the wrong color. They were bluish.

"Wake up!" I yelled. I heard pounding, and I didn't know where it was coming from, but I thought it was in my ears, my chest. My whole body was beating.

I took her hand, but it felt cold and clammy. I dropped it, put my ear to her chest, and I heard something, a heartbeat, but it was faint and not going *da-dum da-dum da-dum* like it was supposed to but more like *da-dum* . . . and then really fast: *da-dumda-dumda-dum*.

I shrugged off my backpack, unzipped the pocket, pulled out the Narcan box, and tore it open. I was always one to read directions first, but there was no time. It was a weird-looking little device, but it had a nozzle that looked just like my mom's allergy spray.

I shoved the tip into Tony's mom's nose, pressed up on the plunger underneath it and heard a *hisssss* as the medicine sprayed out. The next sound I heard was glass breaking just a few feet away from me and the thud of a rock landing on the living room floor. Tony punched at the glass, making a hole big enough for him to get through, though his jacket snagged, tearing his sleeve.

"What are you doing?" he started shouting at me.

I threw him my phone. "Nine-one-one!" I said. "Now!" But Tony wasn't listening to me. He knelt next to his mom and held her hand. "Mom! Can you hear me?"

I couldn't believe it, but she answered, in this soft, scratchy voice. She answered.

"Tony?" she said, and my heart nearly exploded with relief. It was just like that girl, Claire, had said at the assembly, how her cousin had seen Narcan used on somebody, and it was like they'd come back from the dead.

"You're bleeding," Tony's mom said to him, looking at his hands, his arm. "What did you do?" she asked in that tone that all parents get when their kids hurt themselves, apparently, no matter what.

I was wondering whether I should still call 911 when I heard slamming car doors outside and saw a swirl of red lights through the broken window.

"Why did you call?" Tony asked me. "She's *fine*."

"I didn't!" I said, but then the door was pushed in, and two male cops were right up in Tony's mom's face, slipping on latex gloves while they asked her a million questions and shined lights into her eyes. Tony and I stood back against the wall until another cop came in, a woman with a long black braid under her cap, who ushered us into the kitchen. She said the upstairs neighbor had called the police when he'd seen us messing around with the windows.

There were cookies. There was a thermos full of hot chocolate. There was a blanket. Later, I wouldn't remember where those items had come from, only that the police officer, Sharon she said to call her, had seemingly pulled them out of thin air. There were also questions, lots of them, about how we'd found Tony's mom, and about the Narcan, which I had to admit to stealing from the nurse's office. We were sitting at the little kitchen table and Sharon was standing, writing on a notepad. I did all the talking because Tony was crying, his head down on his arms, the blanket covering him.

At one point, Tony raised his head to ask if his mom was

going to be okay, and Sharon said yes, but that she'd "have a long road ahead of her."

"Are you taking her to jail?" Tony asked, his lip quivering.

I played with the dead flower petals. I didn't know if I wanted to hear the answer. I could see how upset Tony was at the possibility and yet I couldn't help thinking that if she went to jail at least she wouldn't hurt herself, and Tony would be safe too, with us. I felt kind of bad thinking that, but then Sharon said she would be going to the hospital, not jail. *Whew.* That was a better option.

"I'm afraid she's going to be in a world of hurt," Sharon told us crisply, but then looked sorry she'd said it. She rubbed Tony's back. "You just love and support her," she said, "but remember, recovery is up to your mom. That's out of your hands."

She looked at me, then back at Tony. "People get better all the time. I've seen it," she said, then added, "Your mom is lucky, you know. If it wasn't for your sister here . . ." She pointed at me, and I didn't even correct her. I just put the blanket back over Tony's shoulder.

-•- ✦ -•-

"How'd you get it?" Tony asked. We were buckled into the back seat of Officer Sharon's police car. She had called our dad. We were going home.

"I used my last five bucks to pay a kid at school to make a scene in the hallway. He pretended to be sick, the nurse ran out, and I slipped in. That was that. Easy-peasy." I couldn't believe how I was talking, like this was just a normal day for me. "Did you really think I went in for my social studies notes?"

"Yeah," Tony said, laughing. "I honestly did." We smiled at each other, and Officer Sharon looked at us in her rearview mirror and smiled, too. Her radio crackled with a woman's voice calling out mysterious numbers.

"What's a ten sixty-two?" I asked.

"Breaking and entering," Officer Sharon replied. She turned the radio down a bit.

I started playing with the straps of my backpack until Tony said, "Are you worried you're going to get in trouble?"

I didn't answer. The truth was, yeah, I was worried. I'd stolen something, broken into a house, and given medical help, which I had no business giving, to someone who was minutes away, I knew, from being . . . dead. Not to mention I'd taken a bus across town without even telling my parents.

"Maggie," he said, "you saved somebody's *life*. Not just somebody's. My mom's. If anybody tries to mess with you over that, I won't let them."

--- ✦ ---

"We're going to have a talk," Dad said. "Tomorrow."

He was crying, and Mom was crying, and me and Tony were crying, and Mittens was yowling because we'd all forgotten about her and her food bowl was empty. Mom fed her, then put out some leftovers for the humans, and we microwaved plates and after that, Dad said we should all just "decompress and get some rest."

"Tomorrow is another day," he said. He was fond of saying that whenever something went wrong, and usually I'd answer, "Well, duh," but I didn't tonight. Tomorrow *was* another day, hopefully a better one.

Later, as I sat in my room checking my phone, I saw that Olive and Rakell had left a bunch of messages, and so had my mom, who had come home to get Grandma's forgotten glasses and found the house empty. Even Mildred at the Shoppe, who knew nothing about any of this, had sent a group text to the BFFs to tell us she'd gotten in a box of lava lamps that were "the grooviest things she'd ever seen." I sat there reading through all the messages, feeling warm and safe and loved, more than ever before.

I played with the items on my desk. I liked to swap things every month or so, rotating other objects into the mix from my prop box. It was good practice. Right now, my items included a little glass bowl filled with flower petals from my mom's yellow chrysanthemums, a wooden clock, and the bronze winged pig. Always three items, the perfect number.

But now as I looked at it . . . the display was almost too perfect. I decided to keep the clock and remove the bowl, but when I lifted it, I accidentally knocked over the pig. Lying on his side like that, the little guy looked quite comfortable, like he was napping.

I decided to leave him that way, thinking he could probably use a rest. After all, he'd been doing a lot of flying. So many impossible things had happened.

Welcome to the Family

The talk came as promised, after breakfast, after the social worker called and Dad spent a half hour on his phone with her in the living room. He was talking quietly, so I couldn't really hear what he was saying, but that was okay. I didn't need a recap of yesterday's events. I'd lived them.

Tony passed me the box of Lucky Charms, and I poured a big bowl. Maybe sugary cereal was our new normal. I wasn't complaining about that part, at least. We were sitting at the island in our usual spots, one empty yellow stool between us. My mom was at the sink, cleaning up the dishes from yesterday.

"We should order another one of these stools," I said.

Mom looked up from her dishes. "Where are we going to put it?" she asked. The three stools fit perfectly, with just enough space between them.

"We can put it on the end," I said, "and tuck it under when we're not using it. We just need to rearrange a bit."

I looked at Tony, and he nodded, his mouth full of pastel marshmallows. He had a bandage on both his arm and his hand from where he'd gotten cut coming through his living room window. I had a bandage on my stomach from where I scraped it sliding into his apartment through the coal door. But other than that, there was nothing different about us—not that anyone could see.

Dad walked in and set his phone on the counter, and Mom turned around and locked eyes with him. *Oh boy*, I thought, *here it comes*. They had probably waited because they were too shocked to deal with us last night, too worried and frazzled by what had happened. It was like, when you jumped off a swing and cut your leg, your mom would spring into action and cradle you gently and clean up the cut. But as soon as you stopped crying? As soon as everything seemed back to normal? She'd scream at you for jumping off the swing.

Mom started in on us first. "You didn't make the best choices yesterday," she said, looking at both Tony and me.

This was my least favorite lecture, the bad choices one.

"You should *not* have gone over there, either of you," Dad added. "You should have called one of us, and we would have helped."

"But there wasn't time," Tony protested.

"Not true," Dad said. "We could have gotten the police to your apartment way faster than it took the two of you to take a bus across town. You should have called as soon as Rachel said she'd gotten your mom's text, Tony. There's a good chance your mom wouldn't have even been there, and then what?"

"But she was," I murmured. "And her name is Rakell."

"And, Maggie, you stole medicine?" Mom added, slightly changing the subject. "How did you even know how to use it?"

"I learned it from watching you," I said.

"What?" both my parents said.

"Your allergy medicine, Mom." I shrugged. "It's the same type of thing."

They looked at each other like they were deciding who was going to speak next. Tony's spoon was clinking against his bowl. Mittens was *meowllll*-ing from the floor by our feet, waiting for an invitation to get up on the counter and lap leftover milk, which my parents did not allow.

"We accept some of the responsibility," Dad said. "We haven't done a good job of laying out ground rules, especially for you, Tony. We're going to make up a list and talk about that next week, and you need to be able to check in with us, so we're getting you a phone—"

"Really?" Tony said, super excited, but Dad squashed him right back down.

"But you'll not be using it, for the time being, for anything except calling home—that's *this* home, to me or Mom—and when you're home, I get the phones. Yours too, Maggie. They'll go right in this basket when they're not charging." He pointed to the basket by the door where he kept his wallet and keys. "And no TV or video games for a week. You're both grounded."

My mouth was hanging open as I listened. This was so weird. Was my dad being bad-cop? I glanced sideways at Tony and could see he didn't believe it either. Yet this was one of those times that I felt anything I said would only get me into even more trouble. One week of being grounded was bad enough. I didn't need to make it two.

As Mom and Dad were leaving the kitchen, they piled even more on us.

"I want you both to straighten your rooms today," Mom said, almost gleefully.

"And I could use some help sweeping out the garage," Dad added.

Once they were safely out of the room, I raised my eyebrows at Tony, and he did the same back at me, and we both started laughing.

"Welcome to the family," I said.

-•- ✦ -•-

"What's your favorite color?" Olive asked Tony.

"Oh, I got this," I said. I pointed to the hoodie he was wearing. "It's blue, right?"

Tony looked down, like he was noticing his favorite sweat-shirt for the first time. "Oh yeah, I like blue just fine. But I wear this because it's so comfortable. I don't really notice the color."

Rakell laughed, and Olive sucked in her breath while she looked over at me, likely waiting for me to launch into a discussion about how color affects mood, even when we're not consciously aware of it. But I didn't think that was necessary, mostly because they already knew all of that. In fact, Rakell or Olive would be perfectly capable of giving that lecture themselves.

I had our roles all wrong, or at least, my belief that we needed super-strict roles in the first place had been all wrong. There wasn't just one way to do things. I didn't always have to be in charge. And a stool with three legs wasn't the only metaphor for perfect harmony. You could find balance in all sorts of different ways, with any number of people.

It wasn't like I was going to wear our awful school color combination of green and brown anytime soon. I mean, a girl's gotta have standards. And I wasn't abandoning design rules. I was just loosening them a little, letting in a little light. Some pretty cool things can happen when you're open to change, in design and everything else, even if that change is nothing you ever could have imagined, not even in your pig-flying dreams.

Tony's closet door was open, so we could see all his new clothes, in a full spectrum of shades but heavy on the blues, that my mom had bought him. Thankfully, the duffel bag and thrift-store stuff were out of sight, so the room didn't smell like old gym socks anymore, nor did it smell like my grandma.

Mom and I had visited her at the assisted living facility recently, and she actually seemed a little happier there than she had at our house. She showed us the big living room she shared with the other residents. She introduced us to a new friend named Beatrice. She did complain about the food, though, and Mom said she'd definitely had some ups and downs with the transition, so it wasn't perfect, but then nothing ever was.

That said, there was nothing wrong with making something better, if you could. This room, for starters, could be so much better for Tony.

"Should we still do this?" Rakell asked, holding up the card with all the paint colors attached. "Since Tony says he doesn't notice colors?"

"Let's hold off on colors for now," I suggested. "Let's do the love-hate."

"Fantabulous!" Olive yelled and clapped her hands. She opened her notebook to a fresh page.

"Why don't you ask the questions, Olive?" I said. "I can take notes."

"Really? Okay."

She handed me her notebook and pen and sat up a little straighter from her spot on the edge of Tony's bed. She looked around the room. I followed her gaze to the floral comforter, to the closet, to the oak nightstand sitting between the bed and the ancient brown chair with the matching footstool.

"Tony," she said, "tell us what you love and hate about this room. Don't think about it too hard. But be honest."

We all leaned in toward Tony, who was sitting in the brown chair. Rakell gave him a little smile, which he returned, like they were sharing some private joke. I thought it was annoying when they did stuff like that, but thankfully, they didn't do it often. And honestly, if Tony was going to have a girlfriend, at least it was someone I liked.

"That comforter," Tony said, pointing. "HATE it!"

"Oh yes, that's a disaster," Olive said. "Did you get that, Maggie?"

"Got it," I said, and wrote, "Comforter = hate."

"How about the chair?" Rakell asked.

Tony shifted around in it a bit, like he was trying to test the cushion for comfort. Then he put his feet up on the ottoman, which was really worn. It sagged in the middle, and the fabric was thin.

"It's pretty comfortable," he said.

"We have to re-cover it." I couldn't help jumping in on this one. The chair was incredibly ugly; I didn't care how comfortable it was.

"Is that in the budget?" Olive asked.

"We have a budget?" Tony perked up.

"A small one," I answered. "My mom said she'd give us a little money, but honestly, the only way we could afford to re-cover this chair would be if we did it ourselves, and that's way beyond my skill set."

"I could re-cover the ottoman, though," Rakell said. "Add a little pop of pattern to that, some kind of fabric Tony likes. It would take the focus away from the chair, and I've done that type of thing before."

"Yes!" me and Olive said together.

"And he needs a desk and chair and a good lamp, for doing homework," Olive added, while Tony groaned.

"She's right," I said. I took out a piece of graph paper and starting mapping out where we could put the furniture. My week of being grounded had passed by quickly, and it felt really good to be working on another project again, especially after losing the contest. Although, as Olive had pointed out to me many times since then, we didn't lose. We came in second, which was hardly losing. I hadn't thought of it that way, but I was going to, from now on.

I heard some laughter coming from my parents in the kitchen, which kind of startled me. It had been a while since laughter was more common than quiet, angry whispers, and it was really good to hear it again.

They were down there working out a menu for Thanksgiving. We'd bring Grandma here from the assisted living facility for the day, and Olive's whole family was coming, and so were Rakell and her mom and brothers. It was usually just the three of us, which was kind of lonely, and we always had plenty of room for more. Now we were going to have a full house.

Dad called up the stairs, "Tony, your mom is going to be calling soon."

Tony said to us, "I'll be back," and he ran downstairs. Right on cue, I could hear Dad's cell phone ringing. Ever since she'd gotten out of the hospital, Tony's mom called him from the rehab house exactly when she said she was going to call, right on time. Next week, Tony and my parents and I were starting counseling. I wouldn't let him walk out this time. Tony was going to be there for his mom, and I was going to be there for him, like he was for me.

"What did I miss?" he asked when he came back in.

"We'll need some objects that inspire you," Rakell said. "For your nightstand."

"How about this?" Tony grabbed his basketball and set it on the nightstand, where it promptly rolled off, bounced across the floor, and out the door.

"That would be a *no*," I said, laughing. "Why don't you look through my prop box? Let me get it."

I came back in with my overflowing box of dollar store and Shoppe finds. Tony knelt down and picked through the stuff. He pulled out the silver frame with the generic photo of the little boy being pushed on a swing by his father. The last time I'd looked at it was on the day I was teaching about tablescapes, the day Tony arrived.

"I like this," he said, "but I guess we need a new picture."

"Oh, I know what we should do," I said, pulling out my cell phone. "Selfie, everyone! How about around the ottoman?"

The four of us got on the floor with the ottoman in the middle. Since Rakell was going to redo the ottoman, this would be a great "before" photo. Maybe I'd take another one when the room was all done. Tony could pick out a hinged frame for two photos, or maybe he could have two hinged frames, so he could also have a picture of him with his mom, plus one of him with Dad and my mom and me.

"Okay, ready?" I said. Rakell beamed her best smile. Olive stuck out her tongue. Tony made bunny ears behind my head.

"Say cheese," Rakell said.

"No," I said, "say BFFs!"

"BFFs!" we all yelled.

Click. I looked around the room. We'd already decided to paint the beige walls the same blue as Tony's hoodie. All the little stuff in the room was going to have to come out; the furniture would be draped with tarps. Yup, things always looked a lot worse before they looked a lot better.

Just then, Olive said, "We haven't done the love part, of the love-hate."

I looked down at my notebook, at the columns I'd made labeled *Hate* and *Love*. Then Tony and I looked at each other. And I guess because we're related and all, I knew what he was thinking. Sometimes the things we love don't need to be written down in a list. Sometimes, the things we love aren't things. For once, I didn't have an exact picture in my mind of our "after" photo, but I knew one thing. It would be fantabulous.

Acknowledgments

Like Maggie, I also have a flying pig. She's made of iron and sits on my office windowsill. I bought her a long time ago, when I was ready to give up on my dream of publishing a novel, and needed a visual reminder to keep trying.

I sent a similar pig to my extraordinary agent, Steven Malk, when this book sold. Steve took a chance on a writer with a single picture book rough draft to her name, and I am forever grateful. I'm so glad he said, in our very first conversation, "You should really consider writing a novel." Thank you to Steve and his team at Writers House, especially Hannah Mann and Andrea Morrison, for their smart and thoughtful editorial feedback through numerous drafts.

My editor at Chronicle Books, Taylor Norman, was a dream to work with, and her vision took this book places I'd never thought possible. She's an absolute master of constructive criticism, so good, in fact, that I'm not sure I've ever worked so hard while smiling so big.

A huge thank-you to Mariam Quraishi for her beautiful book design, and to the whole team at Chronicle for getting my first novel out into the world, especially Mary Duke, Claire Fletcher, Diane Joao, Andie Krawczyk, Margo Winton Parodi, Kaitlyn Spotts, and Eva Zimmerman.

Thanks to Yasmin Imamura who created a stunner of a cover that so wonderfully captures the tension in the book.

My "walking workshops" with Yvette Benavides and Lisa Sharon gave me the confidence to pursue this book when it was just a few notes. I'm also grateful to all the friends who provided keys to their homes when I needed a quiet place to work, especially John and Lee Ann Eyre.

So many friends have encouraged me when the writing wasn't going so well (and celebrated with me when it was!), especially Danni Schantz and Amy Jo Stavnezer, my "egghead" sisters.

Chelsea Churpek, Marlane Kennedy, and Laura Sirot provided tremendous insight and suggestions to make this book stronger. Thank you.

My family is forever indulgent of my decorating whims and never complains when I rearrange the furniture while they are out of the house. My husband, Rick, and children, Lily and Whit, are my first readers, always. A special thanks to Lily and Whit, who were so helpful in correcting my mistakes depicting middle school. Any remaining errors are mine. So happy to celebrate each success with you, no matter how small ("To the car!").

Lastly, to all the amazing people creating children's literature who have inspired my own children, and all of us, to be better humans. It's an honor and privilege to be part of this community.

Marcy Campbell loves to redecorate, when she's not writing. Like Maggie, she also enjoys collecting objects to display, especially cool rocks, shells, and feathers. Her award-winning picture book *Adrian Simcox Does NOT Have a Horse* was an Indie Next Top 10 Pick and a Junior Library Guild selection, and has been translated into eight languages. Marcy lives in Ohio with her three favorite people in the world, plus three cats, and a lovable dog named Turtle. This is her first novel. Visit her at marcycampbell.com.